Shylock's Daughter

Shylock's Daughter

MIRJAM PRESSLER

translated and with an afterword by

Brian Murdoch

Phyllis Fogelman Books New York

First published in the United States 2001
by Phyllis Fogelman Books
An imprint of Penguin Putnam Inc.
345 Hudson Street
New York, New York 10014

Published in Great Britain 2000 by Macmillan Children's Books
First published 1999 in Germany by Alibaba Verlag GmbH,
Frankfurt am Main, as *Shylocks Tochter*
Original German text copyright © 1999 by Mirjam Pressler
English translation copyright © 2000 by Macmillan Children's Books

Designed by Nancy R. Leo-Kelly
Text set in Minion
Printed in the U.S.A. on acid-free paper
1 3 5 7 9 10 8 6 4 2

Library of Congress Cataloging-in-Publication Data
Pressler, Mirjam.
[Shylocks Tochter. English]
Shylock's daughter / Mirjam Pressler ; translated and with an afterword by
Brian Murdoch.
p.   cm.
Summary: Sixteen-year-old Jessica, who longs to be free of the restrictions
of her father and life in the Jewish ghetto of sixteenth-century Venice,
falls in love with a Christian aristocrat and must make choices that will affect
her whole family. Inspired by Shakespeare's play The merchant of Venice.
ISBN 0-8037-2667-8 (hardcover)
1. Jews—Italy—Venice—History—16th century—Juvenile fiction.
[1. Jews—Italy—Venice—History—16th century—Fiction.
2. Fathers and daughters—Fiction. 3. Identity—Fiction.
4. Prejudices—Fiction. 5. Venice (Italy)—History—16th century—Fiction.
6. Italy—History—16th century—Fiction.]
I. Murdoch, Brian, date. II. Title.
PZ7.P921965 Sh 2001   [Fic]—dc21   00-061012

For Barbara:
I might have loved you,
but I couldn't sing your songs
—M.P.

Chapter 1

Jessica lifted up her wide-sleeved pinafore, her *cioppa*, with both hands and stepped sideways around the dead cat that was lying on the street in front of her. She stood still for a moment. It was a tabby cat. It was lying on its side, all four paws stretched out stiffly, and it had a misshapen, swollen belly. Jessica wondered if it had been going to have kittens and they had died with it. There was a swarm of black flies around the dead animal, and one particularly fat one was crawling across one of the eyes—eyes which looked like very green glass marbles.

"Tubal Benevisti is always insisting that Venice is the most beautiful city in the world," said Jessica, and she took a couple of brisk steps so that she could catch up with Jehuda, who had walked on with his head bent.

"Then it's probably true," he said without much interest. "When shall I come and fetch you?"

"Just before sunset, as usual," said Jessica. "So that we can be back in the Ghetto before it gets dark." And in her head she added: And before my father leaves his countinghouse and comes home.

The boy nodded and walked on without a word. He climbed up the steps at the side of one of the high bridges, leaned on the parapet, and waited for Jessica, who came and joined him and looked out along the canal. A covered barge was just going under the bridge and came out again on the other side. You could hear laughing and singing from inside the barge, a cheerfulness that seemed somehow out of place under such gray skies. A couple of seagulls swooped through the air and a black gondola overtook the barge.

"They're having some kind of celebration," said Jessica. "Maybe it's a wedding?" But Jehuda walked on without answering. He's being really strange, thought Jessica. He never did say much, but lately he just seems to have something on his mind. Oh well, that suits me. At least I don't have to worry about him getting too curious.

After they had crossed another bridge, Jehuda turned off to the right, and she followed him. A group of ragamuffins came toward them. The biggest of them had a net with six or seven birds he had caught, and they were trying in vain to move their pinions, to beat their black wings and get away. Their feet had become hopelessly enmeshed in the net, and their trapped bodies could only twitch. The smaller urchins were screeching and catcalling, and the big one was swinging the net round his head the way pious Jews swing the ritual fowl, the *kapora*, round their heads to take away their sins on the day before the festival of Yom Kippur. Jehuda stood protectively in front of Jessica until the lads had passed, and only then did he go on. Three women were sitting on a bench in front of one of the houses, embroidering a green counterpane. "Jews," said one of them, and spat as Jessica and Jehuda went past.

The pair stopped by the house of Levi Meshullam, the doctor. "I'll come and fetch you before sunset, then," said Jehuda. "Peace be with you, Jessica."

"And with you, Jehuda," said Jessica. But the boy had already turned his back and was hurrying off. Seen from behind, his tall red hat looked too big for his narrow shoulders. Jessica felt a sudden surge of pleasure. Without Jehuda, who was easy to pick out as a Jew because of his hat, she felt much more free. She smiled. In the Ghetto she stood out because she wore a light-colored, almost elegant *cioppa*, when most of the Jewish women there wore dark clothes in severe styles. But not here in Levi Meshullam's house.

Jessica went through the gateway to the palazzo. She felt, as she always did, that she was going into another world, a wonderful, beautiful, happy world—one that suited her far more than the Ghetto—a world where she really belonged. And as usual, this line of thought gave rise to a dull sense of shame, as if she shouldn't really think that way, because it went against her father, against Amalia and Dalilah, and against the place in the world ordained for her by the Everlasting One, blessed be He.

The servant at the entrance knew her and stepped to one side with a slight bow to let her pass. Only when she was standing in the entrance hall did she allow herself to think of Lorenzo. For the past few days she had thought about him only when she was alone in her room, for fear that someone might be able to read on her face what was going on inside her head. Now her face was warm with pleasure, and her cheeks were glowing.

She sank into a deep chair by the wall because her legs suddenly felt weak, and she closed her eyes. As she had done so often since that day four weeks ago, she saw Lorenzo as he had come up to her in Levi Meshullam's salon at the garden party. She put her hands up over her face because she thought she could feel his glances touching her skin, running over it like a caress, and she felt once again how he had taken her hand and held it for far too long.

"What a beautiful friend you have," he said to Hannah Meshullam, and the tone of his voice went straight to her heart. "Why have you kept her hidden from me for so long?" And still he did not let go of her hand.

A warmth had spread through her whole body, a warmth she had never experienced before, a feeling that she knew at once was a forbidden one. Forbidden not only because he was a Christian and a nobleman, but also because he was a man. She pulled her hand away from his, turned on her heel, and ran out into the garden. "What a beautiful friend you have," she whispered to herself, over and over again. No man had ever said anything like that about her before. And it sounded quite different from those times when Amalia had said "What a beautiful girl you are, Jessica." Besides, Amalia hadn't said that kind of thing for a long time, and lately she was more likely to make sharp remarks about vanity and frivolity. And now those wonderful words: "What a beautiful friend you have."

Jessica had run down to the edge of the canal, had sat down on the bench under the tree, and had stared into the water. And then, suddenly, he had come and sat down beside her. "I know who you are," he had said quietly without looking at her. "I'm so sorry I startled you."

What a beautiful voice he had, soft and gentle; and how musical, how melodious his speech was, quite different from the language she was used to, which was all drawn-out vowels and half-lisped consonants; his was so beautiful that it made her whole body tremble, and she began to cry without knowing why she was crying or whom she was crying for. And he had taken her hand in his and stroked it with his long, narrow fingers. She had never seen hands as beautiful as his.

That was how it had begun, four weeks ago. Since then his face had been there in front of her every night as she lay in her bed—the beautiful eyes, the broad, high forehead over the straight nose, the softly curving mouth and the slightly jutting chin. However often she might tell herself that it made no difference what a man looked like, and that only his piety and decency really counted, still this image refused to go out of her head. It was as if, without knowing it, she had been waiting for this face all her life, waiting for those hands. In bed at night she lost herself in his eyes and felt the touch of his long, narrow fingers until she fell asleep. And in the morning when she woke up, he was there in front of her again.

That was how it had begun. Since that day not only was her world different, but so was she. The carefree girl had become a woman, full of happiness, but full of fears and worries as well. A Jewish girl and a Christian, a pawnbroker's daughter and a nobleman—it simply could not be.

Every time she came to the same conclusion, every time she told herself so, and yet she still kept going to Hannah Meshullam's to meet him there. To meet him, the one who was so beautiful. To meet him, the one who had filled her boring life with meaning, with feelings that she had never known might have existed. It could not be, and yet it had happened. She had prayed, she had struggled, she had fasted and sworn to be a good Jewish girl. And then she had come running back to him as soon as Hannah Meshullam had sent word.

Jessica let her hands drop into her lap. It could not be, of course it couldn't. But all the same, she was going to see him again now. She stood up, her legs still shaky, and smoothed down the folds of her pinafore. As soon as she went into the salon, she saw him there. He was standing with his back to the main entrance, gazing out of one of the windows that looked onto the canal. Hannah, who had been talking to two young men, one of them clearly a Christian and the other—you could see from the hat he was wearing—a Jew, jumped up as soon as she saw her friend, and the two girls put their arms around each other and kissed. "We were invited to a concert in the Doge's palace yesterday," said Hannah. "I simply have to tell you all about it later."

Jessica nodded, but really all she could think of was: in a moment, in just a moment, I'll be standing there with him. And then she felt the warmth of his hand on her arm, and he whispered close to her ear: "Most beautiful lady, welcome."

She didn't dare look at him for fear she might faint. With her head bowed she followed Hannah and Lorenzo across to the others, sat down on the chair that Lorenzo moved out for her, and listened to their animated conversation without understanding a single word of what was being said. To her ears the words sounded like the splash of waves on an autumn day, just before the first storms came. Lorenzo sat at her side, not touching her, but the place on her arm where he had laid his hand a little while ago still felt warm. How can he talk so easily, as if there was nothing going on, thought Jessica to herself, half curiously, half disappointed. Pastries were served, and water, fruit juices, and wine.

Not until Hannah sat down at the cembalo and started to play a lively little tune did Jessica hear his voice again, once more so close by her ear that she could feel his warm breath. "Come as soon as you can. I'll wait outside for you behind the pavilion." She didn't nod her head, she just lowered her eyes to show that she had understood him. She heard the chair next to her being pushed back on the stone floor and when she raised her head cautiously, she saw him walk quickly through the open doors onto the terrace and disappear.

"Would you like another tartlet?" asked Avital Meshullam, Hannah's younger sister, offering Jessica a silver tray with the little pink pastries displayed on a white cloth with blue embroidered edges.

Jessica shook her head and smiled at the girl, who was really no more than a child. "What's that tune that Hannah's playing?" she asked.

"It's a *canzone alla francese*," Avital explained eagerly. "We heard it yesterday at the Doge's concert. Only it was much better. Hannah can't play it very well, even though she's been practicing it all afternoon."

The little girl went away to offer her pink tartlets to other guests, and Jessica stood up. She strolled across to the window and looked down onto the canal, then moved casually toward the door to the terrace. While everyone was applauding and looking at the cembalo, she slipped out. There were two girls sitting on one of the seats on the terrace, their heads close together, whispering. When they saw Jessica, they looked up. She knew one of them—it was Florina, daughter of Isaac Levi, who owned a big business on the Rialto, and who often had dealings with her father. Florina smiled at Jessica. Jessica nodded and walked on as quickly as she could. She was sure that she could feel the girls looking at her as she went, and she did not feel safe until she had gone around the oleander bushes and could see the pavilion.

Lorenzo took her in his arms. "At last," he said, and laid his face on her neck.

"We shouldn't be doing this," said Jessica, and tried to push him away, but he did not let go. For a moment she had a picture of her father's face, his dark eyes barely visible under the heavy lids, his prominent chin with a beard that had now gone gray, and she thought she could hear his voice saying, "Jew haters, Jew haters every one of them, those Christians," and then she gave in and surrendered to Lorenzo's kisses and to the wonderful feeling that she called love because that was what he had called it.

When Jessica went back, she saw as soon as she came around the oleander bushes that Florina and the other girl were no longer sitting on the terrace, but in their place was Messere Adamo, courtier and tutor to the three daughters of Levi Meshullam, the celebrated doctor. Jessica lowered her eyes as the old man looked at her searchingly, and she bobbed a brief curtsy. As always she felt uncomfortable when he looked at her, although she couldn't understand why. Maybe it was because Hannah had once told her that he knew everything and saw everything, and when she was younger she had thought the Everlasting One, blessed be He, was probably a bit like Messere Adamo.

In the salon Hannah came over to her and asked suspiciously, "Where did you go off to for such a long time?"

Jessica gave a start. Had she noticed anything? she wondered. Quickly she waved her hand in a vague gesture toward the garden, and then at the full vases of flowers that were all around. "The flowers," she said in an embarrassed voice, "you have such wonderful flowers, and we aren't allowed to buy any—I mean, not huge bouquets like that."

Hannah looked at her doubtfully, but then her expression cleared and she nodded sympathetically. "I'll give you a bouquet to take home," she promised. "Come on, though, I really have to tell you about yesterday evening."

Hannah was just describing in minute detail the especially dazzling dress worn by one of the especially dazzling ladies when, out of the corner of her eye, Jessica saw Lorenzo come back into the room and walk lightly across to two young noblemen who were standing talking by the window above the canal.

"Did you see the Doge?" asked Jessica quickly, not out of any curiosity but just to cover up her feelings.

Hannah shook her head. "No, we didn't see the Doge. But we did see the Marquesa, the one they say is his latest concubine. Do you know what 'concubine' means?"

Jessica felt herself blushing, but luckily she did not have to answer the question because, at that very moment, a maid came up to them, curtsied, and said, "Messere Shylock's servant is waiting outside, he has come to fetch the signorina Jessica."

Jessica stood up at once. Hannah walked to the door with her and, on the way, picked up a bunch of red and blue flowers from one of the vases, shook the water off the stems, and pressed them into Jessica's arms. "Here, take these."

Jessica embraced her friend and whispered into her ear, "You have to get a message to me the day after tomorrow." And when Hannah didn't answer her right away, she added urgently, "Please!" Before she turned to leave, she raised her head and her eyes met Lorenzo's. He smiled at her across the great wide room, and she lifted the bouquet and held it in front of her face as she hurried out.

Chapter 2

JEHUDA WAS WAITING at the gates. They set off home without a word. This time Jessica did not even try to start a conversation, she was too wrapped up in her own thoughts—thoughts that became more and more oppressive the closer they got to the Ghetto. The belly of the dead cat was even more swollen than in the afternoon, and now its eyes were shimmering like dirty amber in an evening light that was gray touched with pink. It cannot be, thought Jessica. Lorenzo, why did we do it? What happened to us?

As they crossed the Ponte di San Girolamo—the bridge that connected the Ghetto with the city—Jehuda said, "I've got to get back to the master right away, so he doesn't get angry."

"Yes, you go," said Jessica, "go." She forced a smile. "And if he doesn't ask you straight out, you don't have to say where I have been."

He nodded solemnly. She watched him as he went off toward the countinghouse, removing his red hat as he did so. She lifted the flowers—she didn't know what they were called—up to her face and took deep breaths of their sweet scent until she felt dizzy, and then she went on.

A woman called out, "Jessica."

Jessica gave a start. It was Rachel da Costa, the daughter-in-law of the *parness*, the leader of the community council. Rachel was a fat, ugly woman whose face was pockmarked all over. Of all the people to meet, this tattletale, this witch, the one all the girls were frightened of.

The woman stopped in front of her and looked at her questioningly. "That bouquet," she said, "isn't it bigger than the regulations about luxury goods allow?"

Jessica bowed her head humbly and murmured, "I got them from my friend Hannah, the daughter of Levi Meshullam, the doctor."

Rachel da Costa wrinkled her forehead and looked the girl up and down. "Well then," she said after a while, "I'll let it go this time. But don't forget the rules about luxury goods. It isn't proper for a Jewish girl to be running around with such a huge bunch of flowers. Extravagance is all right for them, but not for us."

Jessica nodded and hurried on. Why aren't we allowed to buy flowers like the Christians do? she thought angrily. Why are we only allowed to buy a little bunch of flowers and no sweets and can't even have preserves? Extravagance—yes, she longed for extravagance, for bright colors, for pretty clothes, for flowers, for excess, for all the cakes and pastries that they served in Levi Meshullam's house. All at once she regretted not having taken one of the little pink tartlets that Avital had offered her.

In front of the ritual butcher's house she almost ran headlong into Marta, Amalia's hunchbacked sister.

"Peace be with you, young lady," said Marta, and put her head even more lopsidedly on her bent neck. She had been born deformed, Amalia had told her.

Jessica turned away. She didn't like this gossipy old woman who would be bound to tell everyone how the daughter of the wealthy Shylock was strutting about with a great bouquet of flowers like a real lady. The malicious chatter would reach her father's ears sooner or later, and that would mean that he would give her another one of his endless sermons on morality. She gave a slight shrug because that was going to happen anyway now that Rachel da Costa had seen her. And anyway, it didn't matter because she would have to face a quite different battle—a fight for happiness or misery, for life or death. It really didn't matter what Marta said.

"And peace be with you too," Jessica answered politely, and nodded to Marta. She wanted to move on, but the hunchbacked woman held her by the sleeve.

"What lovely flowers," she said hypocritically, and then she added in an almost conspiratorial tone, "Is there any special reason for the flowers?"

Jessica felt herself blushing. She understood what Marta meant. If anyone ever bought flowers in the Ghetto, it was almost always for a wedding. Jews were allowed to buy as many flowers as they liked for weddings. "Oh, no," she said quickly. "The flowers are a present from my friend Hannah, Levi Meshullam's daughter." She shook herself sharply free of the old woman's grasp. "Excuse me, Marta, I have to get home."

By the secondhand shop next to the Scuola Grande Tedesca, the synagogue built in the Ghetto for the German and Italian Jews—the Ashkenazim—a little group of Christians were haggling with Chaim Luzatto over the price of a table and four chairs that he had piled up outside the shop. Jessica stopped for a minute and listened to them, then she went on. In front of her own door she stepped around some little children who were crawling about on the street while their mother was filling a water bucket from one of the great stone cisterns nearby.

Dalilah, Jessica's foster sister and servant, opened the door for her. "At last," she shouted, "I was at my wits' end. It'll be dark soon. What would your father have said if you hadn't been home in time? Why do you go to Hannah's so often? You know he doesn't like it when you spend all your time with the Sephardim—with those Spanish Jews!"

Jessica pushed past her and pulled the door shut. What Dalilah had said annoyed her, and much more than that, so had her agitated tone of voice. Who did she think she was? What right did she have to worry about things that had nothing to do with her? "Don't talk nonsense," she said impatiently. "Jehuda took me there and brought me back, and Father didn't mind. Here, put the flowers in the blue pottery vase with the curved handles." She pushed the bouquet into Dalilah's hands and let her light-gray *cioppa* slip from her shoulders. Dalilah bent down and picked it up.

Jessica ran up the narrow staircase to the salon. She grabbed hold of her tapestry work, which was lying on the little table by the window that looked out over the Campo, sat down in the chair, and began to embroider. As she did so, she hummed to herself the tune of the *canzone alla francese* that Hannah Meshullam had been playing. But she made the cheerful little melody sound sweet and melancholy. Why do things always become so gloomy the moment I touch them? Father says I have a melancholy temperament. Perhaps it's because I grew up without a mother. A motherless child in the house of a Jewish moneylender. A poor, motherless child in . . . Jessica let her hands drop in her lap and gazed out of the window onto the square, the Campo, which was thronged with people—women fetching water or carrying vegetables or firewood home, men standing around in groups talking, and here and there Christians who had either come to see one of the moneylenders or wanted to buy something from one of the many secondhand dealers. Jessica saw the three Christians she had noticed before. One of the men was carrying the table, the other man had three of the chairs, and the woman was carrying the fourth. Chaim Luzatto would have made a good profit.

"What are you staring out of the window for?" asked Dalilah, who came into the room just at that moment, the vase with the flowers in her hand. "What's the matter? Why are you being so strange? What was it like at Hannah Meshullam's? Did you see that nobleman again—you know, that Lorenzo, the one with the doggy eyes?"

"Stop asking me questions!" shouted Jessica. "You're not my mother and you're not my teacher. It's got nothing to do with you whom I met. None of it has anything to do with you! Leave me alone!" She saw how Dalilah's thin brown face screwed up, saw her right eye roll so that her squint came back. All that showed how hurt she was. Now Dalilah wouldn't talk to her for hours, Jessica knew, and later on, at the evening meal, her eyes would be red from crying. Poor Dalilah, thought Jessica, and by way of making amends she added, "It was nice at Hannah's. You see the bouquet she gave me."

It was always easy to change Dalilah's mood. She smiled and put the flowers on the table, the one they usually ate from on the Sabbath and on the religious festivals. "Come on, you can tell me," she said. "I saw for myself when the Meshullams had the garden party, how that Lorenzo was making eyes at you. And since then you've been going to Hannah's all the time."

Jessica lifted up her embroidery again and turned her face to one side. "He kissed me," she said, and suddenly she noticed that she had pricked the pad of her left index finger with her needle. A little red drop was slowly forming.

Dalilah clapped her hand to her mouth to stop herself from crying out in astonishment. "You mustn't," she said, "he isn't one of our people. You have to forget all that as quickly as you can."

"No," said Jessica, and sucked the drop of blood from her finger. "No, no. You don't understand. He's told me he loves me. He told me I am the most beautiful and the most intelligent girl he knows. He loves me."

"Love!" said Dalilah. "What's love? He's a Christian. He's a Christian and a nobleman who wants a bit of fun with a Jewish girl. How on earth could you let it happen? He'll be laughing about you with his friends right now. A nobleman!"

"But Lorenzo is a fourth son," countered Jessica. "He said himself that he can't expect to get anything from his family. He said that he'd have to marry a rich woman to finance any change in his life."

"There you are, then," exclaimed Dalilah. "All he wants is your money. Everyone in the city knows your father is rich, even if we don't see much of it because he insists on living modestly. For moral reasons, he says—well, all right, he *is* the master, we're his dependants. But never in his life will he give you permission to marry a Christian. Never! He hates Christians because they despise us and they spit at us and they say we crucified their god." She put her arms around Jessica's shoulders from behind and buried her face in Jessica's light-brown hair.

Jessica caught a faint smell of cinnamon and she closed her eyes. Dalilah had always smelled of cinnamon, even when she was a child, all through the years when they had slept in the same bed. After Dalilah had moved out into Amalia's room, it was that smell of cinnamon that Jessica had missed most of all every morning when she woke up.

"Jessica," said Dalilah quietly and imploringly, "Jessica, please stop chasing some crazy dream. You are one of us, a Jewish girl, your place is here in the Ghetto."

Jessica shook Dalilah's arms away and jumped up. "But I don't want to stop!" she shouted. "I want to get out of here! Just look through that window. A row of houses round a big square, that's all, and that's supposed to be all there is to life? I want to have garden parties too. I want flowers. I want to eat as many preserves as I like. I don't want to be scolded all the time by women like Rachel da Costa. I want dances, I want to go to the carnival. Am I not a girl, am I not just as pretty and just as lively as any of the other girls in the city?" She took a step toward Dalilah. "You've told me often enough yourself that I look like one of them. And you're quite right. It's only an accident that I was born a Jew's daughter—a mistake of nature, yes, just like you sometimes get a white mouse in a litter of gray ones. Yes, I was born into a Jewish family, but what if a husband makes me a Christian?"

"The Almighty, blessed be He . . ." whispered Dalilah, horrified. "You mustn't talk like that, Jessica." She threw her arms around Jessica again with a gesture that was so violent that it seemed as if she wanted to hold her here, in the Ghetto, in this house, in the place where she was supposed to be. "Jessica, calm down. You can't. He's not the man for you. A Venetian nobleman without money or property— he's not in love with you, he's only in love with your father's gold!"

Jessica pushed Dalilah away roughly. "Don't touch me!" she hissed. "You don't know anything. You don't under- stand anything. You don't know what love is." And with a sudden nastiness, to hurt Dalilah and to shut her up, she went on, "How could you know about love anyway, with looks like yours . . ."

Dalilah turned away abruptly and pretended to straighten the folds of the curtain. It was made of a soft, velvety material, blue with gold borders—a blue that looked almost silver when the light fell directly on it, like the sea on a hot summer's day, or the night sky when there was a new moon. This curtain was the most beautiful thing she had ever seen. In all the years since the master, in a sudden burst of extravagance, had agreed to let Jessica fit out the salon, Dalilah had never been able to get her fill of looking at this material, and she never came into the room without finding some reason for going up to the window and running her hands over the curtain. But now the blue grew dark before her eyes and the borders blurred and turned into golden snakes that moved threateningly toward her. . . .

Dalilah shook herself, straightened her shoulders, and tensed her arms. Enough of that, said an inner voice, a harsh, hard one that wasn't the voice of anyone she knew. Enough of that. Don't get worked up. You're an ugly Jewish girl, an orphan without any family, without a dowry. No one is ever going to marry you unless—and only if you're very lucky—it's some poor widower with young children. And he won't have you because he loves you, but because he needs a mother for his children. Stop dreaming. Jessica is right. She's right.

With a rapid movement Dalilah pushed her hair back behind her ears. Her face was as stern as ever, as ugly as ever, and her right eye squinted wildly. She went quickly to the door and walked out firmly, to get some comfort from the sound of her own footsteps, comfort in the knowledge that she had a place here in Shylock's house. That's the way it is, she thought. That's the way it is. Yes, yes. She didn't look around when Jessica called out after her, "Dalilah, wait, please wait! Wait, I didn't mean it like that!"

It doesn't make any difference how you meant it, thought Dalilah, all that matters is what the truth is. The Everlasting

One, blessed be He, has ordered the world and put everyone in their proper place. Who am I to question His holy wisdom. . . .

She ran down the stairs, which creaked under her feet, and kept on thinking, yes, yes, that's the way it is, and went into the kitchen. Without a word she grabbed hold of a dirty iron pot, then got some sand and a cloth. She poured some water out of a jug into the pot and started to scour it. After Amalia's long illness last winter it had been her job to take over any work that the old woman could no longer manage. This meant getting water from the stone cistern, scrubbing the tiled floors, scouring the pots, and anything else that Amalia told her to do. Dalilah looked across at Amalia, who was standing by the stove and clearly hadn't noticed her coming in. As soon as she saw the bent back and the almost-white hair, she suddenly became composed again. Her mouth relaxed, her right eye flicked back so that she was no longer squinting.

Dalilah rubbed hard with the cloth and heard the grinding of the sand, and she settled down gradually into a regular, circular movement that calmed her. There was a sharp, irritating haze in the kitchen, smoke that dispersed only very slowly in bad weather like this, and it made her eyes sting until the tears were running down her cheeks. She worked away doggedly, rubbing the cloth over the dirty surface of the pot and thought to herself, yes, that's the way it is, that's the way it is, and that's the way it should be.

Amalia was standing by the stove stirring a large pot. "Red beans," she said suddenly. "We're having red beans with lots of onion, the way the Spanish Jews eat them." So she had noticed Dalilah coming in after all, even though she hadn't turned around. Now she straightened up and wiped the sweat off her face with her arm.

Dalilah nodded. She had her head bent down over the pot she was cleaning, which had porridge burned onto it. That was happening more and more often too, Amalia letting something burn. Life was getting harder in this household, even harder than it had always been. Amalia had gotten old, she didn't talk much now. Mostly she was wrapped up in herself. Perhaps she was thinking that her days in the world were numbered? That was something Dalilah couldn't imagine. Of course she knew that she wouldn't live forever, but the end was such a long way away. Poor Amalia, thought Dalilah. Poor Amalia, poor Dalilah, poor Jessica. And the master was getting more and more bad tempered and greedy. Suddenly the thought came into her head that really she could understand Jessica, very well indeed. This thought shook her so much that the pot slipped from her fingers and hit the floor with a loud crash.

It made Amalia jump.

Chapter 3

SHYLOCK WAS SITTING BENT over his books in his counting-house on the Campo di Ghetto Nuovo. It was that time between afternoon and evening, and even though it was still daylight outside, he had lit a candle, because he had closed up his counter, and the two windows next to the shutter were too small and the bars across them were too close together, so that the gray light that got in was not enough to let you read and write. The candle flickered a little in the draft that came though the holes in the walls. Outside on the Campo the usual afternoon hubbub was gradually dying down, and you could pick out individual voices. From the house next door came the resounding curses of Jacopo di Modena, the baker. He could never control his temper, and you could often hear his loud voice in Shylock's countinghouse. Shylock listened for a moment, but he couldn't make out what Jacopo was getting so annoyed about, and so he lowered his head again.

He looked over his accounts with some satisfaction. There was nothing that could make him a poor man overnight—not even tax increases or some new levy brought in against the Jews. His funds were getting bigger, his wealth was growing. The grace of the Everlasting One, blessed be He, was upon his business, and he wasn't the kind of man who would throw his money out of the window. His nature or his background had made him thrifty—someone who knew the value of money.

But he still wasn't really happy, and deep in his heart was a gnawing but unspecified fear. How could he not be worried? A Jew was never safe from persecutions, from malice, from jealousy and things worse than those. Pope Pius V, may his name be wiped from human memory, had only been in office for two years and had issued a bull prohibiting any more Jewish settlements. Nobody was sure yet whether the Doge would abide by this. Venice was rich, Venice had colonies, and that made the Doge more powerful than the other princes, more powerful and more independent as far as the Pope and the Church were concerned. Nothing was more important to him than healthy and flourishing trade. In spite of that, Shylock had heard a rumor on the Rialto that morning that Jews who had just come to Venice, mostly refugees from the Inquisition in Spain and Portugal, would no longer be given permits to settle, not even here on the far side of the Canale di Cannareggio. These Jews were mostly Marranos—that is, they had been forced to accept baptism—but in spite of that had still had to put up with persecution and humiliation in those western lands. There were a lot of them living in the city itself, and nobody really knew for sure whether they were Christians or Jews. There were others, however, who had returned quite openly to the faith of their fathers and had moved voluntarily into the Ghetto Vecchio, where the Sephardic Jews and the Levantines lived. And more and more were seeking refuge in Venice. The word was that in the last few days three families had been turned away—two had moved on and the third, a Spanish family, they said, was being put up in the Ghetto Vecchio for the time being because one of the children was dangerously ill.

And what about the Jews who had settled in Venice long ago, most of whom had been living in the city or in Mestre for generations? Even they couldn't feel completely safe. The Great Council didn't take much notice of justice and the law. Wasn't it only a few years ago that the lords had simply cancelled the *condotta,* the settlement treaty for Jews, and not renewed it? And in the year 1565, according to their reckoning—that is, the year 5325 from the Creation—they had suddenly, and for no reason, banned Jews from moneylending and from selling secondhand goods, which was a disaster for all the poor dealers. What were they supposed to live on? At that time a number of families had left Venice, and one of them had made it as far as the town of Zefat in Galilee, in the Holy Land, so they had heard later from a traveling merchant. This merchant had been a guest in Shylock's house and had shared in his Sabbath meal. Shylock couldn't help smiling to himself when he thought of the eagerness with which Dalilah had bombarded the stranger with questions about the land of the Patriarchs. Were camels really so big, and did they really have such a tall hump and such a long neck? And were they really white, like the camel you could see in the stone carving on the wall of the Palazzo Mastelli?

It was true that the ban on moneylending and selling second-hand goods had not been in effect very long, but it was not until a full year after that a new *condotta* had come into force, so there had been three years of uncertainty.

Besides, who could guarantee that the lords in the Great Council wouldn't suddenly decide to take away again the permission given to Jews to live and ply their trades in the city? Especially right now, when Venice was having more trouble with the Ottoman Empire. If there was a war, then Shylock knew that the Jews would be the ones to suffer, would have to pay higher taxes and would be exposed to all sorts of random violence. Whenever the Christian lords got involved in a war, never mind who the enemy was, the Jews always found themselves between the two front lines. It was always the same. You attack my Jews, and I'll attack your Jews. May the Everlasting One be merciful to His people and protect them from misfortune. Shylock made a sign to ward off evil and spat over his left shoulder.

Whatever would occur to them next, he thought, these enemies of Israel? One regulation after another, one restriction after another. It was a good thing that Leah hadn't lived to see it all. With everything that happened, that was always his first thought: a good thing that Leah hadn't lived to see it, or: what a pity that Leah hadn't lived to see it. That hadn't changed after all those years. He even thought himself ridiculous because he—a grown man, a man on the threshold of old age—still talked to Leah when he was on his own, just as if she were still alive. It was the only weakness that he allowed himself.

He looked up at the window, at the little square of sky with the grill in front of it. "Leah," he murmured, and in his mind he saw his wife in front of him, not pale and thin as she had been when she died, but healthy, in her prime. "It's a good thing that you didn't live to see all this. Times are hard. These worries are grinding me down."

How beautiful Leah had been, and how like her Jessica was. The same light-brown hair, the same big gray eyes with the long dark lashes, the same thin nose, not too long and not too short, the same full lips over a round, well-formed chin, the same rosy skin, which he had always compared in his head to the color of young pomegranates, even though he didn't really know what young pomegranates actually looked like. For all that, Leah's face had been softer, less *demanding* than Jessica's. More modest, he thought to himself. She had been a poor girl, and if he, Shylock, hadn't been prepared to take her without a dowry, she might never have married at all.

Shylock wiped his eyes. It was a long, long time ago that she had left him, a bare two years after Jessica was born, but for all that there wasn't a day went by when he didn't think of her, when he didn't talk to her. The few years with her had been good ones. Leah had brought happiness into his life, and laughter and color. The years before he had met her were fixed in his memory as having been gloomy and miserable—a pale, washed-out gray color, as if that time had been part of somebody else's life; some stranger whose fate he had just heard people talk about, and for whom he had, after the event, only vague feelings of sympathy and pity. When Leah had come into his life, when he had seen her for the first time, he felt as if he had been born for a second time, had become a new person, a different person. Maybe it was true. The old Shylock, only son of a poor refugee from England and an even poorer Jewish woman from Mestre, had crumbled to dust, and a new man had come into the world, a lion of Judah. A strong man, a happy man, who got up every morning thanking the Lord from the depths of his heart for the great gift of life. Even when things were going badly for the Jews, even then.

Shylock sighed. When were things *not* bad for Jews? A few years before he met Leah, he had taken over his father's little pawnbroking business, a wretched little undertaking with wretched little customers, mostly Christian laborers, artisans, widows, or abandoned wives, who would bring in some pearls, their wedding rings, amulets, candlesticks, a winter coat, sometimes a fur, and would get a few ducats. His father, driven by Jew haters from his home in London because he would not adopt Christianity, had never amounted to very much in the Veneto. Only he, Shylock, the son, had become a man of wealth and respect in the city of Venice, and for that he was thankful to the Everlasting One, blessed be He. And yet this still wasn't the life he had longed for as a young man. However, was it not written that "A man's heart deviseth his way, but the Lord directeth his steps?"

The way that Shylock would have chosen for himself would have been a quite different one. He would have liked most of all to have studied medicine at the University of Padua and become a doctor, which was one of the few professions still open to Jews as well as Christians. But there just wouldn't have been enough money. And when his father died—two years younger than he himself was now—that had decided his future. He still had two unmarried sisters living at home, and he would have to earn enough to provide dowries for them. Then the younger of them, Jessica, had died of a fever before she could stand under the marriage canopy, and Sarah had moved away to Austria with her husband, a not particularly well-off cloth merchant. Shylock hadn't heard from them for years. He rarely thought of his sister Sarah.

Shylock put his head in his hands. Even when he was young, he had had to look after women, first of all his mother and his sisters, then Leah, and now there were three women living in his house again—Jessica, Amalia, and Dalilah. But only Leah had made him really happy. Later on, a few years after Leah's death, there had been a brief time when he had thought that Amalia might be able to take Leah's place, at least as a mother to Jessica. But Amalia, who was older than he was, had been sent a letter of divorce by her husband before he set off for the New World, a letter divorcing her because she was barren and had never given him a child. And he, Shylock, was one of the *Kohanim*, those who were descended from the ancient priests, forbidden by Jewish law to marry a divorced woman.

Shylock pushed these thoughts to the back of his mind. Things were better as they were. No other woman could ever have replaced his Leah, not even Amalia. Nevertheless he was grateful that she had stayed with him to be his housekeeper and to look after the motherless girl. Still, in spite of Amalia, the years after Leah's death were as gray and drab as the years before he had met her. The only brightness that he had left and the only thing that gave his life a little warmth was his and Leah's daughter, Jessica.

He would have to make a match for Jessica. She was long since of marriageable age, and the agitation that seemed to have come over her lately had not escaped his notice. Up to now his jealous love had stopped him from doing his duty as a father and finding a husband for Jessica—his love and the memory of Leah, which overwhelmed him every time he looked at his daughter.

"Leah," he said, "when I go home and I see Jessica, it's often just as if you had been given back to me." He felt a sudden warmth running through him, and, before his eyes, Jessica and Leah merged into the same person, the same woman. He lowered his head in shame. But then he heard Leah's voice: "You have to get that kind of thought out of your head. You must find a match for Jessica, it's urgent." Shylock's hands went cold. "But not right away, Leah, she's still so young. My house will be empty without her, the light will go out of my life. Surely I can wait a little while longer, can't I? Another year, maybe two. She's only sixteen, after all. You were already eighteen when we married." Leah didn't answer, and he knew what she was thinking. It had been different for her. Her father was a poor man and couldn't give her a dowry. "Perhaps you're right, Leah," he said. "I'll go and see Menachem, the marriage broker, as soon as I can."

But when he thought about the older Jewish families living in Venice, there wasn't a single one whose son would be good enough for his Jessica. And none of the Spanish Jews either; none of them were sufficiently well thought of to be worthy of his daughter. He didn't want to give her to an old man who had already made his name and whose law-abiding piety was beyond reproach—no, not his young, beautiful Jessica. Well, Menachem had contacts in all the countries of the world, his connections ran to Jerusalem and Zefat and northward to the cities beyond the Alps, and surely he could find a suitable son-in-law for him. "But not right away, Leah, not right now," said Shylock. Again Leah's answer was silence.

A loud knocking brought Shylock back to himself in his dark countinghouse. From outside came a loud shout: "Hey, Shylock, are you there? Let me in, I've got a business proposal for you. You won't regret it!"

It was a young, confident voice, the speech of an aristocratic young man. A nobleman who needed cash and who expected to be able to get it from Shylock the Jew. No poor petitioner would ever have spoken so loudly and in such demanding tones.

Shylock closed the books that lay open in front of him on his desk, opened a drawer, and put them in. Only then did he get up, stiffly, and go to the door. When he looked out through the grill, he recognized Bassanio, the son of an aristocratic but impoverished family, who spent much of his time with other young nobles on the Rialto.

Shylock pulled back the heavy bolt until it slotted into its ward with a screeching noise, a shrill, ominous sound. He opened the door, but no wider than was necessary to let Bassanio in. "Come in, my lord," he said, and made a slight bow. "What brings you to my poor countinghouse? Surely not this unpleasant weather that lies so heavily upon the spirit and the soul and makes a man quite melancholy?"

Bassanio came in, took off his plumed cap, and laid it on the table, where it looked thoroughly out of place, like some exotic bird in a poor hut, a bird proudly showing off its bright plumage. Shylock would not have been surprised to hear it crow like a cockerel. Bassanio's well-cut green silk coat and yellow breeches seemed to shine.

The young nobleman fell into a chair, breathing deeply. "I need money, Shylock," he said without any ado, without any of the usual polite formulas, without any explanation. "Three thousand ducats. For three months."

Shylock stroked his beard to gain himself a little time and closed his eyes. He disliked money transactions with these noblemen. The aristocracy made chancy customers, they were less reliable than merchants and artisans, where you could gauge the risk easily, and where you knew what was what. On the other hand, it was just as risky for a Jew to refuse a nobleman anything. And so Shylock hesitated a little as he repeated, "Three thousand ducats. That's a lot, a great deal of money. I'm not sure whether I can raise such a large amount of cash."

"Shylock, stop playacting," shouted Bassanio, and brought the palm of his hand down onto the desk. "Everyone in Venice knows how rich you are. I tell you, you won't regret it. I can give you Antonio as guarantor for it."

"Antonio the merchant?" said Shylock slowly, still playing for a little time. "The Antonio whose ships go to the Indies and to England—"

"Yes, yes, that Antonio." Bassanio jumped up impatiently. "He's asked me to bring you to his house so that you can deal with him directly."

"Perhaps it isn't my place to ask," murmured Shylock without looking at Bassanio, "but all the same, I'm surprised that such a wealthy gentleman as Antonio wants to borrow money from a Jew. Antonio of all people, someone who despises me and my people, who spits at us and mocks us and drives us away as if he were kicking a dog to one side. . . . And this Antonio, of all people, wants a favor from me, the hated Jew?"

"No, it certainly *isn't* your place to ask," said Bassanio angrily, "but I'll tell you again, to protect the good name of my friend and patron. *I* am the one who needs the money, and I need it right away, before Antonio's ships come back with the rich cargoes he is expecting and when he could give me the money I need himself. So come on, Shylock, the gondola is waiting for us."

Shylock put his coat on slowly and with some ceremony, took the red hat that he was obliged to wear outside the Ghetto, and locked up his countinghouse. Bassanio walked briskly across the Campo, the plumes on his hat dancing. Shylock followed his green silk back down to the Ponte di San Girolamo. The gondola was waiting by the bridge, with a liveried servant at the oar. Bassanio had already jumped in and held out a hand to help Shylock on board and then to his seat. The gondola cast off. The servant guided the oar with steady movements. Shylock stared at the man's hands, which held firmly on to the ridged upper part of the oar, while the flat, rounded part moved regularly back and forth in the rowlock. The gondola rocked as it passed along the canal, then turned off right into a side canal until it entered the Grand Canal itself.

Shylock sat there, tense and quite unable to admire the beauty of the palazzi. Seagulls were screeching above their heads, and their cries suddenly seemed threatening and fateful. He had never heard the seagulls cry so loudly since the time when they had buried Leah. He had stood there on the quay and watched the funeral gondola until long after it was out of sight. But he had looked and looked and had been aware of nothing but the cries of the seagulls. He pushed the thoughts of Leah abruptly to one side and looked up at the sky and the pink shimmer of the setting sun.

He sat there rigidly on the seat, his knees pressed close together, his arms by his body. Antonio, of all people, wants money from me, he thought; of all people it has to be that Jew hater. But that wasn't the only reason that he was reluctant to do business with him. Antonio was easygoing and had expensive tastes, and his lifestyle was extravagant. Well, yes, he was rich, his ships took Venetian goods to every quarter of the earth and came back laden with treasures. But still he was not a man you could trust. Why, for example, did he not invest his profits in solid securities—in buildings or shops, say—instead of spending them all on his friends and his feasts, so that when he wanted to load his ships to sail again, he had to finance everything with borrowed money? Shylock was afraid of Antonio. Everyone kept saying how friendly and kind he was. Friendly and kind to young Christian men, thought Shylock bitterly.

Antonio has two faces. Which one is he going to show me now? Isn't there a proverb that says: If a man wants something from another man, he will change his face? What sort of face am I going to see?

Bassanio hummed a little tune to himself and beat time on his knees, in their elegant yellow breeches. Shylock knew that beside this young man he must look like an old raven beside a young peacock. If only the seagulls would not scream so loudly.

Chapter 4

IT WAS ALREADY DARK by the time Shylock stood at last in
the open doorway of his own house looking out across the
Campo, but there wasn't a single star in the sky. Only a
blurred and milky spot marked the place where the moon
was hiding behind clouds. A couple of men were standing
over by the Ponte di San Girolamo, but at this distance he
couldn't make out who they were. Perhaps students from
the Yeshivah, from the rabbinical school, still arguing a
point of interpretation in one of the books of the Torah. A
door opened at the house of Joshua da Costa on the other
side of the Campo, and a man came out with an oil lamp. It
was Ephraim de Pomis, the doctor who lived in the Ghetto
Vecchio. Shylock let his glance wander up to the first floor,
where Sarah da Costa, the old *parness*'s crippled wife, sat
every day. I hope she isn't worse, thought Shylock, although
her death might be a relief, both for her and for her family.

Shylock waited. He had sent Dalilah into the Ghetto Vecchio to ask his old friend Tubal Benevisti to call in and see
him. Just at that moment they came around the corner. In
the darkness, Dalilah looked even smaller and thinner than
usual, gliding along beside Tubal almost like a shadow. Shy-

lock smiled. Gratefully he noticed that the cry of the gulls, which had been ringing in his ears ever since his gondola trip with Bassanio and had continued to echo in his head when he got back to his countinghouse and even on his way home, faded away as soon as he saw Tubal; the strange trembling in his hands stopped as well. And even his feet felt suddenly far less cold.

Tubal was a tall lean man, and like many tall men he had long since affected a slight stoop, as if he was trying not to draw attention to himself. He had to duck his head to get through the low doorway. As he did so, he touched the *mezuza,* the little box with the Deuteronomy passages fixed onto the right-hand doorpost, and brought his fingertips up to his lips. Only then did he take off his hat and place it on the long chest next to the place where the cloaks were hanging. The silver decoration on the blue skullcap he wore underneath it shone in the light of the oil lamp as he turned round. He laid a friendly hand on Shylock's shoulder and greeted him. Dalilah took off the heavy woollen blanket she had placed round her shoulders as a kind of cloak and folded it up.

"Dalilah, bring a bottle of wine and goblets up to the salon," said Shylock. "My friend will be thirsty. And get some bread, some cheese, some olives, and some garlic as well. Oh, and Dalilah, take care not to wake Amalia. She was very tired, and she has already gone to bed."

Dalilah nodded and disappeared obediently into the kitchen, and Shylock turned to his friend. "Thank you for coming," he said, picking up the lamp and leading the way up the stairs. "Jessica," he called, "where are you, my daughter? We have an honored guest!"

Jessica came out of her room. When she saw who the guest was, she was delighted and exclaimed, "Uncle Tubal, how lovely to see you! I haven't seen you for months. How was your journey? I hope it wasn't too exhausting."

Tubal stroked Jessica's cheek. "No, no, my child, no more exhausting than any other trip across the Alps. But I'm happy to be back in our beautiful Venice. The northern countries may be rich, and some of their merchants are quite civilized men, but it's always a bit miserable for the likes of us—we miss the sun and the blue skies and the salty smell of the sea. But let me have a look at you, my child." He stepped back a pace. "You get to look more and more like your mother," he said with a broad smile. "I think that we can at last say that you are not a child anymore! It's time your father started to look for a suitable bridegroom for you."

Jessica blushed. If only he knew, she thought, and lowered her eyes. Oh, Uncle Tubal, if only I could tell you. Tears pricked against the inside of her eyelids. Tubal put his arm around her shoulder and looked at his friend. "She is just as beautiful as Leah—may her memory be a blessing for us both—was when she was young."

Shylock knew that this was true, and he had thought it often enough himself, but he never liked to hear other people speak Leah's name because it always felt like a kind of desecration. It was as if some stranger were fingering his memories, uninvited, and leaving greasy marks on them. He even felt that way when it was Tubal Benevisti, who had, after all, been Leah's cousin, since his mother and her mother had been sisters.

To cover up his private confusion, and not to upset Tubal with an awkward silence, Shylock quickly said, "Thank you for coming, Tubal, you are a most welcome guest. My house is your house—come, sit down, my friend."

There were sounds of footsteps outside on the stairs, and Jessica ran over to the door and opened it. Dalilah brought in a tray with a bottle of wine and the glasses, a plate with bread, salt, cheese, olives, and garlic, and a water bowl, so that the two men could wash their hands before they spoke the benediction over the wine. She put the tray down on the table.

"Thank you, Dalilah, you may go to bed," said Shylock. "I shan't need you anymore. Jessica can serve us."

Dalilah left the room. Jessica waited until she heard Dalilah's footsteps stop at the bottom of the stairs, and the door of the room that Dalilah shared with Amalia shut. While the two men dipped their fingers into the water and then dried them with the white cloth that had also been put on the tray, Jessica went over to the table and poured the wine, first for her father and then for Tubal Benevisti. This was something unusual. Normally her father only drank the prescribed glass of wine on the Sabbath and on holidays, so that he could say the *kiddush,* the prayer to start the holy day.

Shylock raised his glass and spoke the benediction: ". . . *borei peri hagafen,*" thanking the Lord, the King of all the World, who gave man the fruit of the vine.

Tubal took his glass and he too said the blessing. And then he added, "May the Everlasting One grant us many more occasions to sit together like this. L'*chaim!*" He pointed to the chair next to his and said, "Come, Jessica my child, come and sit by me." He looked over at Shylock. "Or is whatever you want to discuss with me not for the ears of a beautiful young girl?"

"Jessica is my daughter," said Shylock abruptly. "I'd like her to stay here. I want her to hear from my own mouth what will reach her ears as gossip before too long anyway." He drank some of the wine and felt how the fluid ran down his throat and spread its warmth through his whole body. "Listen," he began, "to what happened to me today."

Then he described in detail the visit from Bassanio and then the trip to see Antonio, and he didn't hide from them how uncomfortable the young nobleman, the extravagant Antonio, and the whole business had made him feel.

"Three thousand ducats," exclaimed Tubal in amazement. "That's a great deal of money."

Shylock nodded. "That's another reason I sent for you," he said. "I can't raise a sum like that in such a short time. You must help me, my friend. Three thousand ducats, with Antonio standing as guarantor."

Tubal Benevisti moved his head from side to side as he thought. "He's a wealthy merchant," he said, a little hesitantly, "but all his money is tied up in his ships and his trade with Tripoli and with India. He is even supposed to have one ship on the way to Mexico. And another to Hamburg, loaded with the most expensive silks, or so I heard. But all the same—"

Shylock interrupted him. "I know what you mean. A ship can be wrecked, even two, three, or four ships can be wrecked, can go down with all hands and with a full hold, however costly that cargo might be. Or they can fall into the hands of pirates, and there are enough of those scoundrels on the high seas. I raised the very same objections."

Tubal nodded and ran his hand over his well-trimmed beard as his clear gray eyes, eyes that were as beautiful as Jessica's, stared into the distance. He was thinking. Shylock waited patiently. "For all that, Antonio is a man whose bond you can accept," said Tubal eventually. "At least, it would be difficult to turn him down. I think in any case that the risk is a small one. Antonio is one of the most respected patricians in the city."

"A Jew hater," said Shylock bitterly. "Many a time he has cursed me and mocked me. Usurers and unbelieving dogs, that's what he calls us Jews, just because we make a living by lending money for interest. Only last week he said that he himself never takes interest from loans, and when he said that, he looked right at me and spat. And it's true. He has already given that wastrel Bassanio, whom he seems to love like a son, a lot of money, and now he plans to give him even more, though I don't understand why he wants to. And without asking for interest, of course."

"Well," put in Tubal, "you don't take interest from me any more than I do from you. We only take it from strangers. After all, it is written that 'Thou shalt not lend upon usury to thy brother; usury of money, usury of victuals, usury of any thing that is lent upon usury; unto a stranger thou mayest lend upon usury; but unto thy brother thou shalt not lend upon usury; that the Lord thy God may bless thee in all that thou settest thy hand to do . . .'"

Jessica was trying hard to hide her agitation and to present a calm face, as if she were indifferent to what her father was saying, even though what he was saying could not be a matter of indifference to her. She knew Bassanio, he was Lorenzo's best friend and another regular guest at Levi Meshullam's house. She had seen Antonio too, a slightly portly gentleman, no longer in the first flush of youth and always surrounded by a circle of young aristocrats. What is going to happen? she thought despairingly, what is going to happen! With an enormous effort she forced herself to speak. "But, Father," she said, "we all live in the same city, and neither Bassanio nor Antonio are really strangers."

"All Christians are strangers," interrupted Shylock. "And especially all the Jew haters. Shouldn't we be allowed to earn our bread like other people? It's easy for Antonio to talk, he lives off his trade, he doesn't depend on earning interest and so he can lend money to his friends without making any demands. It's different for us. It isn't just that we are barred from other work that could make us a living—no, the *condotta,* the settlement treaty, actually demands that we should be bankers and moneylenders, and it is only because of that that we are given permission to stay in Venice. So we have to make sure that our money increases; it has to grow and bear fruit so that we can live our lives and feed our families. The *condotta* lays down a maximum of twelve percent interest on any bond, and there's talk about lowering it to five percent. How are we supposed to live on that?"

A malicious smile crossed his lips.

"I put Antonio to shame," he went on, with open scorn in his voice. "I showed him that a Jew can lend money without demanding interest, and I sealed a special bond with him. I refused to take his ships as a guarantee, I told him they were too shaky. So he agreed to a pound of his own flesh as a pledge."

Tubal jumped up. "What are you saying? May the Eternal One preserve us and keep us from misfortune. Did some demon possess you that you could make such an arrangement?"

Jessica had turned pale. She stood up quickly and went across to the window. Her shadow was long and narrow and danced against the wall until it was swallowed up by the dark curtain. She pretended to arrange the folds, pulled the curtain aside a little and looked out over the empty Campo. No one must see how agitated she was. The moon came out from behind a cloud and made the water cisterns gleam whitely. Two figures were moving on the bridge over to the Ghetto Vecchio. Only when she felt that she had control of her features again did Jessica close the curtain.

She heard Tubal breathing heavily, and she was aware of an undertone of uncertainty in her father's voice when he spoke again.

"Let me tell you how it came about. I didn't want to accept the commission at all, not with Antonio, but you know how it is—a Jew can't simply turn down a nobleman when he wants something. And so I said that I couldn't take his ships as a pledge, and I put up every argument I could think of against money and goods that had been entrusted to the uncertain seas. Antonio listened to my objections disdainfully, and then he said that the word of a merchant of Venice ought to be good enough for a Jew. I wriggled a bit and pointed out how quickly a serious word can be turned into a mere joke. Tubal, believe me, I didn't ask for it. Only then, that man Bassanio said that many people pledge a pound of their own flesh if they want to show how serious a bond is."

"Yes, I've heard it before as well," broke in Tubal, "but not between Christians and Jews. They don't make that kind of bond."

Shylock nodded. "I said that too. But Antonio insisted on pledging a pound of his flesh as a bond. I think he simply couldn't accept that a Jew wouldn't lend him money on his name alone. And as far as I was concerned, I couldn't refuse again without openly insulting him, so I had to agree. The only way I could shame him was by insisting on lending him the money interest free, and that's what I did. I had to bring him down a peg or two, that fine gentleman who has pushed me aside into the mud time and time again, who crosses himself if he chances to meet me in the Rialto, and spits at me when I am going about my business. Now I shall own a pound of his flesh if he doesn't pay his debts by the appointed time, and it can be cut from any part of his body I choose."

"You shouldn't have done it," said Tubal, "never mind how difficult the situation was. I'm not comfortable with that kind of a bond. Money against some security of equal value, that's how our business works, and that's how it should be. A pound of flesh as security—it's a devilish idea."

Jessica went back to her place, took the wine flask and filled the glasses for the two men. Her hands were shaking and a few drops spilled.

"Devilish," repeated Shylock angrily. "Devilish, you say. And what about the Christians? Do they treat us like human beings? No, they curse us as dogs and as the spawn of hell. And if a demon lends money, then why shouldn't he set devilish conditions?" He took another gulp of his wine. "I am a Jew," he said. "Has a Jew not eyes? Has a Jew not hands, organs, senses, affections, passions? Is a Jew not subject to the same diseases, healed by the same means? If they prick us, do we not bleed? If they poison us, do we not die?" He had lifted up his hands and spoke with his eyes closed. Jessica stared at him. The prophets in the Bible must have looked just like that. Threatening and full of foreboding. Suddenly she felt a fierce love for her father, but the image of Lorenzo came to her at once and pushed her father to one side.

Shylock was silent and took another mouthful of wine. When he spoke again, his voice sounded calmer, almost exhausted. "I heard about a religious tract that is supposed to have appeared in Venice, an anti-Jewish piece of writing called *De Judaeis et aliis infidelibus*. They say it's by a man called Maquard de Susannis."

"Yes, that's true," said Tubal. "I've already read the thing."

Jessica turned to him. "What does the title mean?" she asked. "And what is it about?" She had to clear her throat before she could get the words out, and even then her voice sounded strange in her own ears.

"The book is called *On Jews and Other Unbelievers*," said Tubal. "This man Maquard de Susannis puts up the argument that being a Jew is a crime against God, a crime that has to be punished. Jessica, my child, don't take your father's anger amiss. They have humiliated him too often."

"Yes," cried out Shylock, "yes, and yes again. The Everlasting One is my witness. How often can you let yourself be spat at without wanting to defend yourself? And there's something else, have you forgotten the 'Jew race' that Antonio demanded I should take part in? An insult to every honorable Jew."

In the Venice Carnival the Christian lords forced Jews, often the especially fat ones, to run a race against one another, half naked, while the spectators laughed and catcalled and occasionally helped the miserable objects of their game on their way by hitting them with sticks. It was a shameful, humiliating performance.

Tubal put his hand on Shylock's arm. "I can understand you, my friend," he said, "but if you didn't want to get involved, why didn't you just say that you couldn't raise that much money?"

Shylock gave a short laugh. "Was I supposed to pretend to that wretched merchant that I am a poor man?"

"It was your own vanity that led you to make that bond," said Tubal.

Shylock spoke sharply. "You needn't worry, Tubal my friend. Antonio will never owe me anything," he said. "Antonio is a rich man with rich friends. And besides, what would I do with a pound of Christian flesh? What use would that be to me? It would be less use than a pound of beef or a pound of goose. But you will have to help me, Tubal. You must let me have a thousand ducats by tomorrow. I can only get two thousand together."

Tubal nodded. "You can have the money tomorrow," he said. "I'll bring it to you in the countinghouse at around midday. I am not very happy about being involved in this matter, but I won't leave you in the lurch. But still, with everything that happens I have to think about all Jews. You know as well as I do how they set on our people in other cities, how they stone Jews and turn them out of their houses, and worse."

The oil lamp flickered. Smoke drifted across the light. Jessica stood up and put in a little more oil. She was confused and could think of nothing but what Lorenzo would say about this business. She felt her eyes fill with tears again. "It's the smoke from the flame," she said, embarrassed, and wiped her eyes. "And I'm tired, Father. I would like to go to bed now."

Shylock nodded absently.

"Off you go, child," said Tubal. "Go and pray to the Lord that we all come of out this unscathed."

It was a long time before Jessica fell asleep that night. She lay in her bed, tossed from side to side, and thought about Lorenzo. At their last meeting he had urged her, not for the first time, to speak to her father so that he would agree to their marriage. Jessica turned over again and shook her head. Marriage was impossible. Lorenzo imagined it was all so simple, but she couldn't just speak to her father about it. He would never agree to let her become the wife of a Christian. When she had cautiously tried to explain that to Lorenzo, he had waved her objections aside. "Then you will just have to run away with me," he had said. "If you go away with me in secret, then your father will have no choice, and he will have to give us his blessing and the dowry that a rich man's daughter should bring with her. Once we are married, he'll have to make the best of it. Anyway, he ought to be proud to be getting a Venetian nobleman as a son-in-law."

Proud? thought Jessica. No, he certainly wouldn't be proud. He would presumably give me nothing, and mourn for me as if I were dead. That's what the Torah scribe Simone di Modena did when his daughter Judith ran away from the Ghetto to marry a Christian. If my mother were still alive, maybe she would understand, thought Jessica. But Father? He was a hard, miserly man, he would never give way. And she could forget all about the kind of rich dowry that Lorenzo needed. And now there was this bond with Antonio. With a pound of his flesh as security. He was a wicked old pawnbroker, her father, the kind of man a daughter could only be ashamed of.

If only I had been born as the child of Christians, thought Jessica. Or at least as Uncle Tubal's daughter. Everyone respected him, and he didn't just look more distinguished than her father, he really was more distinguished in every way. What a splendid *zimarra* he had been wearing this evening, that full, well-cut coat with the broad sleeves. Or as Levi Meshullam's daughter. His daughters didn't have to live in the Ghetto, and they enjoyed privileges that other Jewish girls could only dream of. They had lessons from the court tutor, Adamo, and from Aaron ben Avram, and they could speak Arabic, Hebrew, and Spanish fluently. Levi Meshullam was a Sephardic Jew, and the laws that applied to him were different from those for Ashkenazi Jews like her father. He was on good terms with much of the Venetian nobility, and he made no objections if his daughters were friendly with Christians. How good life was in his palazzo, thought Jessica. Oh, if only I'd been born in another house, with a different father. One who loved me and wanted me to be happy.

She pulled the covers up over her head and cried herself to sleep.

Chapter 5

Dalilah . . .

I HATE PLUCKING CHICKENS. I feel sick when I see that pale stubbly skin, never mind the bluey-green eyes that carry on staring at me through those closed transparent eyelids. And those half-open beaks with the dead tongue hanging out! No other animal ever seems to me to be as dead as a dead chicken. I don't have any problems with fish, for example, even though they are slippery and cold, colder than chickens—or at least, they feel as if they are. I can scale and gut fish and it doesn't turn my stomach, and I even prefer the stink of fish to this repulsive sweetish smell. It prickles in my nose and makes my throat tighten.

Two chickens for a good healthy soup, that's what Amalia said, and she sent Jehuda to Israel Yarach the butcher. Not too big and not too small, she said, they've got to be round and plump. And make sure you have a good look at their bellies. White soft down feathers mean that the chickens are not too old. And the feet, Jehuda, the feet! The rings have to be light and yellowish. If they are too dark, then the bird is an old one. And tell Israel Yarach they are for Shylock, and he shouldn't even think about trying to pass off old birds on to him just because I'm not well and can't keep an eye on things.

Jehuda had to go to the vegetable seller near the Scuola Levantina, the synagogue for eastern Jews in the Ghetto Vecchio, because Amalia is sure that the sellers there have better vegetables than ours do, and above all else they have more herbs. He brought back the fresh vegetables—leeks, celery, carrots, and onions—that Amalia told him to get. So that the soup is a really good one, just like the master is used to, that's what Amalia said. And at the end she shouted after him not to forget the marjoram!

Really it ought to be Jessica cooking the soup, she's the mistress of the house, I'm only responsible for helping with the housework. When she puts the food in front of the master tonight, it's a certainty that she will act as if she had cooked it herself. Anyway, she won't contradict him when he praises her for making such a good soup. Only Jessica isn't even at home. She put on her beautiful blue dress, then her light-gray *cioppa,* and got Jehuda to take her to Hannah Meshullam's, and that's the second time this week!

It isn't as if she doesn't know perfectly well that the master wouldn't like it. We Ashkenazim should keep to our own, that's what he always says. We should keep to ourselves, and the Sephardim should keep to themselves, that's how it ought to be. Their ways are not the same as ours. But Jessica has lots of friends among the Sephardic girls. They are richer than the Ashkenazim, and they have more freedom, even when they live in the Ghetto Vecchio. I suppose that's because the Sephardim come under the jurisdiction of the

Cinque savi alla mercanzia, and they get treated as merchants first and Jews second; the *cattaveri,* the officials who control us, are a lot stricter.

May the Everlasting One, blessed be He, make sure that Jessica doesn't meet that Lorenzo at Hannah Meshullam's house. He's got her completely confused. He kissed her! I only have to think about it, and it makes me feel funny. A disaster! It simply must not happen! Not Jessica! Not us! I shall have to speak to her. I absolutely must ask her if she has forgotten Judith, the daughter of the Torah scribe Simone di Modena. Three years ago she ran away from the Ghetto and married one of them, a carpenter who lived near the Great Arsenal. Her father rent his garments and sat *shivah,* went through the ritual mourning exactly as if she had died. Even now he walks around the Ghetto with his eyes downcast. I'll tell Jessica that. And Judith's mother still keeps apart from the other women in the synagogue and doesn't talk to them. Think of the shame, I'll say to her. And they haven't found husbands for Judith's two sisters yet either, even though they've been marriageable for ages. I'll tell her that too. Even Shlomo, the only son, only has Sofia Yarach, the butcher's daughter, for a wife, and he's a Bible student at the Yeshiva and might have expected something better. The whole family is paying for Judith's wrongdoing. What will become of them? What will become of us? May the Everlasting One, blessed be He, preserve our house from sin and shame and put Jessica's crazy ideas out of her head. She's usually so clever, and she's such a know-all when she's talking about other people! I simply can't understand why she has this tremendous blind spot when it comes to that Lorenzo. One of them. A Christian! May the Everlasting One have mercy on us. How are we going to avoid the threat of a disaster like that, and can it be avoided at all?

I suppose that really I ought to tell the master what Jessica said. But I shan't do that; never. Jessica means too much to me. I love her, we grew up together, we were like sisters, and I can't just forget all that. You don't betray your own sister. If only I knew what was the right thing to do, and what I could do to get her thinking straight again. Is that what love is? Does love make you so stupid?

The downy feathers are flying into the bucket like snowflakes. I'll collect them so that Amalia can use them in her eiderdown. She gets so cold these days. She's been in bed with a fever again for two days. At night when I get into bed beside her, the warmth is quite welcome, but then it gets unbearable. Last night I had to get up at around midnight and make myself a bed on the floor with blankets and pieces of clothing so that I didn't disturb her. Because every time our legs touched, her hot ones and my cold ones, it made her shudder. And it was unpleasant for me too. I hope Amalia gets better soon.

I think she suspects that there is something going on with Jessica, but she won't say anything to her. She loves Jessica like a daughter—I suppose because she didn't have any children of her own. In spite of that, Jessica can be quite impossible, not only to me, but to Amalia as well. You never know where you are with her these days. Sometimes she is bitter and arrogant, the next moment she's kind and effusive. And when she's like that, she'll put her arms around

Amalia and kiss her, and she's even nice to me and will say something to make me laugh. But at other times she hardly takes any notice of me, and when she does say something, it's only to give me some order or other. If she has had a bad day, I can't do anything right, however hard I try. I'm either too slow, or I don't pay attention, or I've forgotten to do something she asked me to—I'm not combing her hair properly and so on, or I'm just stupid and clumsy. Like the other day, when she snapped at me for not finding her fan, and all the time she had left it at Rachel's, the daughter of Ezra ben Shoshan. And afterward she never even said she was sorry.

It is really difficult to get out the hard feathers on the back and on the wings, it makes my fingers hurt. Well, I'll just do them one at a time, even if it does take longer. Amalia is much better at it than I am—she can pull out a great handful at one go. Maybe I'll get the knack of it eventually.

I'm sure that it's all the fault of that Lorenzo! Since that garden party at Levi Meshullam's, Jessica has changed; she's getting more and more difficult, more and more arrogant, more and more unpredictable. I used to know what she was thinking, but not anymore. Mind you, she's more beautiful than ever. She is so beautiful that my heart aches every time I look at her, and I wish we could go back to the days when we were sisters, friends. If only we could have stayed children for ever and ever!

When I am lying next to Amalia at night, I often think of the long talks I used to have with Jessica. Especially since Amalia fell ill. And when she is lying there groaning, that's when I long for Jessica. It was such fun when we used to lie in bed and tickle one another and laugh and laugh until our sides hurt.

I curse the day when she turned twelve, and her father said that I had to be her maidservant! It will be your job to serve her and keep a sharp lookout that no harm comes to her, that's what he said. And I've tried for all those years to watch over her. But how can you watch over a bird that is ready to leave the nest and fly away? How do you watch over a cat when it wants to roam? How am I supposed to protect her from a good-looking peacock like Lorenzo if she's set on falling in love? It's the master's own fault, he ought to find her a husband. Why doesn't he? It's his duty as a father, after all.

But the master is a hard one to understand. He often gives her jewelry, and, then, when she dresses up, he complains and preaches at her. Like the day when Hannah Meshullam gave her that bunch of flowers. Rachel da Costa went to see him and opened that great mouth of hers. I just don't understand how a good and decent man like Joshua da Costa got himself a daughter-in-law like that. She's really mean and malicious, and after her little visit, the master was furious with Jessica. He went on and on in a really loud voice about modesty and restraint. We mustn't draw attention to ourselves, he said, we mustn't attract envy and resentment.

And there is already a new storm brewing at home, because yesterday Jessica said to me: Dalilah, go to Shimon ibn Lazar and tell him not to skimp on the material for the sleeves of my dress, nor with the gold clasps on the front and the wrists. And ask him whether he got the gold braid for the bodice.

What does she want a dress with gold braid on the bodice and gold clasps for? Her father will be really angry when he sees it. If she wears the dress when she goes to the synagogue at Rosh Hashanah, he'll make her wear a shawl over it so that no one can see the gold. I'm absolutely certain it'll be against the dress rules of the *provveditori alle pompe*.

Amalia and I get new dresses for the New Year festival as well, and my old one is getting too small for me. Pick out some material, Jessica said to me when we went to Shimon ibn Lazar. I chose a simple green wool. Dark green, like wet moss just after the rain. With red clasps and red sleevelets. I wonder if Jehuda will even notice that I'm wearing a new dress.

The feathers keep snapping off so that little bits of quill stay in the skin like stubble. I'll have to singe them off afterward. What I'd really like to do is to drop everything and just wander off across the Campo. Only I've got to get on with it. I've still got the worst bit to come. Amalia asked me again before I started if I really know how to do everything. Of course I do. Cut the plucked chicken's belly open and draw the giblets, making sure that the gallbladder doesn't get damaged and spill the bile out onto the meat and make it bitter. Then cut the head off and get it ready for salting by chopping it once across and once lengthwise with a kitchen knife, taking out the brain and the skin around it, because that's what it says in the dietary laws. First the one chicken, then the other one. It's already making me feel sick just to think about it.

I hope Amalia will get better soon. What a pity she fell ill again. She stays in bed and hardly eats a thing, just a few bits of *challa*, of soft white bread, when I've soaked them in camomile tea for her, and occasionally a drop of the soup that Marta brings her. I don't like Marta. It's hard to believe that they are sisters. Amalia is friendly and kind, and Marta is nasty and unpleasant. Maybe it's all because she's a hunchback. Maybe it's easier for good-looking people to be nice. Yesterday Marta started to go on about Jessica again, about her being vain and arrogant. But Amalia didn't let her carry on. She made out that she wanted to sleep. But she wasn't asleep, I could see that. As soon as Marta had left the room, Amalia opened her eyes again and asked me to get her a drink of water with some lemon in it. That's what Ephraim de Pomis, the doctor, prescribed for her last winter, when she was so ill that the master called him in. I look in on her as often as I can, but I haven't got time to sit by her bedside for very long because I have to do all her work too. And I can barely manage it, even though Jehuda helps me as much as he can.

He's been living with us since last winter. Actually, he was already working for the master as an errand boy before that, but he used to live with his father, the shoemaker Jacopo Romano. Jehuda got the room between ours and the kitchen. I wouldn't want to sleep there, it's a room without any windows. Before Jehuda moved in, the master used it to store things that people had pawned, pledges he'd brought from the countinghouse. And we had the chest in there too, with all the special Passover dishes and cutlery. We had to carry it all up to the attic and make up a bed for Jehuda. He still runs errands for the master and does other jobs for him as well. And he has to help us too. For instance, he has to go with Jessica whenever she leaves the Ghetto. I wonder if he always tells the master where she's been. I shouldn't think so. He doesn't say much, and he's been especially quiet lately. I'm sure he wouldn't volunteer anything if the master doesn't ask him directly.

Jehuda is a nice looking lad, really still a boy. He only had his barmitzvah two years ago. He's not much taller than Jessica, and he's got brown eyes and brown curly hair. He's all brown, his skin is brown as an autumn leaf. It's only his lips that are red. Fancy a boy having such red lips . . . Dalilah, stop thinking that way, you're a sensible girl, a good servant, and a proper maid to your mistress Jessica, even if you *would* rather still be her friend like you were in the old days. . . .

We used to be together from morning till night. I'd have been happier playing on the Campo with the other children, but Jessica always wanted to wander around the city and see something different. Of course we always did what Jessica wanted. She used to like the palazzi, those lovely houses with all the statues, although we are really not supposed to look at them. Amalia always says that it is written: "Thou shalt not make any graven image or any likeness of any thing." Look away, bow your head, walk past quickly. Besides, naked women are naked women, even when they are supposed to be angels or something.

Jessica never looked away. I did. The only one I never looked away from was my lion, the lion on the Doge's palace, the lion of Judah. The lion is so handsome, so strong, and so positive. He's standing there with one forepaw resting on a book and the Doge is kneeling in front of him. I can't remember when I first saw the lion. I often think it must have been in a dream because the first time I stood there in front of him with Jessica, I was sure that I already knew him. Whenever I'm depressed, I find it a comfort to think about the lion. Back when I was little, I used to imagine him taking me on his back and flying over the sea to the land of our forefathers. The land flowing with milk and honey. He is the savior, who else could be?

At last I've finished plucking the chickens. Now for the next part. I've got to get the board that we use for meat, put them on it, and with one blow of the chopping knife cut off the head of one of the chickens and then the other. It's horrible, the way they keep staring at me through those dead, transparent eyelids! I go cold and the skin on my arms goes goose-pimply. It almost looks like the plucked chicken skin. But my arms are warm and brown and alive. And now the headless chickens have to go over the flames. The pale skin gets sooty patches where the remnants of quill that I couldn't pull out start to burn. They stink. Even when I turn my head to one side I can't get away from the stench. It probably stinks like that in hell.

Now it's time to cut open the first of the chickens. It's soft and pliable and it's hard to get the knife in. Now the belly of the bird is open, and I can see the dark entrails and the yellow globules of fat with the transparent skin around them, and I want to be sick. The inside of a chicken looks horrible. And the guts stink. There's the gallbladder. Cut it away carefully, watch out. Good, I managed it. And now the liver, the kidneys, and the spleen. With the spleen you have to take the skin off and remove the veins before you put it in water. Tonight, when the master comes home, I'll slice the liver into thin slices and cook it over a flame, the way the Law says, and serve it to him with chopped onions before the rest of the meal, just like Amalia always does.

At last I've got the second bird done as well. The worst is over now, and the next bit is child's play. I just have to get the chickens ready for eating. Yes, Amalia, I know, you've told me often enough. Put them into one of the pans that can be used for meat and cover them with water. Take care to clean the insides of the birds, where the blood is, really well, as prescribed by the Law. After half an hour I shall take them out of the water and salt them. You have to rub salt onto all surfaces of the meat and make sure that there are no parts left unsalted, that's what Amalia drummed into me. That's why poultry has to be opened up really wide, so that you can salt the insides properly. It's written in the Law.

As if I didn't know that already! Haven't I watched Amalia often enough when she was making sure poultry was kosher? And when the chickens have been in the salt for an hour, you have to rinse them three times, Amalia said. Don't be sparing with the water, in case, may the Lord forbid, you go against the Laws regarding blood.

I just nodded and inside I prayed to the Everlasting One, blessed be He, to make Amalia well again soon so that she can pluck and draw the next chickens herself and make them kosher. Life is hard without Amalia and the kitchen is cold and forbidding when she isn't there. I miss her. I feel alone and abandoned, even though she is lying in the room facing the Campo and there is only Jehuda's room between hers and the kitchen. I don't know what I would do without her. She doesn't talk a lot, but she's a good soul and she has a kind heart. There were plenty of times when she's put her arms around me and kissed me, or comforted me when the master or Jessica were cross with me. I love her. And besides, I shall be grateful to her for ever and ever.

You see, it was Amalia who persuaded the master to take me into his house when my mother died. I can't really remember, I wasn't even four years old at the time, but Amalia's sister Marta never tires of reminding me of my debt of gratitude, three times a year at least—at Rosh Hashanah, at Yom Kippur, and at Passover. Even when Amalia gets cross with her and says that nobody should take pride in their good deeds, otherwise they are worthless and no more than just vanity. Acts of charity like that, *mitzvoth*, are supposed to be done secretly and not in public.

While the chickens are in the water and then being salted, I'll wash and chop the vegetables for the soup and clean the kitchen. I don't need to fetch water or wood, Jehuda has done that already without even being asked. He's really very helpful. And he has such lovely eyes!

I hope Jessica comes back soon. And I hope the soup turns out well.

And I hope Amalia soon gets well again.

Chapter 6

THAT DAY SHYLOCK LEFT his countinghouse earlier than usual, a good hour before the sun disappeared behind Joshua da Costa's house. Nothing more than a mild pearly haze on the clear blue sky gave any indication that sunset was approaching.

Shylock pushed the heavy key into the lock, just as he did every day, and turned it twice. The door was reinforced with iron, and the lock had been made specially by a locksmith from Padua, the best in the whole of the Veneto. Even so, Shylock took home each night any especially valuable item that he had accepted as a pledge so that he could store it in the attic. They would be safer if they were close by him, or at least, that is what he thought, because he slept too lightly for anyone to be able to break into his house unnoticed under cover of night. Besides, the door to his house was also reinforced with iron and made secure with a particularly good lock.

And today, as he bolted the door of his countinghouse, there stood on the ground beside him a long and broad wooden chest, with ironwork on the corners and iron handles on the narrow ends. A spice dealer from the Rialto, who had had dealings with him before, had pawned it during the day for a considerable sum of money. In the chest were two heavy silver candlesticks and a valuable Chinese porcelain vase, well packed in linen cloths.

Shylock had naturally inquired whether the candlesticks were religious objects or not because, if they were, he would not have been able to take them. The regulations, which the *cattaveri*, the controllers, enforced with such strict attention, laid down that Jews were not allowed to accept items of religious significance, nor could they take books from students. "No, no," the spice dealer had assured him. "They are household effects, just like the vase. You should have heard my wife complaining when I packed the things up! I shan't have a minute's peace at home, she'll go on crying and calling me all kinds of things until the candelabras and the vase are back where they belong. I'll redeem it all in a month, Shylock, by the time the man who owes me money gets back from his travels." And if he doesn't redeem them, said Shylock to himself, then in a year's time I'll be able to sell them on the Rialto for a good profit.

Shylock took the key out of the lock and put it carefully into the brown leather purse that he wore next to his body on a belt underneath his outer garment. "Right," he said to Jehuda, "we are ready."

I'm glad I took the lad on formally, he thought to himself. I'm getting too old to cart heavy chests and things like that around, my back isn't as strong as it used to be. Jehuda is helpful, he's got young bones and fresh blood in his veins, even if I do have to admit that he is a bit small and slight for his age. Shylock suppressed a smile. If the boy had been stronger, then Jacopo Romano the shoemaker wouldn't have given him to me, he thought. He'd have hired his son out as a porter or as a helper in the market, so as to bring in more money. Chaim Luzatto the secondhand dealer and Ephraim dalle Torre the wood merchant had both been looking for a strong young apprentice for ages.

The boy crouched, picked up the chest by one of its handles, and heaved it onto his left shoulder. Shylock bent down and helped him to stand up. Slowly they walked across the Campo, which at this time of the day was still busy and crowded. A lot of people greeted Shylock. He responded with a restrained nod or with a few words, depending upon the person. Whenever he stopped, Jehuda stopped too. Suddenly it struck Shylock that he never walked straight across the Campo, but always chose the path along by the houses. For a moment he wondered why that should be, but then he greeted Simone di Modena, the Torah scribe, who was standing in front of his house, and forgot all about it. Some women were sitting in the last rays of the afternoon sun by the Ponte di San Girolamo, knitting. Shylock gave them a brief glance and imagined for a moment that Leah was amongst them, since she often used to sit knitting with other women on the Campo. But then this idea was gone too, and he thought about what he would have to do that evening.

Around midday a messenger had come from Joshua da Costa, who was the *parness*, the community leader of the Ashkenazi Jews, to ask him to come that same evening to the Scuola Spagnola in the Ghetto Vecchio, the official seat of the Jewish community council and of the administration for the Ghetto. There was to be a *kehal gadol*, a meeting of the great community council to which all Jews belonged if they paid more than twelve ducats a year in taxes to the Venetian senate. The *kehal gadol* was rarely called, usually only twice a year, when they elected the lesser council, the *va'ad katan,* and that wasn't due until next year, just before Passover.

Shylock wondered what could have happened. The last *condotta* agreement had been signed two years ago, so that new rates and taxes were really not likely. It must be something unusual, because the everyday workings of the Ghetto administration were handled by the lesser council, and the *kahal gadol* didn't concern itself with things like that. The messenger, a young Sephardic Jew from the Ghetto Vecchio whom he had never met before, had not been able to give him any more information and had simply been told to pass on the summons. Without noticing that he was doing it, Shylock shook his head from side to side, as people do when they are beset with doubts and forebodings. Well, he would find out. Immediately after evening prayers he would set off for the Scuola Spagnola.

He was so deep in thoughts of his own that he gave a sudden start when Jehuda, walking beside him, tripped over something. Horrified, Shylock grabbed the chest and had a vision of the Chinese vase broken to pieces before his eyes. But things did not turn out quite as badly as that. Jehuda did indeed fall forward, but he kept a firm grip on the handle of the chest, which only slipped onto his back and was protected by his body from crashing into anything hard. The boy groaned. Now Shylock noticed what it was that had caused him to trip. On the paving stones lay a dead pigeon. Simone da Costa, who happened to walk past at that moment, picked it up, went to the canal, and threw it into the water.

Shylock bent down, lifted the chest off Jehuda's back, and placed it carefully onto the street. "You clumsy oaf!" he shouted, his hands still trembling from the shock. "You could easily have smashed that expensive vase! Haven't you got eyes in your head?"

Jehuda was nearly weeping. "I'm sorry, master. It won't happen again." He tried to stand up, staggered, and put his hand to his right knee.

Shylock held out his hand and helped him up. He felt an unfamiliar surge of emotion. "Come on, we'll carry the chest between us," he said gruffly.

The boy tried to object and went to heave the chest onto his back again, but Shylock would not let him. And so they went on, carrying the chest between them. The boy was limping and breathing with short, hard gasps, but he never uttered a word of complaint. Shylock gave him a sidelong glance. Jehuda's handsome brown face was twisted, his full and remarkably red lips pressed hard together. You could see that he was in pain but was trying bravely to stop himself from crying out. He really was so young! Shylock had a sudden surge of sympathy for this slender lad who had been condemned by fate to a life of labor. "It's not your fault that you are not strong enough for heavy burdens," he said in a tone that was far friendlier than usual. "You are too young, and I'm too old. It's the way of the world."

Shylock was surprised by his own sudden gentleness. Why am I sorry for this boy? he thought. He's fifteen; that's more than old enough to work. I had to work as well when I was his age. Mind you, I was already a lot stronger, at least if my memory doesn't deceive me. But Jehuda is obedient and helpful, and that's more than you can expect from most lads nowadays.

Two women came toward them, one of them Rachel da Costa, the daughter-in-law of Joshua, the *parness*. She returned Shylock's greeting with a sour expression on her face. She was clearly still annoyed that he had been cool and dismissive toward her when she came to him to talk about his daughter. Because she was so fat, she had to squeeze against the wall of the house to let Shylock and Jehuda, carrying the chest, get past.

At last they reached their door and could put their burden down. Shylock grasped the iron knocker and banged it hard against the door. Behind the door they could hear footsteps. Jessica opened the door for them. Shylock kissed the *mezuza* as he crossed over the threshold, and Jehuda did the same.

"Good evening, Jessica, my child," said Shylock, and then he turned to Jehuda. "Take the chest up to the attic," he told him, and as Jehuda obediently bent down, Shylock said, "Wait!" He walked quickly over to the kitchen, pulled open the door, and said to Dalilah, "Go and help the lad, he can't manage it on his own."

Dalilah wiped the sweat from her forehead, put down the soup ladle, and ran over to the staircase. Jehuda twisted his lips into a wry smile. Dalilah took hold of one of the handles of the chest, Jehuda the other. They went up the stairs carefully, Dalilah in front and then Jehuda, taking one step at a time. "Be careful," Shylock shouted after them, though he could see for himself that he didn't need to tell them. Of course not. Dalilah was reliable and minded what she was doing.

Shylock took off his hat and straightened his skullcap. "Jessica, the *parness* has called me to a meeting of the *kahal gadol* this evening. Brush my Sabbath coat and get my good shoes ready. But first of all bring me some water so that I can wash."

Jessica carried a bucket of water up the stairs to her father's bedroom, the windowless chamber between the salon, which looked out over the Campo, and her own room, the window of which faced the canal. She lit the oil lamp, then she brought a jug of hot water from the kitchen. Shylock sat down on a low stool and took off his shoes. "Leave me now," he said, and Jessica took the black coat that her father wore on the Sabbath from its hook and went out of the room.

At that moment Dalilah and Jehuda came down the stairs from the attic. Dalilah's face was red and unusually heated. Jessica gave her an inquiring look. She likes Jehuda, she thought, and suppressed a smile, though he's just a lad, a little boy. Suddenly she pictured Lorenzo, who had gone to visit relatives in Padua and would not be back for a week. At once she felt such a violent longing that tears came to her eyes. She quickly hid her face in her father's coat and went down the stairs behind Dalilah and Jehuda, who was still limping.

In the kitchen she took the soft brush that was kept in a box for this purpose and set about giving her father's coat a thorough brushing. It was made of simple woolen cloth, black and without any decoration at all; the elbows were already getting shiny and the cuffs of the sleeves a little frayed. Her father had ordered a new coat for Rosh Hashanah. Bound to be black and boring again, thought Jessica. Why doesn't he have a properly cut *zimarra* made, with wide sleeves, like the one Uncle Tubal wears? He goes around like a starving beggar, even though he is so rich. She brushed furiously at the worn patches on the sleeves. When he talks about modesty, he means miserliness, she thought. I don't care how miserly he is when it's to do with himself. But what about me? And in her mind she said to him what she had so often wanted to say: I want something different from what you want. I want beauty, splendor, a bit of happiness. If only she dared to say it to his face. I'll do it, she thought to herself. One day I'll do it. I don't want to spend my entire life being humble and modest.

Meanwhile, Dalilah was running back and forth, pouring hot water into a dish and tearing a strip from a clean white cloth. She told Jehuda to come and sit on a chair, and she knelt in front of him on the floor. "You've torn open your knee," she said without looking at him. "The cloth and the knee itself. Take your stocking off so that I can clean the wound."

Jehuda did what he was told and gasped with pain as Dalilah dabbed carefully with the cloth to clean the dirt from his bloody knee. Jessica, who had gone across to the window with the coat over her arm, glanced at her. "Why don't you get Amalia's ointment?" she suggested.

Dalilah lifted her head and smiled at her. "Yes, you're right, good idea." She jumped up and went over to Amalia's room.

The old woman was lying on the bed with her eyes shut and her hands resting on the coverlet in front of her. A soft light fell on her face through the window grill. Dalilah was pleased to see that her face, now that the fever had passed, did not look as red and puffy as it had in the past few days. Her cheeks were pale, with a soft pink sheen. Dalilah took a couple of steps toward the bed and ran her hand across the sick woman's forehead. No, she wasn't hot anymore. And her face wasn't that unhealthy red color anymore that meant she was feverish, but it had the gentle color of a ripening apple. Amalia opened her eyes and smiled. She really did seem to be better. Dalilah asked for the ointment to put on Jehuda's knee.

"Over in the cabinet," said Amalia. Her voice too sounded firmer and less quavery than it had yesterday. She raised her hand and pointed across to the cabinet, which was immediately beneath the window. "But don't forget that you have to clean the dirt from the wound first."

Dalilah suddenly felt so relieved and happy that she took the old woman's hand and kissed the wrinkled skin with the brown liver spots. "I've already done that," she said, and turned away to hide her embarrassment.

"What is Jessica doing?" asked Amalia.

"She's cleaning the master's Sabbath coat," answered Dalilah. "He's been summoned to the *kahal gadol*."

"May the Everlasting One have mercy on us," said Amalia. "That can't be good news. Ask Jessica to come and see me for a little while later on so she can read me a few Psalms. And the blessing for recovery after a serious illness. I want to thank the Everlasting One, blessed be He, for His goodness to me."

Dalilah nodded. When she reached the door and turned to have another look at Amalia, she had closed her eyes again and her breathing was even and regular.

But Amalia was not asleep. She was preoccupied with her own thoughts. She was so tired, so exhausted, and she was afraid. Ever since she had been so ill last winter, she had been quite unable to shake off this fear. She noticed with every passing day how old she had become, not just by her failing strength, but by the way her mind returned constantly to the past, and by the gradual deadening of her emotions. She had long since ceased to weep over the fact that she was barren. The pain had gone, and so had the memory of her husband, Leone, the way she had waited with longing every month, and the regular and recurrent misery and disappointment. When Leone had divorced her, she had thought she would die.

Until she met Shylock. Of course he could not marry her, and she had never thought he would, but he had given her the child she wanted—Jessica. What a scrap of wretchedness she had been at the beginning and what a beautiful happy girl she had become, especially after Dalilah came into the house. Amalia had to smile as the image of the two girls came into her mind. They used to wander off into the city so often, and afterward they would tell her all the amazing things that they had seen. Jessica had become more beautiful year by year. She had accepted the admiration that everyone had for her in a happy and carefree way. Nobody could ignore her beauty. Amalia sighed. Jessica probably thought that her appearance was the most important thing of all, and that was her mistake, so much emphasis on something external. The Everlasting One, blessed be He, had given her this gift of beauty, thought Amalia. But there was a danger in it for the soul. It should have been our task to develop in her an inner beauty. Instead of that, we made her vain.

Chapter 7

SHYLOCK HAD PERFORMED THE ritual washing and had said his evening prayers, and now he went down into the kitchen. He was worried about what would happen that evening, and at the same time he felt unusually agitated. He wasn't one of those who came together regularly on the Campo or in a tavern to make big speeches, drink wine, or play games of chance. He kept himself to himself and only met other people on the short way from home to his countinghouse and back, or when he went to the Ashkenazi synagogue, the Scuola Grande Tedesca, in the mornings, on the Sabbath and on the holy days. And even there he was more inclined to keep his distance, and, when the services were finished, at most he might exchange a few words with a business associate or listen to the complaints of members of the various benevolent societies, who usually wanted him to give a donation for the sick, for widows and orphans, to pay for a circumcision, or for the wedding of a poor girl. When people talked to him, it was almost always about money, and he was used to that. But meeting with other Jews on an ordinary weekday, that was something unusual, and the idea filled him with a vague sense of disquiet.

In the kitchen his coat was hanging over a chair, and his boots were next to it. Jehuda sat on a low stool by the stove, his right knee bandaged. Shylock smiled at him and sat down at the table. "Bring me some bread, some salt fish, some cheese and tomatoes," he said to Jessica. "That will be enough for me." He never ate much, he was just as modest and moderate as far as food was concerned, and today he was even less hungry than usual.

Jessica put out a knife and a platter from the set used for milk products, setting them in front of him on the table and placing a drinking cup and water jug next to them, while Dalilah brought the bread, the fish, the cheese, and two tomatoes from the pantry beneath the staircase. Shylock broke off a piece of the bread and said the blessing, the *ha-motzi*, thanking the King of the Universe who brings forth bread from the earth.

When he had had enough to eat, Shylock stood up, put on his coat and also his red hat, even though he was only going from one Ghetto to another, and left the house. Though not before he had impressed upon Jessica that she should bolt all the doors after him and close all the shutters, and to wait up for him so that she could let him in when he got back.

He set off toward the Ponte degli Agudi, the bridge linking the Ghetto Nuovo with the Ghetto Vecchio. Gradually his worries gave way to a kind of pleasure. Of course he would be seeing Tubal Benevisti, who was also a member of the *kahal gadol*. Shylock walked at a steady pace, keeping apart from the other men, who were moving in small groups across the Campo toward the Ponte degli Agudi. He looked up and saw the moon in the sky. It was only a thin waning sickle, and soon they would be saying the prayers for the new moon in the synagogue.

The gateway on the bridge was open. The way from the Ghetto Nuovo to the Ghetto Vecchio was usually open during the night, and it was only the gateways at each end of the Ponte di San Girolamo that were closed two hours after sunset and not opened again until an hour before sunrise. On the Christian side of that bridge were Venetian watchmen—paid by the Jews—who made sure that nobody entered or left the Ghetto without permission. The Christians bolted the outer doorway, the Jews the inner one. Protection and prison, thought Shylock to himself as he stopped on the middle of the bridge between the Ghettos and looked down at the Rio degli Agudi. The reflection of the moon was shattered into bright splinters on the black water. There was a smell of rotting fish. That might mean that there will be more rain, in spite of the clear skies and the summery weather of the past few days. But maybe it was just some fisherman who had caused the stink by tipping his rubbish in the canal here on his way home.

Shylock walked on. The closer he got to the Scuola Spagnola, the more apprehensive he began to feel again. It couldn't be good news if the *kahal gadol* was summoned; it was never a good sign. What could they have thought up now, these Christians, to torment him and his fellow Jews?

When he reached the building, he paused for a moment and looked up. Only the windows, which began on the first floor and reached up over two levels, gave any indication that this was a synagogue. And no stranger would have been able to guess by looking at the outside of the building how magnificently it was decorated inside. That too was according to the rules. The *condotta* treaty permitted the Jews to practice their religion, but their religious buildings were not allowed to be recognizable as such. And so all the synagogues were on upper floors, even the prayer hall in the Scuola Grande Tedesca.

Shylock went in through the decorated archway into the great hall, which was used for the teaching and study of the Holy Scriptures, except on occasions like this when there was an assembly.

The room was crowded with men. Shylock looked around. There were Jews in the long garments of the Ottoman world, while others, like himself, wore clothes that were appropriate to Italy, usually a coat not unlike the Italian *zimarra*. Outside the Ghetto only their red hats made them recognizable as Jews, as the *condotta* required. He soon picked out Tubal Benevisti, who was taller than most and who kept himself, as was his way, a little apart from the rest. Shylock pushed his way through the crowd until he was standing by him. "Peace be with you," he said.

Tubal raised his head and nodded to him. "And with you, Shylock my friend."

A door now opened at the back of the room and the *parneyssim* came in. Of these seven councillors, three were Ashkenazim, three were Marrano Jews from Spain and Portugal, and one was from the Levant. Slowly the room quieted down, but only when it was completely silent did Joshua da

Costa, the oldest Ashkenazi *parness,* a dignified old man with white hair and a white beard, raise his arm as a sign that he was going to speak.

"My brothers," he began, "peace be upon each one of you, and may all who enter this house be blessed." The other *parneyssim* nodded in agreement. "We have called you together," Joshua da Costa went on, "because a rumor has reached us, and we do not yet know if there is any truth in it. But because of its importance, and because it might possibly have bad consequences, we decided to warn you all."

The old man's voice sounded quavery. He spoke quietly, but for all that there was no problem in understanding him, such was the silence that dominated the room, as if every single person were holding his breath. Joshua da Costa swayed a little, and two men—his sons—jumped up from the body of the audience and supported him, one on each side. The old man moved his head from side to side as if trying to shake off an unpleasant vision, but then he got a grip on himself. His voice trembled a little at first, but then it got firmer and firmer as he went on. "Most of you will remember that day in our city fifteen years ago when our enemies, may the Everlasting One punish them, burned our holy books—"

"Yes," shouted out a man in the front row and took a step forward. Shylock recognized him—it was Meir Parenzo, the printer. "Nearly all the books that Daniel Bomberg had printed were thrown into the flames. Especially the Talmud with the Mishna commentaries of our great teacher Bertorino, of blessed memory."

There was a general murmur of agreement. Joshua da Costa raised his arm and there was silence once more. "My brothers, a Jew who does not wish to be named, but who has some connection with an influential Christian, has let us know that there may be another burning of the Talmud. We ask you to hide the holy books if you possibly can. Take them from the synagogues and the schools and from your houses, and put them in as safe a place as possible so that they don't fall into the hands of our enemies. This is all we have to say to you."

"But why?" called out one of the Marrano Jews, recognizable as such by the Spanish clothes he was wearing. "The new *condotta* guaranteed our right of settlement and protection for our community. Are they looking for more taxes and tributes? Where are we to get the money from?"

"It doesn't seem to be a matter of money," said Ezra ben Shoshan, the *parness* of the Levantine Jews, in a calm and cultured voice. How well he has learned our language, thought Shylock. You would hardly know that he doesn't come from Venice. He was remarkably tall and looked impressive and imposing in his dark-red robe and turban.

"What else could it be about?" asked Chaim, the brother of Meir Parenzo, the printer. "Don't we keep to all their regulations? For the past four years, since the Catholic Church set up their Index of prohibited books, haven't we stopped printing the Talmud under its holy name and only put the word 'Gemara' on it? Do we not go along with all their demands? What else do they want from us?"

Now Tubal Benevisti stepped forward. He cleared his throat before he began to speak in his beautifully modulated voice. "Brothers," he said, "my brothers, on my recent travels I heard time and again that certain Christians suspect us of making common cause with the Ottoman Empire, the enemy of Venice, and they even accuse us of spying for the Turks. A letter is supposed to have turned up, written in Hebrew characters, about a plot against the Serenissima, the Venetian Republic itself. I took it all as rumor, one of those malicious tales that our enemies are forever putting about, may the Eternal One punish them for it. But this might be the reason that they want to get at us again."

"We heard about this letter too," said Ezra ben Shoshan, "some months ago. But we thought that it was no longer an issue, since we hadn't heard any more about it."

A Jew with flaming red hair and a red beard raised his hand. "Do they need a reason to persecute us? My brothers, since when do they need a reason for mocking us and dragging our beliefs through the mud? Take me as living proof of what I am saying. You all know me, and you know that I have only been able to walk with crutches since the massacre in Psing, a little town beyond the Alps. I was a boy, my parents—blessed be their memory—were amongst the thirty Jews martyred in the flames. Believe me, the murderers, may the Almighty strike their names from the book of history, had no special reason for the atrocity—the Jews were honest, God-fearing people. The evildoers did it simply for fun."

The speaker was Aaron ben Avram, the cripple. From the waist up he was a broad, strong figure of a man, but his legs were short, thin, and damaged. He wasn't rich, and certainly didn't pay twelve ducats in taxes. The *parneyssim* had presumably invited him because he was an educated and learned man who taught Hebrew language and grammar in the school for Ashkenazi boys. A rabbi who was standing next to him, Rav Shlomo Meldola, laid a comforting hand on his arm.

Joshua da Costa lifted his hands once more. "My brothers, go home and do as we have told you. May the Everlasting One, blessed be He, protect you all. Let the words we have said from time immemorial at the feast of the Passover become reality: 'From generation unto generation have they risen up against us and would destroy us, but the Everlasting One, blessed be He, has delivered us from their hands.'"

With that, he allowed his sons to help him out of the room. The other *parneyssim* followed, except for Ezra ben Shoshan. He called a couple of the other Levantines over to him, and they had a brief discussion before they left the building together. Shylock knew that the Levantines had a secret room built into their synagogue, where, if they knew about a raid, they could hide the Torah rolls, the candelabras, and other religious objects. They were almost certainly going there now to put the books into a safe place.

"Come, Shylock," said Tubal. They left the Scuola Spagnola side by side and walked slowly down the straight street that led to the bridge. In front of them and behind them were other Jews, walking with their heads bent and their shoulders drooping. Only two young men were talking in loud voices and waving their arms about in angry gestures. Shylock knew one of them. It was Ephraim, the son-in-law of Levi del Banco. He and the other young man turned off down the little lane that led to the tavern.

"Have you had any word about Antonio?" asked Tubal suddenly. "I've heard that one of his ships has gone down, somewhere off England they say, in the Channel, where there have been a lot of shipwrecks before."

"Yes, I'd heard that too," said Shylock. "I'm not worried about it, though. Antonio has several ships. If that had been his only one . . ." He stopped without finishing the sentence.

"Forgive me, my friend," said Tubal carefully. "It's just that I still think you shouldn't have made that bond with him. You shouldn't have set that pound of flesh as a pledge."

"He wanted it that way," said Shylock quickly, in an irritated voice. "And Christians do sometimes pledge an ear or a finger."

Tubal nodded. "Yes, I know. They are allowed to, we aren't. If a Christian hurts another Christian, then one of them is to blame. But if a Jew—may the Almighty preserve us against such a thing ever happening—should hurt a Christian, then all Jews are to blame, and all of them have to pay for it. I'm not saying that this is just, but that's the way things are."

Shylock was silent. He found this conversation difficult. Tubal, who had seen that his friend was feeling threatened, kept any other fears and warnings strictly to himself.

They stopped at the corner of the street in which Tubal Benevisti lived. Shylock pulled Tubal into a doorway. "Down in the foundations of my house I've got a secret hiding place," he said softly. "When I had some changes made to the house four years ago, I got a reliable stonemason to cut it out for me. You know that I'm not a learned man, and I don't own very many books. I could hide your most important ones for you. Now, tonight." Shylock said no more. He did not know himself whether he had made the offer out of kindness to his friend or just to divert the conversation from what they had been talking about before.

Tubal seemed not to notice Shylock's confusion. He put his arm around the other's shoulder and said, "Thank you. That is more than I would have dared to hope. How many books can you take?"

"Ten, maybe, or twelve," answered Shylock. "The hiding place isn't very big, but it's safe."

Tubal and Shylock looked at each other. Then they turned into the dark lane, moving more quickly now and walking past other men who were also on their way home, and soon reached the house where Tubal had his lodging on the first floor. Without a word to each other they crept up the stairs on tiptoe, as silently as they could. Tubal opened the door for Shylock and let him go in before him.

An oil lamp lit up the living room, which also served as a study. Cases full of books lined the walls. Shylock felt, as he always did, great respect when he saw the leather- and parchment-bound volumes. Tubal is a learned man. He knows more than I do, thought Shylock. He has read the Greek and Latin philosophers and astronomers. He isn't only familiar with Jewish scholarship, but with all kinds of other areas.

"My hiding place is very small, only about five feet long, two-and-a-half feet high, and four feet deep," said Shylock as his eyes wandered along the spines of the books. There was real regret in his voice. "And of course, it isn't entirely empty."

Tubal smiled. "One counts for all. You do a service to all of humanity if you save one man, and in the same way you save all words when you save one single word."

He went across to a washing bowl that stood on a chest by the table and poured water over his hands from a jug, first over his right, and then over his left hand, and then dried them on a white towel. Shylock did the same. The open veneration of the word displayed by his friend touched him.

Tubal opened one bookcase, took out a book, and laid it on the table. "Look," he said, "that is the Talmud that Meir Parenzo was talking about at the assembly. It was printed here in Venice by Daniel Bomberg. It has the Mishna commentaries by Bertorino—that's our teacher, Rabbi Obadiah of Bertorino. He adapted the works of the great scholar and teacher Rashi, and with the help of these commentaries he put the Mishna, the oral traditions, into a language everyone could understand. May his name live for evermore; he has been of service to Israel."

Shylock ran his fingertips reverently over the pages. Tubal laid other books on the table. "The Mishna," he said, "and here are five more commentaries in manuscript, all priceless. This book is the Talmud edition that Meir Parenzo himself printed. And this one is the *Masoret ha-Masoret,* the *Tradition of Tradition,* also printed here in Venice, and this is the *Sefer ha-Bakhur,* the *Book of Election,* on the problems of the phonology and morphology of the sacred language. Both of these are by the great Elias Levita, from whom a good number of Catholic priests and scholars learned the sacred language. This one is the *Shulkhan Arukh,* the code of laws and customs drawn up by our great scholar Joseph Karo, who is still teaching in Zefat. The book was printed three years ago by Alvise Bragadin under the supervision of Meir Parenzo. As long as the Jews survive, this book will keep its value, and as long as just one Jew is left living, this will still be one of the most important works of the Jewish faith."

Eventually there were fifteen books on the table. "Those are the most important," said Tubal, running his hand softly over the books, as gently as if he were touching a baby. "Do you think we can carry them?"

Shylock nodded. "It's only paper, parchment, and leather," he said. "The holy letters are as light as the souls that float up to heaven. Have you got two large cloths that we can wrap them in?"

Tubal brought out two large embroidered pieces of cloth. Carefully they placed one book on top of another, one pack with seven and the other with eight, and tied the corners of the cloths at the top so that they could be used to carry them. They held the ends of the cloth with both hands, shouldered the books, and left the house. There was nobody to be seen in the lane now, and only from the nearby tavern could they hear loud talking and laughter.

Shylock walked lightly, easily, and felt almost as if he were dancing. He noticed that Tubal was smiling too, and that he was walking in a different way. It must be something to do with the books, thought Shylock; they aren't heavy at all—no, quite the reverse. It's as if they were lifting me up a handsbreadth above the flagstones. I'm almost dancing. He gave a quiet chuckle, laughing in a way he hadn't laughed for a long, long time, and Tubal joined in with the laughter. "Whatever mischief they are planning, those enemies of ours," he called out quietly, "they won't get hold of these books."

It was already nearly midnight when they reached Shylock's house. No lights were showing, and it was dark on the Campo. Shylock gave a gentle knock at the door, and it was opened at once. Jessica had waited, just as he had told her to. She was amazed to see her father and Tubal Benevisti push through the door in such a lively mood, like two boys who had just been playing a practical joke.

"You can help us, my daughter," said Shylock softly. "But mind that you don't make any noise and wake the others. Take the lamp and come with us to the pantry."

Jessica did as she was told without a word and went with the two men, carrying the burning oil lamp, to the pantry under the stairs, which could only be reached from the kitchen.

"Close the door properly," said Shylock. "Nobody must know anything about what we are doing here." His cheerfulness had disappeared, and, glancing quickly to the side, he saw that Tubal's face had become serious again.

Very carefully indeed he put the cloth with the books in it down on the ground. Tubal Benevisti did the same. Then the two men pushed to one side a large flour container. Shylock bent down, and, taking a small chisel, he levered up several of the floor tiles. Below them was a trapdoor that Jessica had not known existed. Shylock lifted it up, and there before them was a rectangular hollow space. Jessica managed to stop herself exclaiming out loud. So this was the hiding place where her father kept gold and jewelry and other valuables. In the pale light of the lamp she could make out quite clearly the outlines of several boxes and jewel cases.

Shylock stepped down into the hole and moved the boxes and cases around until he had made space for one of the bundles of books. To get the contents of the second bundle in, Shylock had to climb out. Kneeling down, he placed the books carefully, almost tenderly, in two piles, side by side, and then covered them with the other embroidered cloth. Jessica stood with the lamp held up and watched him, holding her breath. She didn't dare ask any questions—the seriousness of the two men made that impossible.

"Wait a moment," said Shylock. He took the light and went out of the pantry. Jessica and Tubal stood in the dark. Tubal put his arm around her shoulder, gentle and comforting. They waited in silence until Shylock came back and placed several more books into the hole, underneath the embroidered cloth. Jessica recognized the Makhsor, the festival prayer book for Yom Kippur that her father had received from his father, and her own prayer book, which had been her mother's, and which he had given her with great ceremony when she was twelve years old. Then Shylock closed the trapdoor over the hiding place, put the tiles back into position, and, with Tubal's help, lifted the flour container back to where it had stood before, dusting his hands on his coat when he had finished.

"Jessica," he said, "you must never mention this hiding place to anyone. You must promise me that."

"I am your daughter," said Jessica, and because she was so agitated, she said it with greater vehemence than she had intended.

"Swear by Him who lives forever!"

Tubal laid a reassuring hand on his arm. "No, Shylock, don't say that," he begged him. "It is written: 'Let not thy mouth become accustomed to oaths.'"

Jessica had turned pale.

Shylock looked at her for a long time, inquiringly, and it seemed to her, with a little suspicion. In the light of the lamp she could see the two deep furrows that ran from the side of his nose down to the corners of his mouth, as if they had been carved in wood, and his eyes were dark hollows. "Very well," he said, "then go to bed, child. I shall let Tubal out."

Jessica put the lamp down in the hallway once more, lit a candle, and went up to her room. The candle flame flickered wildly and threw long shadows on the wall.

As she undressed, she thought: Now I know where he keeps his money. I'm sure there is more than enough there for my dowry.

She shuddered and blew out the candle. In the darkness a tremor ran up her back as if a sudden cold wind had blown through the house. It was midnight, the hour for ghosts and demons. Jessica got into bed as quickly as she could and pulled the covers over her head.

Chapter 8

Dalilah . . .

REALLY IT OUGHT TO be raining. Really there ought to be thunder and lightning to strike down the wrongdoers. Really . . . Only the skies are bright blue, and the sun is shining. And here am I, a Jewish girl from the Ghetto, dressed as a boy, on my way to the Piazza San Marco with Jessica and Jehuda.

My head is buzzing and I don't know what to think. I keep remembering what happened this morning. I can see it all before my eyes. They came at first light, the officers of the senate and of the *Esecutori contro la bestemmia,* the blasphemy commission. The master was still in his room, saying his morning prayers when they hammered on the door. Jehuda opened it. They pushed him aside, seven or eight men, and began to search the house, one room after another.

Jessica and I fled out of the kitchen into Amalia's room. She asked me to give her the big light-gray shawl from one of the drawers, the one she usually only has on for the festivals, and she sat up in bed and put the shawl over her head and shoulders. Jessica and I had draped our cloaks over our nightclothes. Jessica was crying, but Amalia wasn't in the least bit disturbed; in fact, she was amazingly calm. She held Jessica's hand and kept saying: Keep calm, my little dove, keep calm. Our lives are in the hands of the one who destroyed Pharaoh's armies and saved our houses.

Then they came into our room too. Jessica hid her head under Amalia's shawl, but I watched them as they opened the clothes chest and pulled out all the contents. I saw with my own eyes the way they trampled on Amalia's clean linen with their great muddy boots, how they held up her caps and underwear and laughed. They tore open all the drawers of the cabinet as well, pulled out everything in them, and threw it all on the floor.

When they held up the prayer book, the one bound in red velvet, Amalia let out a quiet gasp of despair, though she tried to suppress it, but one of the men heard her anyway. Shut your mouth, Jew, he shouted at her, and put the prayer book into a sack that one of the others held out to him. But they didn't take the silver candlesticks on top of the cabinet, the ones Amalia always lights to welcome in the Sabbath and which she has had ever since she was married.

Later Jehuda told us that they forced their way into the master's room as well. He was standing there in his fringed prayer shawl and phylacteries, the prayer strap around his left arm and the *shel-rosh* tied around his head. He refused to let himself be distracted by the intruders and just continued saying his morning prayers. The men took away his prayer books. Jehuda said that there were only two of them, though, and that he didn't know what had happened to the rest of them. Especially he didn't know what could have happened to the Makhsor for Yom Kippur, the one bound in parchment that the master always handles with such reverence.

When they had gone at last, the master refused to eat anything, even though Tisha b'Ov isn't until next week, the day when we fast and mourn in memory of the destruction of Jerusalem and the Holy Temple. Jessica asked him if he hadn't made a mistake with the day, but he just gave her an angry look and left the house. When Jehuda went to go with him, he sent him back and said he didn't need him today and that he was to stay with us.

Amalia sent Jehuda out into the Campo to find out what had happened and whether our house was the only one that the men had broken into. Then she told me and Jessica to tidy up. She sat upright in bed and spoke in such a firm and confident voice that we should not have dreamed of arguing. And so we folded up the clothes, unless they were too dirty and had to be put into the washtub, and we put all the drawers back. Then we went up to the master's room and put everything back in its proper place. There wasn't a single book left in the room, nor in the salon, which they had turned upside down as well. Even in Jessica's room everything had been flung onto the floor.

Not until after we had finished did Jehuda finally get back. He told us that they had searched every house in the ghettos, here and in the Ghetto Vecchio, and everywhere they had taken away the holy books. Before they came into the Ghetto, they had been to the printing houses and confiscated the Hebrew books, so Meir Parenzo had told him. They said that the Talmud was to be burned because it mocked their God, and that only fire could wipe out that kind of sin. Jehuda had tears in his eyes when he told us that.

Then something very odd happened. Amalia got out of bed without even shaking, with no signs of her having only just recovered from an illness, went into the kitchen with us, and set a meal out for us. As she did so, she told us about the day fifteen years ago, cursed be its memory, when the holy books were burned here in our city.

And today it's happening again, she said darkly. I want you to go to the Piazza San Marco and see with your own eyes what they are doing to our people, so that you can tell your own children later on.

Isn't it dangerous to leave the Ghetto on a day like this? I wondered. At least we are more or less safe here.

But Jessica hardly let me get my question out. If we make ourselves look a bit grubby and Jehuda doesn't wear his red hat, no one will know that we are Jewish, she said.

Amalia looked at me rather doubtfully. I knew what she was thinking—anyone can see that I come from the Ghetto. But then her expression cleared. She told Jehuda to fetch a pair of breeches, a shirt, and a jerkin for me. If I dressed up as a boy, nobody would recognize me, she said, and helped me to change. Then she made our faces and hands dirty with ashes, and our clothes too, so that we looked like poor children. She rumpled our hair and sent us off.

That's why I am stumbling along through the city behind Jessica and Jehuda. We know our way around, in fact, and we know where the bridges over the canals lead because, after all, Jessica and I used to go wandering through the city often enough. For all that, we've reached one canal and have to retrace our steps. My feet hurt in these unfamiliar shoes. I stuffed some cloth into the toes because they were too big, and now they are pinching my toes.

Before, in the Ghetto, the air seemed to be humming, as if thousands of bees were flying around our heads, because the whole Campo was full of people who were making a fuss and complaining. But on our way here, we have hardly met a soul. It's only here, near the Rialto, that the streets are full of people.

Jessica looks like the daughter of some artisan, with her grubby face and the dirty dark-blue dress. She isn't walking as proudly and as erect as she often does, but she's suddenly gone back to the hurried easy pace that she had before, when we were children. I shouldn't have put these shoes on. Why didn't I go barefoot? But if I take them off now and carry them, people are sure to look at me.

Every so often we spot Jews on the street. They are hurrying along with their heads bent, keeping close to the houses and looking around nervously all the time. Even without their red hats I would have recognized them by their scurrying movements, their uneasy glances, and the fear in their eyes. It's the same fear that fills me too. They don't look at us. Nobody does. We are just three older children who clearly have nothing better to do than to roam the streets.

Why are the other two walking so fast? Jessica, I shout, and she and Jehuda stop and wait for me. Jessica takes my hand and walks beside me, matching her pace to mine. Jehuda walks a few steps ahead. He seems to be trying really hard to look older. He's walking straight backed and with his head held up. It looks a bit comical from behind because he is still limping.

Jessica holds my hand tight. Just like the days when we were still children. And because of that I get up the courage to ask her a question quietly. Aren't you afraid that Lorenzo might be there?

She doesn't say that that is none of my business, which is what I expected, and she doesn't even get angry. She doesn't let go of my hand, nor does she squeeze mine any harder, so she can't be angry with me. She shakes her head. Lorenzo wouldn't get involved with something like that, she says in a determined voice. Besides, he's in Padua and he isn't coming back for a couple of days yet. Be quiet now, we're nearly there.

We come around the corner and then we can see the Torre dell'Orologia, the clock tower with the passage through it that leads onto the Piazza San Marco. Jessica holds my hand tighter and pulls me quickly onto the square.

We stop next to Jehuda. St. Mark's Square is so huge and beautiful that for a moment it takes my breath away. Although I've been here so often before, I'm always overcome by the sight of it. But it doesn't last long. On the piazza there are great crowds of people in large groups, men, women, and children, and monks in their habits. It's easy to pick out the Franciscans, the worst of the Jew haters, by their brown habits with the hood and the white ropes they use as belts. It's noisy, and happy and excited voices fill the air. A dozen nuns, standing in a group, are singing hymns. On the other side of the square a priest is preaching a sermon, with broad and solemn gestures. But with all the noise we can't make out a word.

Between the groups of people there are occasional plumes of smoke rising, so that must be where the pyres are. Men carrying sacks are streaming across from the piazetta, presumably unloading boats that have tied up at the quays. When they get near the fires, the crowds part and the people form corridors to let the men through with their burdens.

Jessica puts out her other hand to Jehuda. We have to get away, she whispers. Look, Antonio is standing over there.

I look across in the direction she indicated. Which one is he, I want to know.

She points to a portly middle-aged man talking excitedly to others. Come on, he mustn't see me, she says. Otherwise he might recognize me in spite of the dirt on my face.

We push our way through the crowds and stop right in front of one of the pyres. Immobile, silent, horrified. Books are piled up on the burning wood, books flung open and torn, loose pages with Hebrew script on them. Charred leaves are tossed up in the air by the flames. They flutter upward as if they were living, white birds with black wings. But then they sink down slowly into the flames once more and bend upward one last time before they are burned up and the letters turn to black.

The smoke brings tears to my eyes and the letters become blurred. We stand there and stare into the flames, and it is as if we are paralyzed by horror. But no one takes any notice of us. How many stories have I heard of Jews being burned, time and again. The Jews of Blois were burned because they were accused of murdering Christian children for ritual purposes. Jews have been burned in every age, everywhere, in Spain, in France, in Germany, and in Austria. Even the parents of Aaron ben Avram were burned, in some village on the far side of the Alps. And thirteen years ago the Inquisition sent twenty-four Marranos to the stake in Ancona because they had refused to give up their faith. Now they are burning our books, here in Venice, and I am a witness. I am afraid. When will they burn us? I feel dizzy, I can feel my right eye starting to squint, but it doesn't matter, nothing matters—the world is collapsing all around me, and all there is left is the fire. For a moment I feel as if I'm being drawn into the flames myself. It would just take a step, a single step . . .

And then I hear the inner voice again, the one I know so well, a rough and hard voice, and I don't know whose voice it is and it says: Stop that, Dalilah, right now! Pull yourself together!

I cling to Jessica.

There were apparently about eight thousand books found with the unbelievers, says a Franciscan just near us. He crosses himself and says even louder: Eight thousand blasphemies are burning in the holy fire, praise be to God.

Amen, say the men and women around him. Amen, a word that we use as well, when we want to confirm a pious wish. But here, now, pronounced by these people, the word means something different. I feel dizzy.

And then another Franciscan declaims in a voice that is both solemn and threatening: Jewish moneylenders are killing the poor people and making themselves rich on what these people need to feed themselves, and I, who live by alms and from the bread given to me by the poor, should I stay silent like a dumb dog? A dog will bark to defend the one who feeds it, and therefore am I, whom the poor feed, just to watch while they are being robbed of what belongs to them? And stay silent? A dog barks for its master, therefore should I not bark for Jesus Christ?

True, true, shout those standing near him. That's right. May God's judgment fall upon them!

More and more books are brought along, dropped down by the carriers and torn by eager hands out of the sacks, ripped apart and hurled into the flames. In his hurry to get at one of the sacks, a large strong boy pushes a smaller one out of the way. The little boy is pushed too close to the flames and his coat catches fire. A tumult breaks out. Men throw themselves onto the boy, push him to the ground, and roll him over until the flames are put out. The boy cries, but isn't badly hurt. A pity he isn't, I think, and this shocks me. I never knew that such evil feelings had any place in my heart.

I turn around. Over there on the Doge's palace is my lion. There are lots of lions in Venice—the lion is the heraldic badge of the city—but that one there is my lion. We are too far away for me to be able to make it out, but it isn't necessary, and I know what it looks like anyway. The winged lion of Judah, with one paw on a book. The Doge is kneeling in front of the lion. A day will come soon, I whisper, when other people will kneel before you, not just the Doge. One day these Franciscans will prostrate themselves on the ground before you. One day what is happening here will be avenged. The Eternal One, blessed be He, will punish you for what you are doing now.

Jessica squeezes my hand so hard that I have to stop myself from crying out. She pulls me and Jehuda out of the crowds. We make a wide detour to avoid going near Antonio. I give a secret wave to my lion. One day, I whisper, one day . . .

We go past the Campanile and then across the piazzetta to the quay and stop only when we get to the water, silent, still crushed by what we have seen. Behind us we can hear the noise on the piazza, and in front of us, on the far side of the canal, is the Isola di Santo Giorgio Maggiore, with the monastery buildings by it, and the narrow Gothic church tower. The island is green, trees grow there. You can recognize cypresses by their dark color and the way they look like narrow columns. Farther back, in a light haze, is the Lido. That's where our graveyard is. My mother is buried there. I go every year with Amalia on the anniversary of her death on the fifteenth day of the month of Adar.

I don't know if it is the thought of my mother or the contrast between the beautiful picture in front of us and what is going on in the square behind us, but suddenly I start to cry. The tears just run down my face. Jehuda puts his arm around me to comfort me. Don't cry, Dalilah, he says. What they are burning is only paper. They can't burn the word itself. The holy letters are flying up to heaven where the Eternal One, blessed be He, will take them lovingly into His arms. And one day He will send them back to us. They will come back. Always. Not a single one of the holy letters has been lost forever.

On the way home we do not say another word to one another.

Chapter 9

I<small>T WAS THE LAST SABBATH</small> before Rosh Hashanah, the New Year festival. After the midday meal, which they had all taken together, Shylock and Jehuda had gone back to the synagogue and Amalia and Dalilah were clearing the table. Jessica stood up. "The girls are all going to meet today at Rachel's, the daughter of Ezra ben Shoshan. Shall we go along together, Dalilah?"

She noticed how Dalilah stopped in the middle of what she was doing, how the water jug in her hand shook, and she started to squint. How pleased she is, thought Jessica, and suddenly she felt the old tenderness rise up in her again. She put her arms around Dalilah's neck and pressed her face into the girl's short black hair until she could smell the cinnamon. "Yes, do come with me," she said.

Dalilah looked across at Amalia pleadingly for her permission.

Amalia smiled and took the water jug out of her hands. "I'm going to lie down for an hour," she said. "The last few days have really tired me out. And after that I am going over to visit Marta." She put the jug down on the side table and ruffled Dalilah's hair affectionately. "Off you go, I don't need you here. With God's help I'm well again." And secretly she said to herself: Maybe it isn't as bad as I thought. If the two are together, things can't be so bad. Dalilah is a good girl, although I wish I knew what was the matter with Jessica. She looked at the girls as they went out of the kitchen, and then sank exhausted into a chair. If only they could have stayed children forever, she thought.

Jessica went up to her room to change. She took out the blue silk dress, put a gold chain around her neck, and pinned her hair with a pearl clasp. Finally she took her light-colored silk *cioppa*. When she came downstairs, Dalilah was already waiting by the door, and around her shoulders she had the big light-blue shawl made of thin cotton, so light that you could even wear it on warm summer days. I'll order her a real *cioppa* from Shimon ibn Lazar soon, thought Jessica. She still dresses like a child, not like a young woman. And she's only a year younger than me.

"Come on," said Jessica, and opened the door.

"If I'm not at home when you get back," Amalia called after them from the kitchen, "just come across to Marta's and get the key. Peace be with you."

"Peace be with you, Amalia," called out Jessica and Dalilah, and they left the house.

Outside, Jessica turned to the right, so that she could walk all around the Campo. On the Sabbath it was customary to take a walk around the Campo, regardless of where you were actually going. For the young girls it was a welcome opportunity to show themselves off in their festival finery. Jessica looked around her. Dalilah walked a few steps behind her with her head down, still confused. Jessica thought back to how they had always gone along together to any gatherings of the girls. Only in the past few years had that changed. Only on festival days like Purim, or Channukah, or Succoth, when the groups of girls that met together were very big, had she asked Dalilah to come with her. Had Dalilah ever been with her to the house of Ezra ben Shoshan? Jessica couldn't remember.

The *parness* of the Levantine Jews lived in the Ghetto Vecchio in a house with a garden. Amalia had once told them that the other houses in the Ghetto Vecchio used to have gardens, but over the years more and more houses had been built on any open land, because the stream of immigrants from Spain and Portugal simply never got any less.

Most of the newly arrived Jews were Marranos, who had been forced to adopt Christianity by the Inquisition, but a number of Levantine Jews lived there as well. One of them was Ezra ben Shoshan, a rich shipping broker. He had only arrived in Venice three years earlier, but already he was one of the wealthiest and most well-respected men of the Ghetto. People said that he had brought great riches with him from his homeland, and that he still maintained excellent connections with the merchants of the Ottoman Empire.

Jessica felt the eyes of the women they passed looking at her, giving her envious and admiring looks, and she suppressed a smile of satisfaction. She knew that she was beautiful. Her silk *cioppa* rustled against the silk of her dress when she walked, a sound that always delighted her, and the sun was warm on her face. With her head held high she walked proudly and confidently across the Campo, where on this warm Sabbath afternoon lots of people had gathered. Their voices mingled with the screeching of the gulls and the cooing of the pigeons. Men in their best clothes were standing around talking, while others were going into the synagogues, either the Scuola Grande Tedesca or across to the Scuola Canton, hurrying along because it is written: "Let us go swiftly to pray before the Lord."

The women kept to one side, closer to the houses, as if they needed some protection, but they too formed into groups and were talking, some with serious faces, others laughing and joking. They stopped from time to time to call out to their children, who were playing on the Campo, so that with proud and concerned gestures they could push hair away from eyes, tidy clothes, tuck shirts into breeches, or bend down to straighten stockings. The older women wore traditional gray or black clothes. The younger ones had dresses of colored material, but they were still subdued. Jessica thought about the dress she had ordered. People's eyes will drop out of their heads with admiration, she thought. Of course, her father wouldn't like it, and she knew that she would have to prepare herself for one of his sermons, although for a dress like that it didn't seem too high a price to pay.

In front of Shimon ibn Lazar's house a group of women were deep in animated conversation, and one of them was Rosa, the tailor's wife. As Jessica came closer, they lowered their voices and carried on their chatter very softly. As she went past, she caught the words "gold," "extravagance," and also "pride and sinful vanity," but none of this bothered her. Let them gossip away if they hadn't anything better to do! Jessica smiled. If only they knew!

She walked faster and turned off toward the Ponte degli Agudi. Surely Hannah would have some news of Lorenzo to give her today. That was what they had arranged. He must have come back from his journey by now, and tomorrow, with luck, she would see him. She walked jauntily, as if she were already on her way to him, to her lover.

When they left the Campo, the buzz of voices died down. The air was filled only with the cries of the gulls. The bridge was in front of them. The wooden beams sounded hollow under their feet and glittering patches of light danced on the dark water of the canal. Jessica went quickly along the Strada Maestra, and then turned down into the lane that led to Ezra ben Shoshan's house. Not until she reached the door did she stop and wait for Dalilah to catch up.

In the garden there were already ten or a dozen young girls, all Sephardic Jews, all in their best clothes and all with cheeks red with excitement and eyes shining. Jessica greeted them one after the other, exchanged a few words with one or two of them, and waited impatiently to be able to talk to Hannah Meshullam on her own. At last she was able to go off with her friend and sit on a bench that was almost hidden behind a rose hedge.

"Have you seen Lorenzo?" she asked frankly. "Is he back?"

Hannah laughed. "Yes, and he asked me whether he would be allowed to come and present his compliments to you early tomorrow afternoon. And so I hereby invite you to visit me tomorrow in the early afternoon." She put her arm around her friend, and the laughter vanished from her face. "It's a dangerous game, Jessica."

"It's not a game," said Jessica. "It's serious."

Hannah hesitated. "And if your father finds out?"

Jessica shrugged her shoulders with a feigned indifference. She hadn't been able to think of anything else. She lifted her head. A few paces away, behind one of the bushes, was Dalilah, who was looking across at her. Jessica raised her hand and made a gesture of dismissal. Dalilah turned and went.

"Your father has made a very strange bond with Antonio," Hannah went on. "Everybody is talking about it. With Antonio, of all people, who is good and generous and who didn't even want the money for himself, but for Bassanio, the young friend he loves just as much as a father or an uncle would."

Jessica said nothing and looked down at her hands, with their carefully manicured fingernails.

"Do you want to know why Bassanio needs the money?" continued Hannah. "He's gone to Belmont to try and win Portia as his wife. She's a rich heiress. I've heard that he has so many debts that marriage to Portia is the only thing that can save him." She gave a mocking laugh. "Well, he's not the only Venetian nobleman in that position. Mind you, if you want to court a rich woman like that, you can't really turn up as a beggar."

"Do you know this Portia?" asked Jessica.

"No." Hannah shook her head. "But I've heard a lot about her. People tell a really strange story. Apparently her father laid down in his will that a suitor would only be allowed to marry her if he chooses the right one out of three caskets. The first casket is made of gold, the second of silver, and the third one of lead. But there is a cruel condition attached. If a man wants to submit himself to this test, he has to swear a solemn oath beforehand that if he chooses the wrong casket, then he will never be allowed to marry another woman."

"That was a strange will," said Jessica. "Gold, silver, and lead? What does it mean? Gold like the sun, silver like the moon, and lead like a poor man's life? I think her father didn't love his daughter, and didn't want her to have a husband at all. Didn't he want her to marry and have children?"

"I'm not so sure that he didn't love her," said Hannah. "Perhaps he wanted to protect her after he was dead. How many girls know for sure that they have the right one if they are allowed to choose for themselves?"

I would, thought Jessica, and looked at the red blooms on the rose hedge. I'd know perfectly well. But she did not put her thoughts into words.

At that moment, Rachel and two other girls came along. "Oh, there you are, you two," Rachel called out. "Come on, there are fruit juices and sweets and cakes."

Hannah and Jessica stood up and followed their friends to the table that had been set up behind the house, spread with all these things.

The girls ate and drank. They talked, of course, about the burning of the Talmud. Their faces were serious. Then Dalilah began to tell the story of how they had gone to St. Mark's Square. The others listened intently. Dalilah spoke slowly and in a dramatic voice, and when she described how she had hobbled along behind Jehuda and Jessica, she made her audience laugh out loud. Strange, thought Jessica, it sounds as if the tragedy has turned into a comedy in Dalilah's mind after only a few days. But that's the way she is—any story she tells comes out sounding comical. When Dalilah was telling them about the painful blisters that she had gotten on her heels from wearing shoes that were too big, and jumped up to show them how she had hobbled along, everyone laughed. Zipi, the daughter of one of the jewelers on the Rialto, shouted out, "That was really stupid of you. Ordinary street children don't wear any shoes. If you had gone barefoot, nobody would have paid any attention to you."

"Nobody paid any attention even the way I was," said Dalilah, and sat down at the table again. "No one notices a boy on the street. And Jessica looks like one of that lot, so she can move about as she likes."

"That's true," said Rachel, whose father's house it was, and ran her hand through her own black locks, which even the red ribbons that she had tied into them could not keep tidy. "I wish I had fine, light-brown hair like that."

But Jessica was no longer really listening. In her thoughts she was with Lorenzo, and she would see him tomorrow. How long she would have to wait. Then she heard something that penetrated her thoughts and made her listen carefully again. ". . . they say he's been seeing a Christian woman."

Jessica looked up. It was Zipi who was telling the story in a low voice, like a conspirator. All the others were listening, clearly fascinated by what she was saying.

"What did you say, Zipi?" asked Jessica. "I'm sorry, for a moment my mind was somewhere else."

Zipi was only too pleased to repeat her story. "It's Adamo Salmoni, that arrogant jewelry seller who works for Shmuel Levi. You know, the good-looking fop who always thinks he's better than he is. He might be called before the *Esecutori contro la bestemmia*." Zipi gave a malicious laugh. "He's been accused of seeing a Christian woman, a widowed washerwoman with two small children. If he's unlucky, he'll get the maximum sentence, my father says, five hundred ducats and two years in prison. But since it isn't some innocent citizen's daughter that's involved, he might get off with less. What an idiot! What does he want with this Christian woman? Aren't there enough unmarried Jewish girls?"

Jessica felt a pain like an arrow in the breast, but she did not let the others see the turmoil that Zipi's story had aroused in her. She drank some fruit juice and asked, as casually as possible, "What's the penalty for a Jewish woman who gets involved with a Christian man?"

"There isn't one," answered Zipi. "If that happens and the Christian wants to marry the Jewish girl, then she has to be baptized. But if he doesn't marry her, then she just has to live with the shame of it, and it's hard to find a decent Jew who would want to marry her then, never mind how big her dowry is. My uncle Menachem, the marriage broker, he says that there are at least three girls like that in the Ghetto, though he wouldn't tell me their names. Since he told me, I've been looking at people really closely, but I can't find out who they are. Can you imagine any Jewish girl you know behaving like that?"

Jessica quickly popped a little cake decorated with a sugared cherry on top into her mouth so as not to have to answer the question. She chewed vigorously and shook her head. Fortunately, the girls seemed to have lost interest in Adamo Salmoni, and now they were talking about the marriage that had been planned between Sofia, Zipi's sister, and a young Jew from Rome, who was also the son of a jeweler. Zipi gave a detailed account of what the matchmaker had said and what her father had said and what Sofia had said, which incidentally was very little. By all accounts, the young man was good-looking, well-educated, and rich. "Sofia really has all the luck," said Zipi longingly. "And sometimes she can be really horrible."

Jessica put on an interested look, laughed when the others laughed, said "ah" and "oh" when the others said "ah" and "oh," and followed her own thoughts. A life of shame, she thought, I couldn't cope with that. Lorenzo will have to marry me. He really has to marry me, or else I'm lost. If he doesn't marry me, I'll kill myself. But he loves me, he won't let me down.

"Can you move up a bit?" someone said suddenly, just near her. It was Rachel, who had pulled her chair next to Jessica's. "I heard something that I absolutely have to tell you. My father was talking to a business friend yesterday and the subject of Antonio came up. It seems that another one of his ships has been wrecked. It was on its way to Tripoli with a cargo of Venetian lace and glassware."

"What's that got do with me?" Jessica snapped. Was everyone getting at her today?

Rachel shrugged. "Well, then," she said, "nothing at all. I thought you might be interested because of that strange bond your father made with Antonio. But if you don't want to know . . . What's the matter?"

Jessica stood up. "I'm sorry," she said. "I have a headache. I think the best thing is for me to go home and lie down."

She called Dalilah and they left the garden together. The cheerful voices behind them got quieter and quieter.

This time they didn't walk around the Campo. Jessica walked silently, with her head bent. Dalilah gave her a side-long glance, but didn't dare to say anything. Something must have happened.

Jessica's father and Jehuda had returned from the syna-gogue; they saw Shylock's hat and Jehuda's skullcap lying on the chest in the hallway. They could hear Amalia in the kitchen singing a Psalm.

Jessica went up the stairs to the salon, Dalilah behind her. Shylock sat on a chair by the window with a leatherbound book on his knee. Dalilah wondered where he had gotten it from, since surely all the holy books had been burned.

"Father," said Jessica, "I have to tell you something. They were saying at Ezra ben Shoshan's house that another of Antonio's ships has gone down. Seemingly it was bound for Tripoli, carrying Venetian lace and glass."

"I know," answered Shylock, and he looked up. The ex-pression on his face was forbidding and angry. "But it is still the Sabbath, my daughter, and it is our duty to keep this day holy, to receive it with joy in our hearts, and to avoid speaking of business."

Jessica turned and ran out, into her own room. Dalilah followed her in bewilderment. When Jessica had shut the door behind her, she suddenly got hold of Dalilah by the shoulders. Quietly and insistently she said, "You must never go against me, promise me that. We belong together, we two."

Dalilah pulled her shawl tighter around her shoulders. "I promise," she said, and went downstairs. Jessica heard her open the kitchen door. She went to the window and looked out at the canal. The water was a shiny blue-black color, and was moving sluggishly. A gondola went past. On the seat were two women with baskets. The gondolier stood at the end and moved the oar quickly and skillfully. Jessica lay down on the bed and shut her eyes. She really did have a headache. Perhaps it was fear that was causing all the pressure behind her eyes. He has to marry me, she thought. I couldn't cope with a life of shame.

Chapter 10

Shylock counted out fifty-eight ducats and pushed them across the table. Antonia, the artist's wife, took the money and put it into a bag. "Thank you, Shylock," she said. "As soon as my lord abbot pays my husband the money he's been owing him for more than half a year now, I'll come and redeem the jewelry." She shook her head. "The good friars don't know what it's like when you've got seven hungry mouths to fill every day."

Shylock looked at her with something approaching sympathy. Her husband was a painter, a well-known artist, and paintings from his studio, once they were finished and hung in the churches, were the talk of all Venice. Admittedly, Shylock hadn't seen any of them, although there were also some Jews who liked that kind of picture. He had even heard of Jews having their portraits painted and putting them up in their salons. Mind you, they were Sephardic Jews. Few of the Ashkenazim had enough money for that kind of thing. And they were also more reluctant to go against the commandment: "Thou shalt not make unto thee any graven image or any likeness."

Once Antonia had left his countinghouse, Shylock sat

there for a moment immobile. He was thinking about the time when he had himself once transgressed against that commandment. He had taken a painting as a pledge, and for the whole month that he had kept it, before it was reclaimed, he had looked at it time and again, almost greedily. It was a painting of Venus, a goddess rising naked from the waves in front of a clear blue sky. A naked woman with naked breasts that were barely covered by her long hair. He had kept the painting hidden in a cupboard, hoping every day that it would be reclaimed, and had still not managed to stop looking at it. Even now the shameful memory made the blood rush to his face. After that, he had always refused to accept when someone offered him a painting as a pledge.

Quickly he opened the jewel case that the painter's wife had brought as a pledge, and took out the jewels. Necklaces of gold and pearls, of fine workmanship and certainly worth more than the ducats he had given her for them. But he knew that she would come and redeem her jewelry because she had come to him often, and she had always been back on time. She was one of those customers from whom his only profit was the interest.

Shylock weighed the necklace thoughtfully in one hand. Perhaps he would soon have to convert everything he had into cash to be able to repay Tubal the ducats he had borrowed from him. After prayers this morning he had spoken in the Scuola Grande Tedesca with one of the shipping brokers who worked with Ezra ben Shoshan. It was more than a rumor about Antonio's ship not reaching the harbor at Tripoli. It had been a storm, they said, or maybe the ship had been taken by pirates. At any rate, the ship and its crew had gone without trace. For Shylock it was of no importance whether it had been due to storms or pirates. After all, did it matter to a mouse whether it was eaten by a cat or a hawk? And the great nobles didn't care whether they trod on a worm or a snail.

A passage from the Proverbs of Solomon came into his mind: "When thou sittest to eat with a prince, consider diligently what is before thee; and put a knife to thy throat, if thou be a man given to appetite." A dull fear came over Shylock, and he could not shake it off, even when he told himself that Antonio had two more ships. *Was* I too arrogant? he thought. Will the Everlasting One, blessed be He, punish me for my pride? But then he remembered the carnival five years ago. Antonio had insisted then that he, Shylock, should take part in the Jews' race. The horror and humiliation that he had felt when he had had to race half naked against other Jews—he would never forgive him for that. Shylock covered his face with his hands. It was as if it had been only yesterday.

At that moment there was a knock on the door. Shylock took his hands from his face, quickly packed the jewels, which were on the table in front of him, back into their case and closed the lid. The man who came in, his head bowed humbly, was Shimon ibn Lazar, the tailor. He was carrying a large bundle in his arms, wrapped in black cloth.

"What do you want?" asked Shylock in surprise.

Shimon twisted around like a snake. His thin body bent and then straightened up as his hands, still underneath the bundle, waved around in the air. "Forgive me, Shylock," he said in his strangely high-pitched and rather strained voice. "I must beg forgiveness in case what I have to say is out of place.

But Rosa, my wife, thought that I ought to come and see you. If destruction is going to come upon a house, she said, it will start at the threshold, so off you go, she said, go and see Master Shylock and show him what his daughter—may the Everlasting One grant her a long and happy life—show him what she ordered from you."

Shylock had a strange feeling, half uncomfortable and half afraid. Uncomfortable because he found Shimon ibn Lazar and his groveling manner repulsive, and afraid because of what the man was going to say to him. He wondered for a moment whether he should just throw him out, whether it might not be better to know nothing about it. Ignorance prevents ulcers and bad dreams, but it doesn't absolve you from responsibility and protect you from the punishment of the Lord when you had the chance to know what was going on. And so he took hold of himself and said dismissively, "Well, tell me what brings you here."

"Oh, dear, Master Shylock," dithered Shimon ibn Lazar, never ceasing to twist and turn the upper part of his body and wave his hands around with the bundle still in his arms. "You know, no one likes to have bad news by word of mouth."

"Then don't use your mouth, and just show me what you have to show me," said Shylock, barely managing to suppress his anger.

Shimon ibn Lazar stepped forward, put the bundle down onto the table, and pulled back the black cloth. In front of Shylock lay a dress made of dark-red silk with pale-green decoration, gold clasps, a gold-embroidered bodice panel, and flared sleeves with gold braid. He stared at the dress.

"What's this?" he asked, although he knew there could be only one explanation.

"Your daughter, Jessica, ordered this dress from me," mumbled Shimon. "My wife said I ought to show you the dress before your daughter gets it." Shimon drew breath noisily, licked his lips, and went on: "My wife is a poor, ignorant person, but she does have a certain amount of common sense. She says that when people start talking, it's easy to lose your good name, however moral you might be really. A well-brought-up Jewish daughter can lose her reputation all too easily, she says, because there are plenty of wagging tongues around here too, though Heaven knows there shouldn't be." He hesitated, wriggled a little more, and carried on, "There was something else she said I had to tell you. Some Jews are saying, may the Lord stop their loose tongues, that the young lady has been seen unaccompanied outside the Ghetto. When a fledgling bird is ready to fly, says my wife, then you have to shut the cage door so that it doesn't fly away—"

"That's enough," interrupted Shylock. "Take off the bodice panel and change the gold braid for ordinary silk ribbon. I don't know what color would suit it. Consult your wife and do whatever she tells you. And now go, I'm busy."

Bending down so as not to show his agitation, he reached out his right hand for his accounts book and quill. Anger and irritation had filled him so much that he thought he was about to explode.

Shimon ibn Lazar wrapped the dress up in the black cloth again and backed away toward the door, twisting and turning in his usual manner, until he backed into the wood itself. "A single crumb of leavened bread, says my wife, can spoil all your efforts to keep the Passover pure, by which she means—"

"Be off with you," said Shylock. "Remember me to your wife, and give her my thanks. Tell her that even a tongue that wags too much sometimes tells the truth."

He didn't look up to see Shimon ibn Lazar leave the countinghouse. But as soon as he heard the door close, he put his head in his hands. "Leah," he said. "Leah, we are in trouble. I don't know what it is, but I can feel how the dark clouds are gathering over our house. There will soon be thunder and lightning and I shan't be able to prevent the storm."

Leah remained silent and gave no answer, even when he asked: "Leah, are you there?"

Jehuda found his master deep in thought; his face was gray and the deep furrows that ran from his nostrils down to his mouth seemed to have gotten even deeper. Jehuda thought of something his father often said: Worries usually show themselves first in your face. For the first time in his life he had hard evidence of the proverb, and this nearly made him smile. But that soon passed, and Shylock told him harshly to go and ask Amalia what things she needed for the feastdays. "Get a move on, or I shall be after you. And don't go dawdling around on the Campo again, or you'll be sorry!"

Downcast and struggling with the most confused thoughts, Shylock went home. He had to speak to Jessica and get the anger out of his heart before he could devote himself to his prayers. "Come upstairs with me, daughter," he said after he had taken off his hat and put it next to Antonia's jewel case on the chest of drawers.

Jessica followed him upstairs with some hesitation. Her father wasn't the sort of man who raised his voice when he was angry, but she could tell from his harsh, dull tone how upset he was.

"I have two things to say to you," he said when she had come in and sat down at the table in the salon. "Shimon ibn Lazar the tailor came to see me in the countinghouse today and showed me the dress that you ordered for the New Year festival."

Jessica became red with anger. "How could he dare to do something like that behind my back?"

"How could you dare to order a dress like that behind *my* back?" Shylock snapped at her. His face had reddened as well.

Jessica stood up and walked back and forth in the room. Here it was, happening again. Here he was going on at her with his reproaches, and it was her duty to listen humbly to his sermonizing. That was how it was supposed to be and that was what she had always done. Only later, when she was alone, had she cursed him in her own heart and made all the reproaches that she would have liked to make.

"I do not allow my daughter to wear dresses decorated with gold," said Shylock.

With that, Jessica suddenly blurted out: "Why not? I'm young and my whole heart is craving for beautiful things. I want to dress up like other young girls. Even in the Ghetto there are girls who dress much more splendidly than I do, and some of them have fathers who aren't nearly as rich as you."

"The great prophet Jeremiah said: 'Let not the rich man glory in his riches.' It's right and proper that a Jewish daughter should be modest."

Jessica knew that she ought to bow her head, but she simply could not do so. "Modest, modest!" she shouted. "Am I supposed to dress in gray or brown or black as if I were an old woman? Why did the Eternal One, blessed be He, create beauty? Why did He give our dyers the ability to produce colorful materials? If God had wanted us to go around in gray, He would have given us fur like mice."

Jessica looked almost pleadingly at her father. She was afraid of what would happen now, but at the same time she felt a curious sense of liberation. For the first time she had spoken openly the arguments that she had lined up against him time and again in her head.

Shylock saw the expression of despairing longing on her face, an expression he had often seen on Leah's face too, especially in the year before her death. Jessica looked as if she would be prepared at that moment to give anything, even her life, to be able to say the right thing now, or do the right thing. But then the expression was gone again. Suddenly a shadow came across her face as if a cloud had appeared in the sky. Why can't we talk to each other properly anymore? thought Shylock. She and I, one human being to another. Why are we always trapped in these roles as father and daughter? But this thought was no more than a fleeting one in his mind too, and then he was the angry father again, the justifiably angry father, trying to take something burning out of his child's hands because she was too young and stupid to realize the dangers. "I've told Shimon ibn Lazar to take away all the gold and put in simple cords and silk," he said in a hard voice.

Jessica ran to the door, but her father held her back. "Jessica!" This time his voice sounded loud and sharp. So loud that Dalilah, who was standing downstairs in the hall, could hear it. Quickly she picked up the jewel case that the master had left next to his hat. She could use it as an excuse if anyone found her on the staircase. She crept cautiously up the stairs.

The door to the salon was ajar, so Dalilah, while she could not see in, could hear every word clearly.

The master was speaking in a voice that was harder and angrier than she had ever heard. "And what's more, people say that they have seen you outside the Ghetto," he said, "unaccompanied."

"What if they have?" shouted Jessica. "Am I a prisoner?"

"A girl can very quickly lose her good name, and that is the surest road to misfortune," said Shylock. "From today you are no longer allowed to leave the Ghetto without accompaniment. And you will stop visiting the house of Levi Meshullam. I should never have let you go there. But no more! Do you understand me? I shall tell Amalia and Dalilah to watch you very carefully to see that you don't disobey my order. Or am I to feel ashamed of myself whenever I meet the other Jews? Am I to cover my face when anyone mentions the name of my daughter?"

"I'm not your slave!" shouted Jessica at the top of her voice. The door slammed shut and, before Delilah could get away, Jessica appeared at the top of the stairs.

"You betrayed me," she shouted. "Your tongue is forked

like an adder's. You promised me your loyalty and what did you do? Betrayed me!"

Dalilah ducked and hunched her shoulders. As ever she felt helpless in the face of Jessica's anger. She did not dare to contradict. Jessica spat, and the spittle landed at Dalilah's feet. Then Jessica ran into her room. Again the door slammed, and the bolt was pushed home.

Dalilah went downstairs slowly and put the jewel case back next to the master's hat.

Chapter 11

Dalilah . . .

THE DAY AFTER TOMORROW will be the first day of the month of Tishri, and tomorrow, as soon as it gets dark, the New Year festival will begin. For days we've been cleaning and polishing the house, just like every year. As far as Amalia is concerned, everything being spotless is part of Rosh Hashanah. It's one of her things, and not all the women take it quite so seriously. Lots of people buy new clothes, though—that's usual. At Rosh Hashanah you try your best to get around the dress laws of the *provveditori alle pompe.* If you can afford it, you buy at least one new item of clothing. Even if it's just a shawl or a pair of shoes.

We are not a poor household, although to tell the truth, compared to others, we do live as if we were. Living modestly, that's what the master calls it. Jessica has said often enough that what he calls modest living is really miserliness. When Amalia hears her say things like that, she gets cross with her and says that it isn't miserliness, and that the master knows how hard it is to earn a living and therefore he turns every copper *soldi* over three times before he spends it.

It isn't my place to say so, but actually I think Jessica is right. But I'm not completely sure what the difference is between miserliness and thrift. How should I know something like that?

Yesterday Shimon ibn Lazar brought our new dresses. To get around the dress laws, which lay down how often you are allowed to buy new clothes, the dresses had small things wrong with them when he brought them. This is to be on the safe side, so that nobody could say that they were brand new. But nothing was terribly serious. Some of the hem on Jessica's dress was undone. Amalia sewed it up immediately. There was a little patch on mine, but I soon got rid of it. All I had to do was to pull on a thread and it came off. With Amalia's dress, which was gray, like all her clothes, there was a dirty mark just above the hem where ashes had been rubbed onto the cloth. We washed it out and by evening it was dry again. Even the master had a new coat made this year. Mind you, it looks exactly like the old one, but it hasn't got the worn patches.

My dress is lovely. As green as fresh moss. I laid it out on our bed this morning and as often as I can I open the door and have a quick look at it. I wonder if Jehuda will like it. We didn't order anything for him from Shimon ibn Lazar because he is still part of his own family, and he'll be spending the feast days in his father's house. But he'll see me when I go to the synagogue. I'm sure he'll see me.

Still, until then I'll have to do as Amalia tells me and get on with the cleaning. Just before feast days she becomes the mistress of the house, since she's the cook, and you have to do whatever she tells you to. And in the days before Rosh Hashanah that means cleaning, as far as she is concerned, almost as thoroughly as for Passover. Every single item is picked up, turned around and upside down to see what needs to be done to it. For example, yesterday I spent the whole day polishing the pots and the kettles in the kitchen until they were gleaming and my fingers were sore. I cleaned the brass fittings on the doors and the windows and their surrounds, the ordinary candlesticks and the silver ones we use on the Sabbath, and even the candelabra we use at Channukah and the big seven-branched menorah in the salon. I polished the silver kiddush cups, and also the boxes for scented herbs and the havdalah cups we use at the end of the Sabbath.

Last year Jessica and I did the cleaning together. The work was much more fun then. Everything is more fun when you share it. We called Amalia names behind her back and we thought of all kinds of excuses to try and get out of doing the work, even for a short time. This year Jessica is being a grand lady. She's staying in her room and not taking any notice of the housework that still has to be done.

First of all I was surprised that Amalia let her, and then I got angry. But in the end I thought, well, let Jessica do what she wants, and I threw myself into the cleaning.

Working hard is almost a relief because it helps take my mind off my darker thoughts a little. I've never longed so much for a family of my own as in this past year. Of course I'm grateful to the master for taking me in and looking after me when I was just a poor orphan, may the Everlasting

One, blessed be He, reward him for it and count it as a *mitzvah*. But living in this house has never been easy, and now it's harder than ever.

I keep on having arguments with Jessica in my mind, time and again. Since that evening when the master was so angry, Jessica hasn't said a single word to me. If I try to explain that I didn't betray her and that I never said a single word to the master, she tells me to shut up, or she just turns around and walks away. She doesn't seem to notice how unhappy she is making me. It didn't use to be like that—she always saw when I was upset. Often she would say: When you squint, it shows your feelings, Dalilah. Perhaps the Everlasting One, blessed be He, gave you that blemish on purpose, so that everyone around you would know how you were feeling inside. And once she even said that she envied me that squinting right eye. If she'd had that, maybe her father would have treated her differently. That was the time, years and years ago, when she brought a little dog home. The master ordered her to get rid of it and said that he wouldn't tolerate any unclean beasts in his house. It was a reddish-brown dog, and very small and awkward. I cried too when Jessica took it away. She took it back to St. Mark's Square and left it there. I wonder what happened to it.

Since the big argument, Jessica won't talk to anyone anymore, not even her father. When he asks her something, she just answers yes or no. She'll say "shalom" formally when he comes into the house, but not another word crosses her lips. She doesn't say anything, but the expression on her beautiful face is forever changing. Sometimes it's gloomy, sometimes thoughtful, then sad and depressed again, or angry. Looking at her, you get the impression that some kind of conflict is going on inside her all of the time. Who is it with? With her father? With Lorenzo? I always used to know what she was thinking, but not anymore. She doesn't know what I am thinking either. And what is Amalia thinking? And the master? How little we know of one another.

The master said that we were responsible for seeing that Jessica didn't leave the house alone anymore. How does he think that is going to work? Are we supposed to lock her in? Are we supposed to tie her up? When I tried to talk to Amalia about it, she just snapped at me to mind my own business. But what *is* my own business? How can I keep apart from what is going on in this house? Don't I live here as well? Aren't I part of it all?

Yesterday morning, for example, a servant came from Levi Meshullam with a message for Jessica. She read the note and said that Hannah was expecting her that afternoon. Amalia didn't look up from her work when she said: You are not allowed to go, your father has forbidden you to.

Well, then, if my father insists on keeping me a prisoner, I'll go and see Rachel, Ezra ben Shoshan's daughter. Rachel lives in the Ghetto, so surely he can't object to that.

Take Dalilah with you, said Amalia.

I stopped polishing the big copper pot that I was cleaning at the time, but Jessica snorted in scorn and said in a voice that turned my heart to ice in my body: That snake! Take me there yourself if you won't let me go alone.

You know perfectly well that I am not as good on my legs

as I used to be, said Amalia. If you won't take Dalilah, you'll just have to stay at home. Her voice sounded strict, much stricter than she usually is.

Jessica eventually agreed to let Jehuda take her there and come and fetch her afterward. Jehuda is as innocent as a child and it's easy to distract him. At any rate, he hasn't much idea of young girls and their crafty tricks. Jessica only wanted to visit Rachel so that she would help her get a message to Lorenzo, of course. And naturally she didn't want me to go with her. I'd have known what she was up to, and she'd have known that I knew.

What's going to come of it all? How can we start the New Year with quiet hearts? How are we to get through the days of penance until Yom Kippur? How can we give an account of ourselves before God, yes, how can we keep the Day of Atonement properly if there is discord in the house? It is written: "Yom Kippur takes away the sins between God and mankind. It cannot take away the sins between people until they are reconciled one with another." How can we become reconciled?

The *shofar,* the ram's-horn trumpet, has been sounded regularly since the beginning of the month of Elul to call the faithful to their prayers. At the start I was pleased when I heard it, as I am every year, only now every time I hear the sound, I'm filled with horror. The sounding of the shofar signifies ten things. We had to repeat them so often at school that I know them by heart: "Remembrance of the creation, the turning to God, the revelation on Sinai, the words of the prophets, the destruction of the Temple, the sacrifice of Isaac, a warning in times of danger, the call to judgment, the redemption of souls and the resurrection of the dead." I used to like thinking about the creation, how everything was void and without form, and then the world was made. When I hear the sound of the shofar this year, all I can think of is the threat of danger, and I can't see what that danger can be. How can you protect yourself from the threat of danger if you don't know what the danger is?

Amalia is clattering around with the pots and pans in the kitchen. She's working all the time as well. Yesterday Jehuda brought half a lamb and sacks of vegetables and fruit, and ever since she's been busy roasting, stewing, and boiling. The whole house is full of the nicest smells. It will be a marvelous meal—on feast days we always have something especially good. Tubal Benevisti will be our guest. And perhaps one or two strangers that the master will bring home from the synagogue. After all, it's a *mitzvah* to invite strangers to a festival meal.

I've hardly finished one job when Amalia gives me something else to do. She has just told me to clean Jessica's room. As if she couldn't do it herself. I tried to get out of it. I said that our rooms weren't clean yet either, and nor was Jehuda's. But there's no talking to Amalia when she's got an idea into her head. If you do everything in order, you won't get into a mess, she said. Go and clean upstairs. Maybe Jessica will help you.

Jessica won't help me, that's for sure. She's bound to be sitting by the window with her embroidery, playing at being a lady. She'll just look down on me the way you look down on an insect crawling across the floor; it ought to be grateful that it doesn't get trodden on.

I open the door to her room and look across to the window. But the chair is empty. The window is open, the curtain is moving in the breeze. Jessica is not there. She isn't sitting by the window and she isn't lying on her bed. Her *cioppa* isn't hanging on its hook. For a moment I stand there numbed. She's gone. She must have slipped out of the house secretly. Should I behave as if nothing is wrong, or as if I haven't noticed? But then I'd be an accomplice. And so I go down to the kitchen and ask Amalia if she knows where Jessica is.

In her room, says Amalia. Isn't she in her room? Her face has turned pale, I don't need to say anything more, she knows. Although it is quite unnecessary, she rushes through the whole house herself, looking for her. Of course Jessica isn't there.

Amalia, I say when we get back to the kitchen and I've gathered all my courage. Amalia, I think Jessica has gone to meet a man.

Amalia looks at me and I can see that her face has gone hard. Shut your mouth, she snaps at me sourly. Shut your mouth and don't interfere with things that have got nothing to do with you.

I'm not the one who's done wrong! I've been in the house all day doing everything she tells me to. I've been friendly and helpful and Amalia has no reason at all to be angry with me. Quite the opposite. But I keep quiet. I don't tell her how unjustly she is treating me. I don't let her see how hurt I am. Without saying anything I go up to Jessica's room and start the cleaning.

Later on I go downstairs to tidy up our room. My green dress is lying on the bed. I run my hands over it and picture how nice I shall look in it. The sleeves and the ties aren't too bright a red, are they? I take the sleeves and spread them out. At that moment I hear the main door being opened very quietly. Jessica is back.

Amalia has heard it too, and calls out: Jessica, come into the kitchen.

I wait until I hear the kitchen door close behind Jessica, then I creep out into the hall and press myself against the doorpost.

Where have you been? I hear Amalia ask her.

That's got nothing to do with you, snaps Jessica.

I can't make out what Amalia replies. But I can hear Jessica's answer quite clearly when she says: You're not my mother, you've got no right to criticize me.

Now Amalia raises her voice. Somebody has to worry about it when you lose all your sense of duty. I owe it to your father and to your poor dead mother, may her memory be an honor to you, to watch over the good reputation of their daughter. And you know what your father said. If you dare go out again without somebody with you, I shall have to tell him.

So tell him, then! shouts Jessica. It couldn't make things worse. This house is a nightmare, the house of a miserly, malicious Jewish pawnbroker. Oh, if only I'd been born somewhere else and not shut up in the Ghetto. Prison couldn't be any worse than this.

She starts to cry, and quickly I run back to our room. I know that now she will run up to her room, throw herself onto her bed, and cry herself to sleep. She always does. That's what she used to do whenever someone got cross with her as a child. I often used to go and sit with her and stroke her hair and her back. If I didn't know that she'd tell me to go away, I'd run upstairs to her now.

Instead I go into the kitchen. Amalia is sitting at the table, her legs apart and her hands in her lap. Tears are running down her face. I kneel before her on the ground and take both her hands and bury my face in her soft palms. She has to stop crying or I shall be in tears as well.

Whatever will happen? says Amalia.

I don't know the answer, and so I don't say anything. I just kiss her hands.

Why did she say "shut up in the Ghetto" says Amalia. Why did she say "Prison couldn't be any worse"? I've never looked at things that way. As far as I am concerned, the Ghetto protects us.

But we *are* shut in, I say quietly, without raising my head. The gates are locked from the outside at nightfall.

Amalia has stopped crying—I can tell that from her voice when she contradicts me. They aren't just locked from the outside, but from the inside too. For us Jews the Ghetto means protection against violence and attacks. I was a little girl when they founded the Ghetto, and I still remember how we celebrated the day we moved in.

Tell me more about it, I ask when she stops speaking.

She strokes my hair and says softly: There isn't much more to tell, child. The Ghetto was set up in April 1516, according to their calendar, that means in the month of Nissan, 5275. We were all moved into the Ghetto in the space of three days, into these houses around the Campo that they call San Girolamo. The new iron foundry was here, that's why it's called the Ghetto Nuovo, even though it was the first one. And the Ghetto they founded later was where the *old* foundry used to be, and that's why it's called Vecchio, the "Old Ghetto," even though it's actually newer. Before that, the Jews lived scattered all over Venice, and you were never safe from attacks by the Christians. It was never safe for a Jew to show himself on the streets on their holy days and, especially at their Easter, they often used to break into houses and drag the men out and beat them to death. It was a bad time. Believe me, Dalilah, we Jews are only safe when we are with other Jews, and the Ghetto offers us security and the possibility of living our lives according to the Torah. If only Jessica would understand that.

She starts to cry again. I'm afraid, Dalilah, she says.

That hits me like a blow in the face. If Amalia is afraid, what hope is there? She is the only person who can offer me any security. Who else could? Amalia, I whisper, Amalia, I love you. Amalia, help me, don't leave me alone.

My sole memory of my mother comes into my head, a very blurred image of a woman who is carrying me across a square. I've always thought that it was the Campo, but suddenly I realize that it wasn't our Campo, it was the Piazza San Marco, and I can see the famous bell tower clearly on one side and on the other my winged lion. Now I know that I didn't dream it, I saw it. I'm being carried by a woman whose skin is as warm as Amalia's skin, who smells like Amalia, who looks like Amalia. I'm cold, but the woman's body is warm, and I press close against her. Amalia, I ask, what do you know about my mother? Where did she come from?

Amalia puts both hands around my face, lifts my head, and looks at me. I feel quite weak under her glance. Oh, child, child, she says, I knew that one day you would ask me that. But I know very little, and it is my own fault. She was a sad woman, a widow, who turned up from somewhere. I don't know where from. Perhaps I've forgotten, perhaps I never knew. She was already ill when she came to Venice, and she was taken in and looked after by a benevolent society for the sick, the *Visita gli ammalati*. Dalilah, you will never know where you come from or who your family were. Your mother was a foreigner, a silent foreigner who hardly spoke our language at all, and who was ill. She didn't look like you, she was much lighter-skinned, and she had blue eyes. Maybe she came from the far side of the Alps, maybe from one of the western lands. At any rate she had a bad time. She was very ill. I visited her a few times, and I'm still sorry that I didn't ask about her family and your father. Forgive me, Dalilah, you were a baby, and I didn't bother about you. I was only concerned about your mother. I was sorry for her, not you. Only after she died did I realize that I had failed to do something that couldn't be made good anymore. Everyone, even the helpless child of a poor sick woman, has the right to know where they come from. Perhaps I would have thought of it in time if I had had children of my own.

Her eyes are large and gentle, the brown of the iris merges with the white. Like drops of water that fall into light sand and slowly spread out. Now I know that I shall never find out. Now I know that I really am alone. I never dared ask the question because I was afraid of the answer.

And now? Now the answer has proved to be exactly what I expected it to be: I am alone.

Amalia, I say, and I can hear myself how despairing my voice sounds, Amalia, maybe you are my mother. Why can't you be my mother?

Her hands run over my face, gently, so gently, and then she says: Dalilah, you don't need to be afraid. You are a good girl, you'll be able to cope with your life, perhaps better than Jessica will, who has all the things you envy. Believe me, you are strong and you have much love in you, and the Everlasting One, blessed be He, will make up for the suffering you will have to go through. I wish I *were* your mother; you are the daughter I should have liked to have.

I press her to me and weep with happiness and with relief. But then she takes hold of herself, wipes the tears away, and stands up. That's enough, she says. We've got work to do. Everything has to be spick-and-span for the feast days. Outside and inside.

What did she mean? In the house and in the heart?

Chapter 12

SHYLOCK WALKED AWAY from Scuola Grande Tedesca with
a measured and unhurried pace. He loved the New Year's
service. When the ram's-horn trumpet was sounded after
the reading of the Torah, he felt at one with God and with the
people of Israel, and then he felt aware of the beginning
of things, the creation of the world, and that he could see
ahead to the end and the redemption. He felt the hope of
the Messiah and the rebuilding of the Temple, soon, in our
lifetime.

Men, women, and children were pouring out of the great
portals. Everyone went to the synagogue on Rosh Hashanah, and the only people who stayed away from the service were the very sick, or those who had to look after
someone who was seriously ill. Shylock looked around him.
Everywhere he could see faces that he recognized, but which
on this day looked quite different. There was a strange glow
over the Campo, a light that made this day different from
all the rest. He looked up. Even the weather was festival
weather, with only a few strips of cloud drifting across a sky
of blue silk, like some strange symbol of holiness, and even
the seagulls seemed to be quieter than usual.

Mendel ben Meir came out of the Scuola Canton with his people, followed by Simone di Modena, the Torah scribe. Shylock greeted them politely. Then he bowed to Joshua da Costa, who had just come out of the Scuola Grande Tedesca, walking with a stick. Behind him came his sons, carrying the chair on which sat Sarah da Costa, the crippled wife of the old *parness*. It had been years ago when she had suddenly collapsed, unconscious. She had stayed that way for three days before she woke up again. She had lived, but she could no longer walk. Every morning her sons carried her to the window and put her into a comfortable chair, and every evening she was carried back to her bed, and this had been going on for years now. She could no longer speak, and nobody knew whether she understood anything. She sat by the window with her mouth half open and looked out over the Campo, and every so often a member of the family, a daughter-in-law or a grandchild, would come in and wipe away the saliva that dribbled from her half-open mouth.

Today, on this high holy day, her sons had carried their mother to the synagogue. Perhaps she does understand a little after all, thought Shylock, and made a deep bow to the old lady. Behind her came the whole family, the daughters-in-law and the grandchildren. Joshua da Costa's daughter Esther had come from Mestre with her husband, a rabbi, and their children, for the feast days. Four children, and Esther was pregnant again. Even Rachel da Costa's pock-marked face looked less surly and spiteful than usual. Shylock nodded to her. She started, then nodded back. Joshua da Costa's second daughter-in-law, the wife of his younger son, was also pregnant. She carried her great belly proudly, and, as she walked, she supported herself on her eldest daughter, Sarah.

Right behind them came Rosa ibn Lazar, the tailor's wife, and her sister-in-law, who was married to the baker. Rosa was wearing a dark-blue *cioppa* with a colorfully embroidered train. She got worked up about Jessica's dress, thought Shylock bitterly, and she's wearing a train that is certainly too expensive to be in line with the regulations. For all that, he smiled at her in a friendly fashion. "God cannot reconcile sins between men until they have reconciled themselves with each other."

Shylock looked at Tubal Benevisti, who was standing beside him, stooping slightly, dressed very formally in his black *zimarra*. He was talking to a stranger, a merchant who had come from one of the countries on the far side of the Alps and who had been unable to return home in time for the feast days. Gershom ben Jacob was his name, and yesterday he had been the guest of Manuel Todesco, the cantor in the Ashkenazi synagogue. Tonight he had been invited by Shylock to the New Year dinner, according to the words of the Psalm: "Hear my prayer, O Lord, for I am a stranger with thee, and a sojourner, as all my fathers were."

Shylock felt both happy and grateful that the Everlasting One, blessed be He, should have granted him a day like this one, which gave him such a deep and inner joy. Leah, he thought, Leah, you'll see. From now it will all be different. I'll make my peace with Jessica. I'll show her how dear she is to me and how much I value her, my greatest treasure, my most precious thing, your future and mine, our link in the chain of the generations of Israel. And after Yom Kippur I'll send for Menachem the marriage broker.

There they were. Dalilah came first, in her moss-green dress, her head held high, and behind her walked Amalia in her dark-gray dress with the light-gray shawl around her shoulders. What was it Jessica had said not long ago? Amalia in her eternal dark gray! That color has become so much part of her that the light-colored shawl that she wears when she goes to prayers on holy days looks as colorful as a peacock's feather. Jessica is right, he thought, Amalia has gotten old. For an instant he had in front of his eyes the image of the young, vigorous Amalia, an Amalia with strong arms and a cheerful face, but then she became the gray old lady once again. Dalilah and Amalia came toward him. His eyes wandered to the doors of the synagogue, but he couldn't see his daughter anywhere.

"Where is Jessica?" he asked.

"She went home right after the early-morning prayer," said Amalia. "She wasn't feeling well, and went to lie down."

Shylock's face darkened as a shadow fell on his holiday mood, but he took hold of himself and turned to go. Tubal Benevisti, Gershom ben Jacob, and the two women followed him. He walked more quickly than usual, driven forward by an indistinct fear. Tubal kept up with his fast pace for a little while and laid a hand on his arm. But Shylock took no notice. He could think only of Jessica. He didn't believe that she was ill; she had looked far too healthy and rosy faced for that this morning. Surely, vain as she was, she had gone off to show someone her new dress. But whom? Had she perhaps walked over to the Scuola Levantina to show her friend Rachel the dress? Probably. She'll certainly be back home by now.

He had hardly opened the door when he called out, "Jessica, Jessica!" There was no answer. He forced himself to keep calm and unruffled and to fulfill his duties as a host. Politely he invited Gershom ben Jacob and Tubal Benevisti to come up to the salon, where the table was laid already for the festive meal. Only then did he leave the room with a murmured excuse, hurry across to his daughter's room, and tear the door open, full of terrible foreboding. Jessica was not there. The anger welled up in him, rage and fury at her for leaving him in the lurch precisely when there were guests in the house. She would really catch it when she came back, holy day or not.

He shut the door behind him more forcefully than he had intended. I have to control myself, he thought. I mustn't spoil things for my guests, and it's my duty on a day like this to avoid anger and sadness, as it is written: "Glad and merry in the heart and full of certainty that the Lord in His mercy has attended to the voice of our prayers and the sound of the trumpet." Shylock forced a smile. He knew that it was his duty as master of the house to offer his guests not only food for the body, but also to let them feel the joy and delight in the festival as food for the soul.

By the time he came back into the salon, he had mastered himself. "My daughter offers her apologies," he said casually, without giving a reason for Jessica's absence. What could he have said without telling a lie?

He avoided Tubal's questioning look and offered his guests the water to wash their hands himself, holding out the towel so that they could dry them, and then he sat down with them for the meal. Shylock said the kiddush over the wine, then the *ha-motzi*, the prayer before food, and he felt his mood of celebration gradually coming back.

Meanwhile, Amalia and Dalilah had brought in the food, offering the hors d'oeuvres, then the lamb with rice and vegetables, and then the purée of pears and honey that Amalia had prepared, as she did every year at Rosh Hashanah. The guests praised the meal extravagantly and Amalia, who had by now come to join them at table, blushed with pleasure. Dalilah filled their wineglasses and the mood was cheerful and contented.

They talked about the year that was just beginning today, the year 5328. "May it be a good year for us and for all of Israel," said Gershom ben Jacob. "May it be as sweet as your excellent pears-and-honey."

Shylock and Tubal nodded and said, "Amen."

After the meal Dalilah and Amalia withdrew. Tubal Benevisti and Gershom ben Jacob left as well. Tubal wanted to show his guest from the north some of his rare books before they returned to the synagogue to read Psalms until it was time for the late-afternoon service. "Give Jessica my best wishes," said Tubal, before he put his hands on Shylock's shoulders and gave him the traditional New Year's greeting: "*Leshana tova tikatev*, may you be inscribed for a good year, my friend."

"And may you also be inscribed for a good year," answered Shylock, "and, sir, to you, Gershom ben Jacob. May you have a safe journey, and may you find your family in health and peace."

He escorted his guests downstairs to the door. When they had gone, he did not bolt it. He wanted to spare Jessica the shame of having to knock when she came back. Slowly he went upstairs again. He was intending to sit in the salon by the window and read the passage in the Bible about the birth of Isaac, which was customary on the first day of the New Year holidays, with the story of Isaac's sacrifice as the reading for the second day. But he felt too depressed, and his holiday mood had disappeared from his heart with the departure of his guests.

He opened the door to Jessica's room, sat down on her bed, and put his head in his hands. He thought about what he would have to say to her later, when she came back. He would treat this as a most serious matter, and he would point out the holiness of these days, the ones just before the great celebration of the Day of Atonement. He would tell her that the Everlasting One, blessed be He, looks at all His creation on New Year's day and determines the fates of all men. It is the divine judgment, and therefore all men are called by the shofar to repentance and betterment. During these holy days the fates of all men are inscribed by God in a book. The names of the good are inscribed for life on the good side, those of the wicked are expunged from the book of life. But for the many who are neither completely good nor completely wicked, there is one hope, that's what he would say to her. The final judgment over them remains pending until the Day of Atonement, on which—depending on the level of their repentance—their fate is finally determined. Ten days of penance, Jessica, and you can plead for mercy before the Everlasting One, blessed be He.

Shylock raised his head and looked around. There was something odd about the room, something missing. What could it be? And then suddenly he knew. Of course, the silver candlesticks he had given Jessica on her twelfth birthday. He sprang up from the bed and pulled open the first drawer in the cabinet. Her jewelry was gone too. He pulled the wardrobe door open quickly. It was empty, apart from her everyday clothes and the bed linen.

He began to cough, as if the avenging angel had put his hands around his throat. Breathing hard, he dropped heavily onto the bed, propped his elbows on his knees, and put his head into his hands. "Leah," he said, "I'm glad you didn't have to see this. The storm has broken, it has happened." He really wanted to weep—the pressure behind his eyes was unbearable—but his eyes stayed dry, even though his body shook back and forth as if he had been possessed, and he could not stop it.

"What has happened?" asked Amalia at the doorway as she came in. "Where is Jessica?"

He did not raise his head, but just went on shaking. He heard her walk quickly across to the cabinet, and he knew that she would look into the drawer that he had left open and that she would understand everything. She cried out, shocked and shrill, like a wounded animal, and then he felt her come and sit on the bed beside him and put an arm around his shoulder to comfort him. But no comfort was possible. His daughter had made the decision to leave her father's house, and he had lost his only child.

"Go and see the *parness*," said Amalia suddenly. "Get him to send people out to look for her. Do something, Shylock. Please get something done. We can't just sit here being miserable." All at once she was speaking to him again in the old familiar manner.

Shylock shook his head. "No," he said. "You can't keep a bird in a cage when it wants to fly away. It's too late. Amalia, what did we do wrong?" Only when he had spoken did it occur to him that he had also gone back to the familiar "we" that they had used in the old days.

They sat there for a long time. "Only yesterday evening, after the kiddush and the prayer over the bread, Jessica dipped her piece of apple in honey and ate it, just like we all did," said Amalia suddenly. "The symbol of hope that the New Year is going to be a sweet one."

Shylock knew what she meant. Jessica must already have known yesterday evening what she was going to do today. She must certainly have planned how she would run away, because she did it so cleverly. On the morning of New Year's day the Ghetto would be like a ghost city because everyone would be in the synagogue. It would be the only time when she could get away without being seen. And it still struck him as very strange that she should have chosen this particular day, that she should have robbed him and his household of any joy and delight in the festival. Robbed . . .

A thought came into his head like a bolt of lightning, and he started to tremble. The blood drained from his face and his hands went cold. "Amalia," he said, "take Dalilah and go with her across the Campo and down to the bridges, right down to the Canale di Cannaregio. Have a good look around and see if you can't perhaps find some trace of her."

"Dalilah can go on her own," said Amalia, concerned. "I'll stay here with you."

"No, no," he cried out, "go, please, don't say any more, don't ask questions, just go."

Amalia stood up. She and Dalilah had hardly left the house when Shylock went down, his legs shaking, to the pantry. The flour container was heavy, but this was not the first time he had had to push it aside on his own. The chisel shook in his hand as he levered up the tiles. Then he opened the trapdoor and looked into his hiding place. Empty. It was empty. The jewel cases and boxes had vanished, and so had the bag of ducats. He had only put the bag in a few days before, when he and Tubal had taken the books out again. He stood there, numb, staring at the rust-colored tiles. The lines of gray mortar swam in front of his eyes. Weakly, incapable of gathering his thoughts, he closed the trapdoor, replaced the tiles, and pushed the flour container back into place.

Only then did the full realization hit him. She had robbed him. His daughter had stolen his secret savings. Now the tears ran down his face, his body shook, and his heart felt as if it was on fire inside him. Driven out of his mind, he ran through the door without bothering to close it behind him—what was there left to keep safe in his house? He ran across the Campo by the shortest route, rather than walking along by the houses as he usually did, to the house of Joshua da Costa, the senior councillor of the Ashkenazim, and knocked loudly on the door.

One of the sons took him into the salon. The old man was sitting there in an armchair by the window with a book open on his lap. Without looking at it Shylock knew that Joshua da Costa would be reading the story of the birth of Isaac. "What's the matter, Shylock my friend?" asked the old man in his quavery voice and held out his hand as he did so.

Stopping every few minutes because of his tears, Shylock managed to tell him what had happened. "My own daughter has robbed me," he said when he had finished. "My own flesh and blood. I have lost not only my daughter but my money, the fruit of my labors. I beg you, send messengers out to fetch her back."

The old man raised his hand and laid it on Shylock's arm. "You know that it is beyond my powers to do that," he said softly. "You can make a complaint of theft against her, but first you would have to find her. You could petition for her excommunication to the council, to the *va'ad katan*, because she has done you a very serious wrong. But whether the *esecutori* would let you do it is another matter. And there's yet another thing: Do you really want to hand your daughter over to Christian justice?"

Da Costa stopped and waited, but when Shylock made no reply, he went on. "You have lost your daughter. Mourn for her, rend your garments just as if she had died. The Everlasting One, blessed be He, has imposed this on you as a test, just as He ordered our father Abraham to sacrifice his only son. Abraham was obedient to his God, and he was rewarded. Do not forget that."

The soft, frail voice of the old man had a calming effect.

Shylock was ashamed that he had wept in front of him. Slowly he stood up. "The year 5328 will be my year of misfortunes," he said as he took his leave of Joshua da Costa.

"May the Everlasting One comfort you," said the *parness*. "Peace be with you."

Chapter 13

THE COACH RATTLED ON over bumpy streets and lanes. The coachman, an ugly fellow in a brown coat and a dark cap, sat up on the box and urged the horses onward with his whip. Jessica looked out of the window at the landscape as it rolled slowly past her.

In the woodlands that stretched away to the horizon behind brown fields, the leaves were already showing the bright colors of autumn. And the gnarled and twisted branches of the olive trees at the edge of the road stretched up to the almost turquoise-colored sky like an old man's fingers raised in prayer. Like her father's fingers.

Every time the thought of him came into her head, fear flowed over her like a great wave. She didn't want to think of him, didn't want to see his face, and didn't want to hear his voice. But she kept on being reminded of him. For example, she had found out yesterday that three of Antonio's ships had gone down. Lorenzo had told her with dismay about the misfortune that had befallen the friend who was like a father to him, but this had only made her think of her own father, how it would affect him, and what he would say. Three ships, fully laden with the richest of cargoes, and if something were to happen to the last of his ships, then her father would lose three thousand ducats in addition to what she had taken—she did not dare even to *think* the word "stolen"—out of his hiding place when she had left.

Jessica closed the curtain, snuggled down deeper into her new fur-lined *cioppa,* and put her head on Lorenzo's shoulder. He was asleep. His mouth was slightly open, his lips drawn into a gentle smile, like a baby that has just been fed. Moved and full of tenderness, Jessica looked at his handsome face and wondered to herself how he could manage to sleep in such an untroubled and carefree manner. How confidently he trusted the coachman—who was after all a stranger, quite unknown to him—not to throw his passengers out of the coach and simply run off with their bags, bags that also contained the ducats and the valuables that she had taken with her from her father's house. Perhaps that's the difference between his people and mine, she thought, perhaps I shall have to give up always expecting the worst. Perhaps Christians don't behave badly toward other Christians.

The coachman's back moved from side to side with the irregular movement of the coach. How would he behave if he knew that I am Jewish, wondered Jessica. But at once she corrected herself. She was no longer Jewish, not since that evening in Padua, immediately after they had taken the boat from Venice. The very same day Lorenzo had made her a Christian. He had married her.

The blood came to her head when she thought of the huge gloomy church, and of the fat priest wrapped in his black habit, whose face in the light of the flickering candles looked almost diabolical. He looked like an evil spirit—an evil spirit to whom she felt she had been sacrificed, powerless to help herself, when he put his hands on her head. Confused and helpless she had repeated the words of the priest, had felt the cold water run over her hair, and had, in a cloud of incense, cut herself off from the God of her father and sworn loyalty to Lorenzo's God, without knowing what kind of God that was. "Religious instruction can come later," the priest had said. "What is important now is that she is set free by baptism from her Jewish birth." Set free, Jessica had thought, now I'm free. For a moment her father's face rose up before her inner eye and she felt as if the shadows on the dark walls were moving threateningly toward her. But then that too had passed, and so had the hasty marriage ceremony that had followed the equally hasty baptism.

Later, when they had drunk a bottle of wine at the inn, so that they would have at least a small wedding celebration, Jessica had put the empty glass on the floor and asked Lorenzo to step on it and break it, as every bridegroom in the Ghetto had to do when standing under the marriage canopy as a sign of mourning for Jerusalem. Not until she heard the splintering of the glass did she feel that she was really married.

Jessica knew hardly anything about her new religion and had never given it much thought before now, even though she had been quite clear, of course, that in deciding upon Lorenzo, she would also be deciding upon a new God. But only now did she begin to realize that in the future she would never go to the synagogue again. Never again would she stand in the gallery with all the other women, never again would she breathe in that familiar smell from the people around her, never again say the prayers in a Hebrew that she could barely understand. And she would no longer have the feeling when she was with other Jews of being one of them, one with the people of Israel, one with their God. She could think even of a woman like Rachel da Costa with a certain affection.

In the future she would have to breathe in the numbing incense of Christian churches, and look at pictures of crucifixions and martyrs. With a slight shudder she recalled the crucifix in the church at Padua, the wooden Christ, bleeding from the wounds of the nails in the hands and feet, and from a lance thrust in the side. "Thou shalt not make unto thyself any picture or graven image." That was what was written. From now on she would *have* to worship images.

With loud cracks of the whip and shouted threats the coachman drove his horses uphill, and Jessica pushed away from her mind the thought of her shamefully secret wedding. Lorenzo had married her, that was the most important thing, and he had saved her from a life of shame. The days were gone now when she would have to be worried about the *cattaveri* looking at her too closely, or about the *Esecutori contro la bestemmia*. Even the *provveditori alle pompe* had lost their importance as far as she was concerned. In the future she could have the most splendid dresses made, and eat preserves to her heart's content. She could buy flowers and parade about in dresses with gold on them, and she could dress up without an ugly woman like Rachel da Costa being able to criticize her for it.

She was happy, of course she was happy. A whole string of relaxed days had followed that first evening of secrecy, nights in which Lorenzo celebrated with his friends his good fortune in getting himself a rich wife. Nights during which he swore to her his love and his faithfulness. And many more feasts lay before her, a life of glitter and without any cares. The money and the jewelry that she had taken with her would make sure they could live well for a good while, Lorenzo had said, and at some time or other he would find a trade or take up a good position in the business of one of his friends, maybe with Antonio or with Bassanio, if the latter did indeed manage to win the hand of the wealthy Portia. And besides, he had said with a satisfied smile, she, Jessica, his lawfully wedded wife, his little golden girl, could still expect a rich inheritance. Because, obviously, what she had taken from the hiding place wasn't everything that Shylock had. There were all those outstanding payments, worth a whole lot more, on money he had lent out.

And now they were on their way to Lorenzo's relatives. Always new faces, thought Jessica. She pressed closer against Lorenzo. A beam of sunlight came through a gap in the curtain and lit up the gold brocade on her *cioppa*. She ran her finger over the gold material and smiled. She was an Italian noblewoman now, her clothes proved it. She had cast off her nondescript and modest Jewish chrysalis and had taken up the bright colors of the aristocracy. The gray caterpillar had turned into a butterfly. She just had to get used to it.

Lorenzo moved in his sleep, slid a little deeper into the corner, and gave a soft, contented gurgle. Jessica stroked his hand with the long, beautiful fingers. Then she leaned back and closed her eyes.

The coach rattled on, from time to time there were the sounds of peasant voices from outside, or a cow mooing or a dog barking. Strange noises, different from those she had been used to in the Ghetto. Everything was different, even the smells. The Christian world looked different from the Jewish world, sounded different, and smelled different. Of course she had known that, because, after all, she had wandered through the city often enough as a child, with Dalilah. But now she was positively assailed by the different smells, her nose just as much as her ears and eyes open to the constant stream of new impressions. Even with her eyes shut she could tell when they were driving past farmhouses because the stench from the dungheaps gave it away.

Not only were the smells different, the colors were too. In the Ghetto gray, black, and blue had been the predominant tones, whereas outside the Ghetto there were besides these colors lots of purples, green in all shades, and yellows. Lorenzo's friends and their wives wore colorful clothes, decorated with gold and pearls, and rings gleamed on their fingers. And they were all surrounded by sweet, heavy scents that Jessica found very unusual.

Maybe I smell different to them? wondered Jessica. Perhaps they can tell by the way I smell that I'm not one of them, just like the individual animals in a wolfpack know one another by scent, and use their teeth to drive outsiders away. Perhaps this is why they treat me differently from their own people. She decided that in Genoa she would buy the same sorts of perfumes and creams that the rich ladies and gentlemen used.

Only when he sat up and closed the curtain to the other window did Jessica notice that Lorenzo was awake. She had been so deeply buried in her own thoughts. She felt herself softening under his glance. "Sleep a little more, my darling," he said, and pulled her closer to him. "When we reach Genoa this evening my relatives will be holding a feast in our honor, and you need to be rested."

A feast, thought Jessica, and her spirits sank. She hesitated, but then, in the dark of the coach, she brought out what she had not been able to say in the light of day. "Lorenzo," she said, "I'm not much of a wife for you. I hope you're never sorry that you married me. Your friends treat me strangely, they look straight past me and hardly say a word to me. You deserve a different kind of wife, Lorenzo, a radiant and charming one who can dance, and who can make conversation about everything. I'm just a shy girl from the Ghetto."

"I don't want to hear anything like that again," said Lorenzo firmly. "You are my wife, and because of that you belong to my class." He took her in his arms and kissed her neck. The blood rushed to her head, and she pressed herself closer to him. "It's only because you're so serious," he murmured, although he didn't stop kissing her. "You ought to laugh more, be happier, more outgoing. But don't worry, you'll soon learn how to behave like one of us."

She froze. Like one of us. She had surely not misunderstood his form of words. Even to him she was still the outsider, the stranger. For an instant she was afraid, afraid that it would always be like that. Perhaps she had exchanged a life of shame for a life as a stranger. "Lorenzo, dearest," she whispered. "Hold me tight. Please hold me tight."

The feast in their honor was to take place, just as Lorenzo had said it would. Jessica sat in the room they had given her, having scrubbed herself thoroughly in the bath, while the maid sent by the mistress of the house helped her to dress and do her hair. The maid, a buxom jolly girl with black hair and dark skin, rubbed rouge into her cheeks, smoothed her eyebrows, and put up her hair into an elegant style with golden combs. Jessica sat in front of the mirror and stared at the unknown young woman who looked back at her. She was a stranger. Of course she was a stranger, she was a stranger to herself.

When Lorenzo came to fetch her to lead her downstairs, she had to steel herself not to cry. More than anything she would have liked to crawl into bed, into her own bed in her father's house and she would have cried herself to sleep. But she pulled herself together. She allowed herself to be introduced, she smiled, and curtsied just like the other ladies curtsied. When they sat at table, she observed them, how the other ladies ate, how they took little pieces of food from the plates with elegant gestures, how they dipped their spoons in the soup, how they raised their hands to put something into their mouths.

Jessica found it hard to eat. It was hard for her to put the first piece of bread into her mouth without saying the prayer of thanksgiving. It was hard for her to take any of the meat without thinking: "And the Lord spake unto Moses and

Aaron, saying unto them, speak unto the children of Israel, saying, these are the beasts which ye shall eat among all the beasts that are on the earth. Whatsoever parteth the hoof and is clovenfooted and cheweth the cud amongst the beasts, that shall ye eat." Even if the meat had not come from a pig, she still felt some revulsion because it would not have been slaughtered according to the ritual, not washed, salted, and drained. And when she saw milk and meat dishes next to one another on the table, she thought: "Thou shalt not seethe a kid in his mother's milk." And she turned her face away when even Lorenzo, while he was eating meat, popped a piece of cheese into his mouth from time to time. Jessica had to force herself to eat, fighting against a feeling of sickness and revulsion.

A man in a splendid scarlet *zimarra* and green breeches came up to their table. He bowed to Jessica and said something that she didn't understand, looking at her questioningly. The man's looks were unabashed in their open curiosity. Jessica lowered her eyes.

The man turned to Lorenzo and bowed to him. "My greetings, Cousin Lorenzo," he said. "I have news for you. Your friend Bassanio has married Portia, the rich heiress from Belmont. He invites you to join him and share in his good fortune."

"Did you hear that, Jessica?" exclaimed Lorenzo in delight. "Bassanio did it. He chose the right casket, and he's won himself a wife and money. We'll set off to see him in a day or two."

Jessica smiled, which was what was expected of her, and lowered her eyes once more. Off we go again, she thought to herself. Am I supposed to spend my whole life in a coach?

Cousin Paolo went on staring at her. "Your little heathen is really very beautiful," he said softly to Lorenzo, but still loud enough for Jessica to pick it up. "But is she always so quiet? Can't she speak?"

Lorenzo's answer was a sharp one. "My little heathen, which it pleases you to call my wife, Jessica, is as clever as she is beautiful. She can read, she can write, and she can handle figures. She just needs to settle in, and I think it is not too much to expect from an Italian nobleman to allow her some time to do so."

Jessica heard the anger in his voice, but at the same time the undertone of dissatisfaction. Although he now put his arm around her waist to make it clear to Cousin Paolo that they were very much together, she still had the feeling of having somehow failed again. She had done something wrong, even if she had no idea of what it was. She didn't understand the rules of the game. Where she came from, men and women knew exactly how to behave toward one another. A man would never have looked at a married woman in that way. And certainly not at an unmarried one. When shall I ever know? thought Jessica despairingly, when shall I really be the wife that Lorenzo ought to have? She picked up her goblet of wine and drank it in one gulp.

Even the wine tasted different from the wine in her father's house. It ran down her throat with a pleasant, sweet taste. I shall have to be livelier, she thought, more cheerful and outgoing, that's what Lorenzo said. You can't start a new life without new experiences and without having to learn new things. What does it say in the Book of Ecclesiastes? "To every thing there is a season and a time for every purpose under heaven. A time to be born and a time to die, a time to plant and a time to pluck up that which is planted . . ." What made me think of that just now? she wondered, and then it dawned on her. At the end of the list of all the things there are the verses: "I know that there is no good in them, but for a man to rejoice, and to do good in his life. And also that every man should eat and drink, and enjoy the good of all his labor, it is the gift of God."

Jessica laughed as Lorenzo poured her another glass of wine. "Drink up, dearest," he said, "the dancing will start soon. Do you know how to dance the *passamezzo*?"

Jessica shook her head. Her father had never allowed her to learn to dance, even though some well-off men in the Ghetto had engaged dancing masters for their daughters. Dancing was not an appropriate activity for a decent Jewish girl, he had said, and besides, why did you need to know how to dance? At weddings, yes, but as far as they were concerned, the basic steps you learned for round dances as a child would do.

The wine really tasted good, much better than the wine her father used to say the kiddush over. She was thirsty. "All things have their season, Lorenzo." She said, "There is even a time to dance," and she laughed at the astonishment on his face. How handsome he was, and how happy she could count herself to be for having gotten such a husband.

When the musicians began to play, she let Lorenzo lead her to the dance floor. She danced and danced, enjoying the music, the movement, and the mild confusion of her own senses. Faces swam past her—eyes, so many eyes—and it all began to spin around, first gently, then faster and faster.

Someone asked her something—it was Paolo—and once again she didn't understand what he said, only Lorenzo's name. She looked at the cousin, and his face became blurred before her eyes. "A bundle of myrrh is my well-beloved unto me, that lies betwixt my breasts," she said. She was quoting verses from the Song of Solomon. "My beloved is unto me as a cluster of camphire in the vineyards of En-gedi." She couldn't stop herself from laughing. "He stays me with flagons and comforts me with apples, for I am sick with love." Lorenzo was there. She held tightly to him. "It is the voice of my beloved," she called out. The eyes of the people around her turned into birds flying across a pale-blue sky, the world spread out and became wide and still wider. "Behold, he cometh leaping upon the mountains, skipping upon the hills," she cried. "My beloved is like a roe or a young hart."

Lorenzo said something, but there was such a rushing and a roaring in her ears that she didn't understand a word. It wasn't important anyway—nothing was important anymore. "A bundle of myrrh is my well-beloved unto me, that lies betwixt my breasts," she said. The light from the great chandeliers dissolved before her eyes and became a fire that threatened to consume her, a wild roaring fire. She tried to run away from it, but her legs crumpled beneath her.

Lorenzo picked her up and carried her out to the garden, where she was sick.

Chapter 14

Shylock shuffled along like an old man past the houses on the way to his countinghouse. His feet felt heavy, his back was bent. Days and weeks had gone by, but his pain had not lessened. Time, which had always before covered everything up with its veil, making things easier and dulling the emotions, refused to do this service for him because his sadness and his anger were too great. It was only shame that prevented him from showing the pain that was in his heart.

His anger at Jessica for betraying and robbing him only rarely came to the surface, and then it was at once pushed aside by another thought—the thought that it could not have been Jessica herself who had thought up the deceitful plan, not his daughter. It was the enemies of Israel who were behind it. They had chosen an innocent girl, not much more than a child, to do him the worst harm that anyone could do to him, to cut him out of the chain of the generations of Israel. Fate had decreed that he should only have a single child, a daughter. Now fate had robbed him of the possibility of a grandson, who would say the *kaddish,* the final prayer, for him when he died. The loss of his daughter had meant the loss of his only hope for a future.

Jessica's image was constantly before his eyes. He saw her there wherever he went, in the house and outdoors, by day and by night. When she had still been with him, he had often been angry with her, but it was only now that he had lost her that he realized how much he loved her. He felt it in a hundred ways, every day, every minute. But his sorrow had made him dumb, as the Psalm says: "I was dumb with silence, I held my peace even from God, and my sorrow was stirred."

His very existence had become as gray again as it had been when he was a child and a young man; a monotonous gray, broken only by the harsh lightning-flashes of hatred and fury. Only at those times did he feel that he was still alive.

A young girl overtook him, a basket on her arm, and she hurried along in front of him. She was wearing a blue *gamurra*, a simple garment like the one that Jessica often used to wear on weekdays. The skirt swung back and forth in the rhythm of her steps. Her movements were easy and relaxed, happy and free, fully conscious of the fact that she was both young and beautiful. Shylock stopped and watched her go into Chaim di Modena's bakery. The pain went through his heart like a knife. Jessica had moved like that, youth moves like that. He lowered his head, afraid that somebody might be able to read his thoughts and see his sudden envy of the girl's parents, parents so fortunate that they could still delight in their daughter. And then this surge of emotion in him had passed again. "To every thing there is a season," he thought, "a time to plant and a time to pluck up that which is planted . . ." But how could you just pluck out the flesh of your own flesh?

When he had reached his countinghouse and taken off his coat, Shylock got down his account books, as he did every morning, and counted out a number of ducats from a heavy bag, putting them into the cashbox that he used for current transactions. Since that accursed day he had carried out his business like a sleepwalker. He went to the synagogue in the morning, as he always had, said the words of the morning prayers with an empty heart, words which said nothing to him anymore and no longer had the power to move him. If anyone greeted him, he would nod without speaking, and he never answered a question. Several people had already stopped acknowledging him at all. During the day he sat in his countinghouse, dealt monosyllabically with his customers, took pledges almost absentmindedly and without examining them, and gave loans without haggling over the amount.

Yesterday evening he had checked over the pledges that had not been redeemed because, when the period of credit had run out, he could sell them with the help of his business friends on the Rialto. The job of checking the unredeemed pledges, which in the past had always given him great pleasure because of the good profit he anticipated making, had this time been just a burdensome chore that he had to get done somehow. Still, he had finished it, and in the morning he had sent Jehuda to the Rialto with a message.

Shylock slumped down into his chair behind the counter and opened the book that contained the names of the debtors, the sums advanced, the pledges, and the loan period. He still kept his books with scrupulous accuracy—that was now in his blood and in his bones—but he had never had so little interest in his business.

When there was a knock, he stood up and shuffled over to the door. But it wasn't a customer who desperately needed money. There stood Tubal Benevisti. Shylock beckoned to his friend to come in. He wasn't surprised to see him, indeed he had suspected that he would come to talk to him today, because today was the day on which Antonio's loan was due for repayment. From today the arrogant merchant was in the hands of the Jew.

They sat facing one another. Tubal Benevisti opened the conversation. "I have to talk to you, Shylock my friend."

Shylock nodded and wiped a hand across his eyes, as if he had to wipe away a veil of mist, then put his head on his arms. He knew what his friend wanted.

"I presume you already know that Antonio's last ship went down as well," said Tubal, and when Shylock nodded he went on. "The worst has happened, then. Antonio has nothing left, he's been completely impoverished."

"That is a punishment from the Everlasting One, blessed be He," said Shylock. "And it is written: 'I will subdue all thine enemies.'"

Tubal now asked him directly, "What are you going to do?"

Shylock avoided looking at him, pulled open the drawer and brought out a piece of paper. "I have a bond with him," he said. "He was to have paid back the money by today, that's what the bond says."

"That bond is the work of the devil," put in Tubal. "You cannot possibly insist on holding him to it, that would be inhuman."

"Am I not a man, in spite of everything they have done to

me?" asked Shylock. There was a burning in his throat and a burning in his eyes. "I'm only doing as they do, Tubal, I'm a good pupil. Are they any more humane toward us? No, any hope of finding humanity in them is pointless. Doesn't the prophet Yirmiyahu, the one they call Jeremiah, say: 'Can the Ethiopian change his skin, or the leopard his spots?'"

Tubal shook his head helplessly. "In Solomon's Book of Proverbs it says: 'When thou sittest to eat with a prince, consider diligently what is put before thee. And put a knife to thy throat if thou be a man given to appetites. Be not desirous of his dainties; for they are deceitful meat.' Think about it, Shylock."

"And it is also written," said Shylock, "'Thou shalt not respect the person of the poor, nor honor the person of the mighty, but in righteousness shalt thou judge thy neighbor.'"

Tubal's voice was imploring and he tried to put all his friendship and affection for Shylock into his words when he said, "I beg of you, Shylock my friend, don't lash out in your anger. The Christian merchants of Venice are bound to try and raise the money and repay his debt, you just have to wait a little. It would be proper for you to show them that you are patient and magnanimous."

Shylock grew red in the face as the blood rushed to his head. "Patient! *I'm* to be patient and magnanimous!" he shouted. "Haven't they taken my only child away from me? Haven't they stolen my money? How often do I have to turn my cheek so that they can hit me? How many more humiliations do I have to put up with?" And then his expression changed, the anger had gone, and when he carried on speaking, there was a great seriousness in his tone. "I want justice, Tubal, nothing more. I did not force him to sign that bond, he insisted on it himself. And I want to hold him to it. I demand justice, Tubal. I shall submit a plea of complaint today."

"Shylock," cried Tubal, and grasped his friend's hands and held them tightly. "Don't let yourself be guided by anger and revenge. Anger and revenge are poor teachers. Don't put in a plea, please don't do it. If you do, the law will take its course and nobody will be able to stop it. Don't let things come to court, Shylock. Be more magnanimous than they are."

Shylock turned his face to one side but did not speak. Tubal waited for a while, but when he saw that Shylock would not talk anymore, he stood up. Before he left the countinghouse he begged Shylock with urgency in his voice, "Promise me that you'll think about what I've said. Promise me that you'll be ruled by caution."

Shylock bolted the door after him, went to his counter, and sank heavily into his chair. "Caution," he said. "Leah, did you hear that? Caution? They've robbed me of my daughter, they've stolen my money! And I'm supposed to be cautious? Magnanimous, that's what Tubal said. It would be proper for me to be patient and magnanimous. I ought to wait, he said."

"Perhaps that would really be better," answered Leah's voice from inside him. "Then at least you would get the three thousand ducats back."

"What do I want three thousand ducats for?" exclaimed Shylock. "I've got all I need to go on living, and I don't need much. Jessica has done me a great wrong, but she didn't make me into a pauper. The shame of it—a daughter who has betrayed her father! I would rather she were lying dead at my feet. I'd rather have buried her with all the jewels and all the money than live in the knowledge that she is with those Christians, with our enemies, an apostate from our holy faith."

It was quiet. "Leah?" asked Shylock. "Leah, are you still there? Leah, say something!"

After a long silence he heard Leah say, "Shylock, if she were to come back, if she were suddenly to appear in front of you, would you forgive her and love her again?"

In fright, Shylock almost dropped the inkwell, which he had just picked up. He raised his head in agitation. "What are you asking?"

"I want to know if you would forgive her," said Leah.

He set the inkwell down onto the table and put his head in his hands. "I don't want to hear that kind of thing," he murmured. "Don't say things like that to me, Leah. Jessica, our daughter, she betrayed me. I've got nothing left in the world, my enemies have taken my child away from me, they have robbed me. I want revenge. I shall demand that the bond is upheld. Let that Jew hater find out for himself what it is like to have the most valuable thing you have cut away from your own flesh. His pain will be my revenge, his pain will make mine easier to bear. Nothing else can help me, nothing. . . ."

Shylock sat up, took pen and paper, and began to write. He wrote carefully, forming the letters one after the other, and with every word that appeared on the paper he felt better. When he had put his signature at the foot of the page he folded it, sealed it with wax, and placed it in front of him on the table. For the first time in a long while he smiled, but he could feel himself that it was not a friendly smile.

He sat there for a long time without moving, going over the conversation with Tubal Benevisti in his head, word for word, everything his friend had said, and with what he had answered him, until at last Jehuda came back from the Rialto with the times when he could take the unredeemed pledges to be sold there. Shylock pushed the list aside without really looking at it and gave the boy the sealed letter, telling him to take it to Joshua da Costa, the *parness*, at once. Jehuda took the letter and went.

Shylock stood by the window and watched him as Jehuda ran past the timber yard of Ephraim dalle Torre. Ephraim's teenaged son and two daughters were putting planks of wood into an orderly pile. The rivermen had clearly landed stocks of timber at the rafters' quays this morning. Then Jehuda went past one of the three water cisterns, where three women were doing the washing. They were filling buckets with clean water from the cistern and taking the dirty water down to the Canale degli Agudi and tipping it in. Jehuda disappeared behind the women and could not be seen anymore. In his mind Shylock followed Jehuda's steps, and saw him stop in front of Joshua da Costa's house. Now he was knocking at the door, and one of the sons was opening it and taking him into the room just by the door, the one with the window that looked out over the Campo, where the old man conducted his business. Jehuda was bowing respectfully and handing over the letter. Shylock held his breath. This was it. The *parness* was taking the letter in his trembling hand. Now the deed was done, it couldn't be altered, the decision had been made. Shylock let his breath escape with a loud hissing noise.

It was not long before Jehuda was back. "I delivered the letter, master," he said.

"Did the *parness* say anything?" asked Shylock.

"Yes, he said I was to remind you of a verse in the Psalms: 'Many are the afflictions of the righteous; but the Lord delivereth him out of all of them.'"

Shylock nodded absently and could only think of one thing: The letter with the plea of complaint was with the *vaad katan* and the council would have to send it on to the court of justice in Venice. "Did you hear, Leah?" he murmured. "Now there's no going back."

"Who are you speaking to, master?" asked Jehuda in surprise.

But Shylock didn't answer. He put on his hat, draped his outdoor coat over his shoulders, and opened the door. "We are going home," he said, and turned the key in the lock.

Home. Before, that used to mean seeing Jessica, taking pleasure in his lovely daughter, even if she did often make him angry because of her vanity and frivolity. But now there would be nobody waiting for him except Amalia and Dalilah. Amalia, the gray old woman who was becoming quieter and quieter, and now hardly ever gave any signs of her former powers, and Dalilah, who was trying in vain to behave as if nothing had changed, but still couldn't stop herself squinting more often than before. Even Jehuda, the well-meaning lad, seemed to have lost his youthful good spirits. Quiet and serious looking, he did whatever was asked of him, but only rarely did a smile cross his lips. It was as if light and joy had disappeared with Jessica out of the whole house, and out of the lives of those in it.

Shylock's back was bent, his shoulders stooped forward. He had lost everything that he loved, first Leah and now Jessica as well, and his life had become meaningless. But then he straightened himself up and a little of his earlier strength came back to him. His life did have some meaning. Revenge. He would get his revenge. Suddenly his head felt clearer, his confused feelings had disappeared. At last he was able to think of something other than what he had lost. Of revenge. And it was a sweet feeling.

Chapter 15

Dalilah . . .

THERE MUST BE WATER over at the back there. There, where the grass is longer and greener. I'm sure I'll find water there. The sun is high in the sky, it must be midday. And it's time that I had a wash. I don't want to get to Jessica as dirty as I am just now. She mustn't be ashamed of me. There is a wood not far behind that green patch of grass. I'm sure I can find a place where I can undress. There's nobody around anywhere. I only have to get the position of the church tower firmly into my mind, and the way the path bends around, so that I don't lose my way later. That would be terrible now that I am so near! It's only four hours to Belmont at the most, that's what the woman in the last village told me, and she smiled at me. Keep going east, lad.

Four hours. And I must have been walking for two already. I'll certainly get to Belmont this evening.

The grass is really getting longer, it's almost up to my knees. And I can hear running water already. I was right, it's quite a broad stream. The water is so clear that you can see the stones on its bed.

It's lucky that it's such a warm day. The sun is burning in the sky. It's one of those autumn days that makes you think of the summer that's just gone. Or of next year. It's only because of the sun that I thought about washing. I daren't take my clothes off here in the middle of the field. But over there the stream bends round before it disappears into the trees, and there are bushes and shrubs growing in front of it. Come on, Dalilah, just this bit and you can take your shoes off and cool your feet in the water.

At last! A clearing, as if it were made for me, open to the meadow so that I see right away if there is anyone coming. There are rocks beside the stream too, so I can spread out my wet clothes to dry. I drop the heavy coat onto the ground and throw my bundle, which by now is nearly empty, into the grass.

The water is clean and clear, with a fast current, so that you can drink it. You must never drink stagnant water, Tubal Benevisti kept telling me before I set off. Only running water. I kneel down on the ground by the stream. The earth is wet here and my knees get damp. But it doesn't matter as I'm going to wash out the breeches anyway. With cupped hands I get some water and drink it. It is surprisingly cool and tastes fresh and good, much better than the water from our cisterns.

In front of me a couple of tiny greeny-gray fish flicker past through green stems that grow right into the stream itself. Above the shining water a dragonfly is buzzing. How blue its long thin body is. Over on the other side there is a bird with gray and white feathers, standing in the shallows by the shore. A bird with long, thin orange legs. I don't know what it is called, of course—I don't know what most animals are called. And I've never seen a bird like that. It has turned side-on and is looking at me. I move slowly so as not to startle it, take my shoes off, and sit down on the bank of the stream. Now the seat of my breeches gets wet as well. The cold water does my aching feet good, and they stop burning. The bird lets out a long, wailing cry, flaps its wings, and takes off into the air. I watch it until it disappears behind the trees.

All kinds of noises can be heard coming from the wood just near me. Noises that I have become used to in the last few days. Leaves whisper in the wind, and every so often there is a rustling, presumably some animal running through the undergrowth. And occasionally a bird will whistle, or another one will make a trilling noise. I put my head to one side so that I can hear better. No, no human voices, no footsteps, and there is no one to be seen. And so I can put the moneybag down as well now; the bag Amalia tied on to my belt underneath the jerkin. It's still practically full. Amalia will be proud of me.

I undress down to my underclothes and set about washing my shirt and breeches. Four days ago Jehuda brought them to me, at Amalia's request. Amalia! I would never have expected it of her. Not her, the one who is always so cautious, and who would really have preferred us all to be permanently locked in, inside the Campo. You've got to find Jessica and beg her to come back, she said to me.

Never mind what has happened, the child must come back or there will be a disaster. Otherwise the master will be destroyed.

The breeches are so dirty that the water turns a browny-gray color, but it soon clears again. Now for the shirt. It's hard to get the milk stains out, and I have to rub at them for ages. Why didn't I look at what I was doing when the woman at the farm gave me that jug of milk just after she'd milked the cow? Well, yes, I was watching her in fascination. After all, it was the first time I've ever seen milk coming directly out of a cow. Actually, in the last three and a half days pretty well everything I've seen has been for the first time. Proper roads for the first time, with wagons and coaches driving along them. Fields and meadows for the first time, as far as the eye can see. A farmer with an ox plow in the field for the first time. A hedgehog for the first time, rolling itself up into a ball so that it looked almost like a huge horse chestnut. And yesterday I saw for the first time those beautiful, light-brown animals with the long thin legs, the ones I think are deer. There were five who came out of the wood suddenly. I stood very still. They were a long way off, but even if they had been nearer I don't think I would have been frightened of them.

The shirt is clean now. I climb up, still in my underclothes, and spread the breeches and shirt out on the rocks, after I have wrung them out. The things are bound to dry quite quickly. I'm not going to wash the jerkin, it's too thick. I'll get the stains off with some water and spread it out on the stones too.

There's no sign of anyone around. Quickly I take off my underthings and slip naked into the stream. The water almost comes up to my thighs. I bend forward and wash my face and my body before I start to shiver with the cold.

I'm not sure whether Amalia was only talking about the master when she talked about being destroyed. I'm afraid she's being destroyed, too, with Jessica gone. Anyway, she looks drained and exhausted, as if she had become ill again. Or as if she'd never got better. And to be honest, I miss Jessica more than I had expected. Amalia and the master are old, and Jehuda is a boy and, anyway, he's the silent type. I miss the conversations that Jessica and I used to have when she was in a good mood. I often think now that she was in a good mood much more frequently than I thought at the time. Anyway, I wish for my sake too that she'd come home.

I hope she really *is* at Belmont, this Portia's house, as Hannah Meshullam said. After Hannah came to see us Amalia got quieter and more thoughtful by the day until eventually she came up with this plan.

The sun is so warm that I shall soon be dry. But isn't it strange to feel the air, the wind, and the sun on your naked skin? A new and unusual feeling and so pleasant that I'm ashamed. Why should I be, though? Look away quickly, Amalia would say. A naked woman is a naked woman, even when she is supposed to represent an angel. Well, I'm not an angel. But I'm not a proper woman yet either. Sometimes that bothers me and sometimes it doesn't. "To every thing there is a season."

Quickly I slip into my underclothes and drape the coat over my shoulders so that I'll be sufficiently dressed if anyone does come along. I don't need to wash the undergarment, as nobody will see it under Jehuda's shirt and the jerkin.

Jehuda would much rather that he had gone to Belmont instead of me, but Amalia said that would be impossible. After all, his job is to help the master. And besides, Amalia said, I'm the only one who could convince Jessica. If she'll believe anyone, she said, it will be Dalilah. You could see quite clearly how disappointed Jehuda was. But in spite of that he got hold of clothes for me. At the last moment he even brought along this coat with the sheepskin lining—it belongs to his brother Ephraim. It's getting cooler already, he said softly, especially in the evenings and at night. And on top of that he got me a pair of good solid boots from his brother Samuel, and they fit me wonderfully. It's a good thing that Jehuda has younger brothers.

Amalia had planned out my journey in every detail before she even said a word about it to me. She discussed it with Tubal Benevisti, the master's friend. He gave me a map with my route marked out very clearly on it, with all the places and roads. I didn't understand very well at first, but Tubal Benevisti explained to me very carefully how to use the map and not get lost, so that I would get to Belmont in one piece. Now that I'm so near I don't need the map anymore. It's in my pack, and that's nearly empty. Amalia had stuffed it full of bread, cheese, and olives for me to eat on the way. There were even a few tomatoes. Tubal Benevisti had said that I would need three or four days for the journey.

Amalia had really thought it all out. When I suggested that we should ask the rabbi, Rav Shlomo Meldola, what I would be allowed to eat on the way if my provisions ran out, she already had an answer. No, this time we shouldn't ask the rabbi, she said. We can decide for ourselves. The need to save a human life doesn't only override the rules about keeping the Sabbath as a day of rest, but also the dietary laws. You know that. And as far as this journey is concerned, it's about saving the master's life, and so you can eat everything, whatever you like, only keep away from the flesh of the unclean beasts.

I must have looked completely amazed, because she stroked my hair and said in a firm voice, "I'll take your sins upon myself, child. Just get on your way and bring Jessica back."

Then she put both hands on my head and said the blessing that the master used to say over Jessica on a Friday evening before we sat down to the Sabbath meal: *Yesimekh elohim ke-Sara, Rivka, Rahel, ve-Leah.* May God make you like Sarah, Rivka, Rachel, and Leah. It almost makes me cry to think of it. I would have loved to have her as a mother. No girl could want a better mother than Amalia.

May the Everlasting One, blessed be He, protect and keep you, Amalia said. And only talk to strangers when you have to. Keep apart. Mind what you say and how you say it. It's better to look simple. Never mind what anyone thinks about you. The main thing is not to be noticed. Then she laughed and said: "Simple lads never get noticed." She's right, I've seen that on my journey. Nobody has taken any notice of me, and I was glad about that, only then I thought to myself that nobody would take any notice if I fell overboard either, and I stopped being so glad.

I was only really afraid for the first time when I got to the mainland. I had never left Venice before, and everything was strange. The streets, the people, almost everything I've seen on this journey. Insects that crawl along the ground or fly through the air. And I had never heard so many different birds. In Venice, apart from the seagulls, pigeons, and sparrows, there aren't many birds. At any rate, I've very rarely seen or heard any other kind.

For the first few hours on the road toward the west, heading for Padua, I was so frightened that I didn't have to make any efforts to put a stupid look on my face. My head was full of terrors. This was mainly because I was dressed up as a boy, like on that day of accursed memory when the holy books were burned. But that day Jessica and Jehuda were with me, and this time I was completely alone. Over and over again I thought how right Amalia had been about the Ghetto when she said that we Jews are only safe when we are with other Jews, and that the Ghetto gives us protection.

It's odd—now I can move completely freely and be at ease with nature, whereas at the start everything just frightened me. But how long can you go on thinking of your own fears and nothing else? Once I had gotten a little bit used to the road and nature and everything, then my eyes practically popped out of my head with astonishment. Tubal Benevisti is always saying that Venice is the most beautiful city in the world. Perhaps it is, he's seen lots of other cities. But I know now that meadows, woods, and fields under an open sky are also beautiful. Perhaps even more beautiful than the city. Just as it is written: "And the Lord God planted a Garden eastward in Eden and there he put the man whom he had formed." I was sorry that Amalia couldn't see all this. I kept on thinking, if only she could see this as well.

Those of us in the Ghetto Nuovo get more sun than many of the rest of the people in Venice. Our Campo is so big that the sun reaches all the houses and warms them. Nevertheless, the sun is different under open skies than when it shines on you between houses. Not warmer, but somehow wilder, untamed. And then all the different trees and bushes! I don't even know the names of most of them. Yes, I can recognize olives, pine trees, and cypresses. But what those trees growing over there behind the bushes are called I have no idea, for example. They look nice, with their big, jagged leaves. The colors go from pale corn yellow down to a dark tomato red. I've never before seen such thick banks of moss like the one I'm sitting on now either. The moss that grows on stones and wood in Venice, above the water level, is thin and slimy and nobody likes to touch it. But this moss is soft and tickles the palms of my hands. I must note everything carefully so that I can tell Amalia about it.

A green shimmering beetle crawls out of the moss over my left foot. Its carapace twinkles in the sunshine and its tiny legs are tickly on my bare skin. Never in my life have I ever seen such a beautiful beetle. In the Ghetto you only get cockroaches, and they are horrible. The beetle has just reached my instep and is slipping down onto the other side. It has fallen onto its back and is waving its legs despairingly. I tip it over and watch it disappear like lightning into the grass.

How quiet it is.

I've learned now that "quiet" doesn't always mean the same thing. In the Ghetto it is never really quiet. During the day you can hear voices wherever you are. At the timber yard they are hacking and sawing, dough is being kneaded at the bakery, shopkeepers are haggling with their customers. You can hear the murmuring from the synagogue. Mothers are calling their children. Children are falling down, banging their noses and yelling. And someone or other will be having a loud argument with someone else. During the day it is really *never* quiet. Not even on the Sabbath, or on feast days when nobody is working. On those days people talk all the more. It calms down a bit in the evenings. But even at night it isn't completely quiet. When Amalia and I leave the window open, and that is nearly always except in winter because Amalia coughs less if we do, we can hear everything happening on the Campo. The students at the Yeshiva always go to bed very late. They sit and discuss things for ages by the Canale degli Agudi. Their voices gradually become singsong, the words merge into one another and you can't understand them. A lot of men sit around and play games, and others go to the tavern and don't go home until after midnight. But even when there isn't a soul left on the Campo it isn't totally quiet. You can hear the neighbors snoring, or coughing, and there is always a child crying somewhere.

It's different in the country. During the day you hear sheep bleating, cows mooing, and dogs barking. People shout to one another in the fields, carts squeak and rattle. It's exactly as a friendly farmer told me. And besides all that he forgot the chickens, the geese, and the pigs. They're not exactly hard to hear. But once you have left the houses behind and you are really out in the natural countryside, then it *is* quiet. Between the individual noises, the twittering of the songbirds, the croaks of the ravens, or the ringing of a church bell in the distance, it is so quiet that you can hear the softest breath of wind. It is so quiet that you can be frightened by your own footsteps, your own heartbeat, your own breathing. It is so quiet that you think you can hear your blood rushing in your veins. Until you realize that it isn't your blood, but the wind blowing over the land.

You are never alone on the great roads. You meet all kinds of people, journeymen, wandering players, small-time merchants, and farming people. . . . Once or twice people have spoken to me and said, Well, young fellow, where are you off to? Then I quickly put on my simple expression and just mumble like a halfwit the name of one of the places on my map. My fear of being discovered as a girl was greater than my curiosity. But gradually I became more confident. Why should anyone who sees a child dressed in a boy's clothes think even for a moment that it is actually a girl? And if I'm not wearing a red hat, why should anyone think that I'm Jewish?

I only really spoke to the one farmer, on the second evening. The sun was already low in the sky, and I knew that I had to find somewhere to sleep pretty soon. The fears of the first night were still in my bones. So I was looking to see if I could find another empty barn when I heard a rattling noise behind me and I turned around. It was a donkey cart, and it was coming slowly toward me. The beast was thin and bony, but it was pulling the cart well, and there was a farmer sitting on it. He had his head in his hands as if he were asleep. I wondered if the donkey knew its way back to its stable by itself. But when the cart drew alongside, the farmer looked up and pulled on the reins. Whoa! he shouted.

The donkey stopped, and at once started to graze the grass at the side of the road. The farmer looked me up and down. Well, little fellow, he asked, would you like to ride a bit with me? Jump up! Too much walking gives you sore feet and a rumbling stomach.

He looked so friendly that I am sure Amalia would have liked him too. So I got up and sat down beside him, with my pack on my knees. He asked where I came from and where I was going. I had a story ready in case this happened. My name was Carlo, I said, and I was from Venice. Because I'd been ill for a long time and was a bit sickly anyway, my mother was sending me to my uncle, who had a little farm near Belmont. I was to build up my strength with the good country air and good food. I'd said this story over to myself so often that now it came easily and fluently to my lips.

The farmer laughed out loud, but then he became serious. Yes, yes, he said, good country air. What townspeople think life in the country is like! They talk about peacefulness, but the reality is quite different. You hear sheep bleating, cows mooing, and dogs barking. People shout to one another in the fields, carts squeak and rattle. Every day brings new worries and problems, the seasons change, you have to plow the fields and look after them, tend to the vines and water the meadows. The animals need feeding every day. You have to reckon up, sow, harvest, thresh. Sometimes it rains too much, sometimes not enough, sometimes the sun burns in the skies for weeks, and then sometimes the crops rot in the ground because it hasn't been shining at all. There's never any lack of things to keep you busy, worried, or depressed.

He stopped talking and I thought: So not all Christians are better off than us, and I repeated his words to myself so that I could remember them and tell Amalia. With us too there is never any lack of things to keep you busy, worried, or depressed.

When we reached his village, the farmer said: "It's nearly nightfall, Carlo. Do you want to bed down in the hay in my barn? It's not good to be out at night, when all kinds of riffraff are wandering around."

That's exactly what Amalia had said to me. I accepted his offer gratefully. His house was small, not much more than a cottage—really just a kitchen with a part for sleeping. His wife, a plump red-faced woman, received me kindly and gave me buttermilk and black bread for my supper. Nothing from an unclean beast. I was hungry and started eating right away. Afterward she even put a straw palliasse down for me in the kitchen, and I didn't have to sleep in the barn.

Lying there on my palliasse I was almost happy. I had never seen and heard so many new things in the space of two days. Suddenly I understood why people like to travel, even though there are hardships too, of course. Mostly I was surprised that I was not afraid, even though usually I am very nervous. Perhaps I was simply too preoccupied with all the new things to be afraid. Then again, perhaps I had just got used to traveling. The first night had been very different indeed.

On the first afternoon I had left the main road at the Trattoria Il Tiglio, the Lime Tree Tavern, which was marked on my map, and I had been walking for a long time down a road that went between fields. I met hardly anyone, and I wondered for a while whether I should be pleased about that or not. Being so isolated there made me feel very lonely. And then the sun set. The sky had a reddish-golden glow. Far and wide there was nothing to be seen except woods and fields. Amalia had said that in the evening I was to go to a farmhouse, knock, and ask politely if I could sleep in a barn or a stable. At any rate, she would prefer that to my spending the night at an inn. You never know what riffraff are wandering about, she said. But in an emergency you have enough money for that, she said.

So I was all alone under a fiery sky, and there wasn't a house in sight. I began to run, and I was almost crying at the prospect of having to spend the night in the open. Amalia, I thought, what shall I do? I don't even know if there are any wild animals around here, wolves or foxes and things. I only know the names, and I don't think I'd even recognize any of them. But most of all I was scared of snakes. On top of that, all sorts of stories about thieves and murderers came into my head, and everyone knows that they do their wicked deeds under cover of darkness. And all the ghosts, witches, and demons—you're not even safe from those in the city, let alone out in the open. It was terrible. The more I tried not to think about that sort of thing, the more insistent the thoughts became. . . .

Then, after a bend in the road, I suddenly saw it—a barn in the middle of a field. I ran over to it and, because it was indeed empty, I thanked the Everlasting One, blessed be He, for helping me. Especially after I had climbed up a ladder to the hayloft, where there was enough hay for me to make a soft bed and keep out the cold. I ate my provisions until I had had enough, and then crept deeply into my unfamiliar sleeping place. How thankful I was to Jehuda for bringing me the coat, because it had got really cold. Even the hay would not have been enough to keep me warm. Outside, an owl hooted. The hay smelled so strong that its scent almost made me dizzy. First I thought that I wouldn't be able to sleep, alone in these unfamiliar surroundings with all the new smells and noises and because I was so frightened. But the walking had clearly made me so tired that I slept deeply and dreamlessly until the next morning. Until a ray of sunshine coming through a crack in the roof woke me up.

My clothes are more or less dry by now and it won't be long before I can get on my way again. I'm hungry. The chunk of bread that the friendly farmer's wife put into my pack yesterday morning was eaten up long ago. And all I had for breakfast this morning was some milk. But I've got a couple of apples left in my pack that I picked on the way.

I'll be seeing Jessica soon.

I hope I can find this Portia's house. And I hope Jessica is actually there. What shall I do if she has gone off somewhere else meantime? I'm not even going to think of that. I have to find her, I have to talk to her.

I'm going to tell her frankly and honestly how things are with us all, especially her father. Especially now, after all the ships belonging to that Antonio have been wrecked and the master has lost so much money. Three thousand ducats.

I'll have to find the right words to touch her heart enough to make her come home. I'll describe his face, the deep furrows that run from his nose down to the corners of his mouth, his hollow cheeks, the way his eyes have become sunken and dark, and the way his beard is getting whiter every day. I'll tell her how he goes about his daily business more like a ghost than a man and takes no pleasure in his meals. It *has* to work.

What shall I say when I get to Belmont? Maybe simply the truth. I'm looking for Jessica, my mistress, and I've lost her, that's what I'll say. She is supposed to be staying with a certain Portia. Could you possibly help me find her, *madama,* or *messere?*

Yes, from now on I'll tell the truth. Or nearly the truth. After all, my clothes are lying, and I'm not really a boy. Certainly not a Christian boy. No one must know that I'm from the Ghetto.

My clothes are dry, or as good as dry. I'll put them on, get an apple out of my pack to eat on the way, and go back until I reach the road that goes to Belmont again. In two hours, three at the most, I shall be there.

Chapter 16

A LIVELY THRONG OF JUGGLERS, acrobats, and playactors had gathered in the garden of the palazzo. Portia had hired them to entertain her guests, and later they would be presenting a *commedia dell'arte* play. Jessica felt a childlike pleasure when she thought about that, just like the way she had felt two years ago when they put on the Purim play of Esther and Mordechai on the Campo in the Ghetto Nuovo. She and Dalilah had talked about nothing else for weeks, and afterward they had performed passages from the play to each other over and over again. She would have liked to tell Lorenzo about it, but she suppressed that idea at once. Whenever she told him stories from the Ghetto his face always darkened. By now she had come to realize that it was better if she didn't even mention the Ghetto.

Today Jessica had dressed especially carefully in her best finery, on account of Lorenzo, who was very proud when his wife was admired by everyone. He had more and more reason for being proud too, because she had learned very quickly how a lady should behave at feasts. Without her even thinking about it, her lips now formed themselves into a gracious smile, she inclined her head prettily to one side when a man paid her a compliment, and answered him with a pleasantry. Her shyness in front of strangers was getting less all the time, and she often felt that she had become a different person, without knowing whether she was happy about this or not, nor at what cost this had come about. She sometimes shuddered when she thought of how young she still was, and how many different parts she would have to play between now and the end of her days, now that she had cast off so violently the role that had been assigned to her when she was born.

A jester in his colorful costume blew on a trumpet to announce that there would now be a mime show of the Twelve Labors of Hercules. Lorenzo and Jessica found a place amongst the other guests who were milling about in front of the terrace. Then a dwarf appeared on it. With a mixture of disgust and curiosity Jessica watched the misshapen man, who was much smaller than the few midgets and deformed people that she had seen in the past, and suddenly she saw in her mind's eye Marta, Amalia's hunchbacked sister. The dwarf bounced about. On the top of his slender body sat a huge head with a domed forehead, a small nose, and a strikingly strong chin. He waved his thin little arms and legs around and turned cartwheels to amuse the audience. Then he started on the Labors of Hercules, which was really a parody and was received with great laughter. His battle with the nine-headed hydra got an especially large round of applause. The ladies and gentlemen clapped and shouted out "Bravo!" and "More!"

When he had completed the last of the labors, the dwarf brushed his dark hair aside from his face and took a flying leap down from the terrace. He looked around questioningly, and then ran toward Portia, the hostess, bowed to her and put his hands up to his face as if dazzled by her beauty, then started blowing her kisses. Portia didn't encourage him, but she didn't drive him away. Only when he—to the loud laughter of the men—made an obscene gesture with his hand between his legs did she turn her head from him and wave him away.

Jessica felt herself blushing at this offensive behavior and turned away quickly. Coarseness like this was as foreign to her as some of the remarks that Lorenzo's friends made from time to time. She was, after all, a child of the Ghetto, and neither her father nor Tubal Benevisti had ever made offensive comments. But Lorenzo had laughed out loud too, although she would have preferred him to have reacted with disgust.

A gypsy woman from the troupe of players came up from behind her, an old woman in a brightly colored dress. "Pretty lady," she said in a hoarse but pleasant voice, "pretty lady, give me your hand and you'll find out what the future has in store for you."

Jessica shook her head and hid her hand behind her back. The old woman scared her, and, in any case, she really didn't want to know what the future had in store; she was afraid of the future. But Lorenzo, who had been standing beside her, laughed, fished in his pocket, and gave a few copper *soldi* to the gypsy woman. "But for that you'll have to prophesy something really nice for my lady," he said, taking Jessica's hand and holding it out to the woman.

The woman took it, turned it over, and studied the lines

on the soft surface of Jessica's palm very carefully. She was silent for a long time. The touch of her hands was strangely warm and dry, quite different from what Jessica had been expecting. She watched the dark, wrinkled face of the old woman and saw her shut her eyes suddenly, her mouth twisting as if she were in pain. But almost at once her face cleared and took on the expression of professional interest again that she had had before.

"Come on," exclaimed Lorenzo impatiently, "what can you foretell? What will the future bring for her? Sunshine in the summer and rain during the winter?" He laughed at his own joke and repeated it loudly, "Haha, sunshine in the summer, eh?"

The features of the gypsy woman hardened and with a bored, indifferent voice she said, "The lady can expect a long life with health and happiness. She will come into a rich inheritance and have at least four sons, but she should beware of snakes and serpents." Hardly had she finished speaking than she dropped Jessica's hand and moved on to tell the next lady's fortune.

Jessica stood there in bewilderment staring at her hand, which she was still holding out in front of her as if it didn't belong to her at all. Had the woman's face twisted because of a sudden pain or had she seen something that she didn't want to mention—a misfortune, a catastrophe? Or did a Jewish palm simply look different from a Christian one? Her hand began to tremble.

"Don't pull a face like that," said Lorenzo to her impatiently. But when he saw that there were tears in her eyes he put his arm around her shoulder. "You'll live a long and happy life by my side and have at least four sons," he said. "What more could you want?"

Jessica leaned against him, struggling against the disturbed and dark feelings that had risen up in her. Perhaps the old woman really *was* a witch, perhaps she had seen something unspeakable. A shiver ran down Jessica's spine. Lorenzo kissed her hand to wipe away the gypsy woman's touch. She's just an old woman who earns a living with a game, thought Jessica, and I'm sure she says the same to all the ladies. For a few *soldi* everyone gets a long and happy life and lots of sons. She laughed, but only halfheartedly because suddenly she was exhausted and really felt the need to retreat for a little while to the quiet of her room. "I'm tired, and I'm going upstairs for a little while," she told Lorenzo. "Please make my excuses to Portia and say I'll be back soon."

Lorenzo seemed relieved. He nodded, stroked her cheek with a quick gesture, and turned to talk to a gentleman whom he had introduced to her earlier as an old friend from Padua, from his student days. Before, at Hannah Meshullam's, he wouldn't have just let me go like that, thought Jessica with a sudden pang.

As she was crossing the terrace to go into the salon, Portia's maid came up to her and curtsied. "There is a young boy at the back door who is insisting on speaking to you," she said softly. "I've told him that we have guests and that he should come back tomorrow, but he won't go away."

"A boy at the back door?" asked Jessica in surprise. "Take me to him."

She followed the maid through a long corridor to the back entrance that only the servants used. The boy was poorly dressed, standing head bowed in the shadow of the chestnut tree. She didn't know who it was and was about to ask impatiently what he wanted when she heard a voice that was all too familiar to her. "Jessica, it's me."

"Dalilah!" she cried, and a warm feeling of pleasure came over her. She held her arms open and Dalilah ran into them. Jessica hugged and kissed her friend, then turned to the maid, who had stepped back a pace and was waiting, and called out happily, "This is not a boy, it's a girl. She'll be hungry and thirsty after the long journey she has behind her. Bring something to eat and drink up to my room for her."

The maid curtsied and left. "Just bring cheese, no meat," Jessica called after her. Then she took Dalilah by the hand and led her upstairs. When they had closed the door behind them she flung her arms around Dalilah's neck. "I'm so happy to see you," she cried. And then she had a sudden thought. She grabbed Dalilah by the arm and pushed her down onto an upholstered seat by the window. "Why are you here?" she asked in great agitation. "Is it something to do with my father? Has something happened to him?"

Dalilah shook her head. "No, he's not dead, if that's what you mean, but he's not really alive anymore either. He wanders through the house like a ghost, never speaks and hardly eats. He looks terrible, like a very old man. With hollow checks and lines on his face. Amalia is afraid for his health and his life, and says that it will destroy him if you don't come home. And it will destroy Amalia too. Come home with me, Jessica, please."

Jessica got up and walked quickly across to a wardrobe that was set into the wall and pulled the door open. "I can't come home," she said, standing with her back to Dalilah. "Even if I wanted to, I couldn't come back. Tell my father to mourn for me as if I had died. He should tear his clothes and weep just like you do when a child dies. He's not the first man to lose a daughter."

She took a dress out of the wardrobe and tossed it across to Dalilah. "Here, put that on. You mustn't be alone with me here dressed as a boy, because people would talk. Get changed."

Dalilah undressed down to her underclothes and lifted up the dress. It was a *gamurra,* the plainest that Jessica could find, but Dalilah had never worn such a richly decorated garment. Quickly she slipped it on. The *gamurra* was a little too big for her, and fell down in loose folds from her waist. She looked down, delighted, and when she sat down again she smoothed the skirt with such a gentle stroking gesture that Jessica thought involuntarily of the times her friend had stroked her, when she had been ill or sad.

Jessica pushed the boys' clothes to one side and sat down next to Dalilah. "And there's something else too," she went on in a quiet and downcast voice. "How could I ever stand in front of my father again after everything I did to him? Don't you know that I robbed him?"

"Yes, I know that," answered Dalilah, and went on stroking the soft blue material. "But Amalia said: 'What are ducats when a father's love for his daughter is at stake, or a daughter's love for her father?' Of course the master was angry at first, and raged and cursed. But he doesn't put all the blame on you, Amalia thinks. He says that the strangers led you on to do it all. Come home, Jessica. I'm sure he'll forgive you."

"I can't," said Jessica violently, and lowered her head. "I can't, Dalilah, it simply isn't possible." She folded her arms, as if she needed to protect herself against her friend's words.

There was a knock, and the maid came in and put a tray of fine white bread and various kinds of cheese on the table, together with a jug of lemonade. Dalilah, no longer able to restrain herself, stood up and began to eat hungrily.

Jessica waited until her friend had had enough, and then she said the words that she knew would make such an impression on Dalilah. "I can't come back to you all, even if I wanted to. I'm married." She stood up and walked across to the high window onto the garden and looked out. Down below a juggler was performing his tricks. When Jessica turned around again, she saw that Dalilah was crying. Tears were running down her familiar brown face.

"Amalia hadn't thought of that," said Dalilah through her sobs. She knew what the word "married" meant—namely that Jessica had been baptized, that she had cast off her Jewish faith and really couldn't come back again.

Jessica sat down next to Dalilah and put her head on her old friend's shoulder. She caught a whiff of the familiar smell of cinnamon, and, suddenly, for the first time since she had left her father's house, she had to cry. The two friends held on to each other just as they used to do when they were children.

But then Dalilah sat up straight. "The Marranos," she said hesitantly, "they were baptized, and they could still go back to the Jewish faith."

"They had baptism forced on them," said Jessica in a tired voice. "I took it of my own free will."

"But anyone can make a mistake," cried out Dalilah. "The Everlasting One, blessed be He, is always prepared to accept the contrition and the penitential return of His people. Why should He not accept your contrition and penance as well? Come home, Jessica, please. Since you've been away there has been nothing but misfortune over our house."

Jessica put her finger to her lips. "Not so loud," she said. Then she ran her hand over Dalilah's face. "Your eye is squinting again," she said with a small smile. "I've often been unkind to you in the last few months. I'm so sorry. Please forgive me."

"Oh, I forgave you that long ago," said Dalilah, and kissed Jessica just as she had always kissed her. "On Yom Kippur I prayed that you would forgive me and we'd be reconciled in the sight of the Everlasting One, blessed be He."

"Did you fast for me as well?" said Jessica with a trace of mockery in her voice. "How do you manage to fast for two, anyway?" But in a moment she was friendly again and put her arm around Dalilah's shoulder. "Never mind," she said, "we'll talk about all that again later on. Now come over to the window."

For a long while they watched the juggler balancing rods on his head while he spun rings on his arms, without dropping any of the rods or breaking the rhythm of his arm movements. Jessica drew Dalilah to her and laid her cheek against Dalilah's short black hair. "Later they are going to perform a comedy," she said. "Do you want to see it? Do you still remember when we watched the theater people on the Campo at Purim?"

"Of course I do," answered Dalilah. "I can remember Esther and Mordechai very clearly." Then she asked curiously, "What feast day is it today?"

"It isn't one," answered Jessica. "They have a feast here practically every day, or we are invited to feasts at other people's houses. You can't imagine. I couldn't either. These people are different from us, completely different. 'But they count our life a pastime, and our time here a market for game,' as it says in the Book of the Wisdom of Solomon."

She smiled at Dalilah's bewildered face. "Come over to the mirror," she said. "We have to make you up and get you ready so that you won't stand out."

Jessica put cream on Dalilah's face, then rubbed rouge into her cheeks, plucked her bristly eyebrows, and did all the other things to make her beautiful, things she had learned by now. Dalilah stared at the mirror with her eyes wide open, watching her own transformation. Suddenly she asked, "Do you live here all the time as Portia's guest? Have you been here long?"

"We've been here for a few weeks now," answered Jessica, stroking Dalilah's hair with a golden comb. "Lorenzo isn't making any efforts to leave. He wants to stay with Bassanio—they are best friends."

"And you?" asked Dalilah. "Are you happy here? I mean, is it what you wanted?"

Jessica paused, shaken, looked at Dalilah, and then suddenly burst out: "Sometimes I get the idea that Bassanio is more important to Lorenzo than I am. When I once said that to him, he told me that I wouldn't understand that sort of thing and that friendship between men is quite different from the love of a man for a woman. Male friendship is more durable, he said, and above all it is more selfless and therefore has to be set higher. He told me that he loves me, but that as his wife I have to understand that his friendship for Bassanio is part of the supreme good in his life." Jessica stared into the mirror, the comb in her raised hand. Her eyes sought Dalilah's, as if she could help her.

"What's so bad about that?" asked Dalilah. "Your father and Tubal Benevisti are friends too, aren't they? Friendship is a beautiful thing, nobody can deny that."

"With Lorenzo and Bassanio it's a different sort of friendship," replied Jessica. "Lorenzo called it a divine friendship. Can you imagine that with my father and Tubal Benevisti?" She put the comb down, and her voice changed in tone when she said, "But that's enough of that, there's no point in talking about things that can't be changed."

She fetched an elegant, bright-yellow *cioppa* from the wardrobe and helped Dalilah to put it on. "Now look in the mirror," she said. "You must admit that you look completely different now. Like a lady."

Dalilah's eyes opened wide with amazement. Her boyish looks had vanished, and instead a dark-skinned, delicate woman looked back at her. She was no longer the ugly little thing that she had always been. Jessica fetched a pair of pointed shoes for her, white satin ones, and said, "Good, now we can go down."

Dalilah started to giggle.

"What's the matter?" asked Jessica, astonished. "Why are you laughing?"

"I just thought what Amalia would say if she could see me like this."

Now it was Jessica's turn to laugh. "She'd say: That is not appropriate for a Jewish daughter."

"Vanity is a sure road to misfortune," said Dalilah.

And Jessica added, "When destruction is going to come upon a house, it will start at the threshold."

"A respectable Jewish daughter can lose her reputation all too easily."

"Rouged cheeks are Satan's apples of temptation."

"Even if they are like meadows of beauty, they shall still vanish away like smoke."

Jessica and Dalilah looked at each other, two young and beautiful girls, and opened their arms at the same time. Jessica pressed a kiss on Dalilah's red cheek. "I shall introduce you as my cousin, so as to avoid any long explanations. Come on, then, little cousin. Even if your heart is aching, here you always have to have a smile on your face, that much I have learnt. So be happy, even if you have to go home with your mission unfulfilled."

As they went through the door they heard the jester blowing his trumpet down below as a sign that the program was about to continue.

Chapter 17

FROM THE DISTANCE CAME the sound of church bells. Tubal Benevisti stood up. Shylock looked at him. For the first time in all those years he saw incomprehension in his friend's face, almost rejection. Tubal looked back at him, but he seemed to look right through Shylock into the past, or maybe into the future, but at any rate, not at the present. His close, gray eyebrows, which grew together over the bridge of his nose, formed a thick, straight line. Shylock looked at his friend with his clear gray eyes—so familiar to him because Leah and Jessica had them as well—and his carefully trimmed beard so that he would be able to recall them later; as if he were going to have to leave him and wanted to imprint his features on his memory one last time. Tubal, on the other hand, looked as if he had already taken his leave of Shylock and looked right through him, as if he were already trying to forget the other man's face while it was actually still there before him.

" 'No man should ever go into a place of peril saying unto himself: I shall presume upon a miracle,' " said Tubal darkly. "That is what is written. And think too, Shylock, that we shall all be made to pay for it. An important man like Antonio in prison and all because of a Jew." He hesitated, then went on in a strangely different voice. "If you persist in this, no one will be able to help you—not me, nor any other Jew."

"I know," murmured Shylock. "No one can help me anyway."

"That's not true!" cried out Tubal violently. "It's very simple. All you need to do is accept the offer of the Venetian merchants to collect the money on Antonio's behalf and the matter will be settled. Then your plea of complaint is nullified and Antonio will be let out of prison."

Shylock shook his head. "No, I insist on justice," he said. "Right is on my side." He picked up the bond that Antonio had signed and held it up. "Here, it's his own signature. He was the one who wanted that contract, not me."

Tubal Benevisti went to the door, but before he opened it he turned back once more. "Justice," he said, almost scornfully. "Justice! You think you have right on your side, Shylock, my friend, but in the end you'll find out that it is only a Jew's right. You are sitting down to eat with princes. Be careful not to show too much appetite and don't forget to put the knife to your own throat." He opened the door. "Peace be with you, Shylock."

Shylock had been listening to him with his head bowed. "Peace be with you too," he murmured, without raising his eyes. The door closed.

Shylock stayed where he was, sitting with his head in his hands, and gave himself up to his own thoughts. The demand that he had laid before the *va'ad katan* had not been without its consequences, and Antonio, unable to meet his debt, had been thrown into prison. He was to stay there until the trial. Shylock formed his lips into a malicious smile. Once again he pictured Antonio, as he had done so often, all alone in his dungeon, deprived of his young friends and of the chance to dress up in his usual manner. His light *zimarra* and the white hose he always wore were gray now, and however much he tried, the stains would never disappear. Just as the stains on my life will never go away, thought Shylock. "Antonio," he said to himself, "where are they now, your pride and your Christian arrogance?"

The thought that this noble gentleman was experiencing at firsthand what it was like to be humiliated and shamed gave him a feeling of warmth in his breast and in his back. Once again he pictured himself putting the knife to Antonio's bared breast, but as always he saw only the horror in the face of his enemy, his mortal terror. He never pursued the image because he could not imagine cutting with his own hands into the body of a living person. It was something quite different from slaughtering a chicken, and he'd never even done that. But when it came to it, he'd be able to do it, he was sure of that. His hatred would help him. You didn't need to anticipate such a deed in full.

He raised his head. "I won't have my rights taken away from me," he said out loud. "Not by Tubal, nor by Joshua da Costa, nor by Ezra ben Shoshan, not by anyone. Do you hear me, Leah?"

A sudden draft chilled him and left him shivering. Frightened, he raised his head again. Had someone come in? No, the door was closed and bolted. How could there be any wind here in an enclosed room, he thought, and then he heard Leah's voice saying to him, "Go home, you've no time now for delighting in other people's misery and none at all for self-pity. Go and look after Amalia, she needs you."

Amalia had been ill again for a week and had taken to her bed just after Dalilah had returned. Shylock had no idea where the girl had been, and it was of no interest to him anyway. Not until she had come back did it occur to him that he hadn't seen her for a few days. The thought did come into his head that perhaps she had been ill and that nobody had told him, but he was too indifferent to ask. She was there again, and she could help Amalia, that was all that counted as far as he was concerned, especially now that Jehuda had gone home. His father had cut himself on the hand, a particularly bad wound, and Jehuda had to help him out for the time being as the shoemaker had five younger children to feed.

When he got home, Shylock went—and this was his usual practice nowadays—to see Amalia first, before he ate anything or said his evening prayers. How quickly you can change your habits when outside circumstances change, he thought. After only a few days he had felt that this was what he had always done on coming home: entering the house, putting down his hat, taking off his coat, opening the door to Amalia's room.

Amalia lay in the bed and looked at him with large eyes that had an unhealthy sheen to them. She was very pale, but on her cheeks were the red flecks of fever. She had always been a powerfully built woman with strong arms, but now she looked thin, almost transparent, and the outline of her body under the cover was so small and flat that you might take it for that of a child. "Shylock," she said, and started coughing again.

Shylock sat down on the chair next to her bed. "How are you feeling today?" he asked. "Did Hannah Meshullam send the medicine that her father promised?"

She nodded, her head wobbling on her thin neck. "Thank you, Shylock," she said, "but you shouldn't waste your money on me, I'm beyond medicine now. My life is in the hands of the Everlasting One, blessed be He."

"You mustn't talk like that," he said fiercely. "As long as there is life, there is hope. And the Everlasting One, blessed be He, has given us responsibility for our own life, with the commandment that we have to keep it as long as possible."

"But it is also written: 'If it should be that the soul desires to leave the body, then no man may hold it back,'" said Amalia. The words had exhausted her, and she closed her eyes.

Shylock did not know what to say. What was the best thing? If he talked to her cheerfully and did everything to encourage her and give her a renewed will to live, then perhaps he could prevent her from talking about her death and giving him her last wishes. But if he agreed with her, he might push her deeper into sadness and weaken her, and that might hurry her death on. While he was still thinking about this, Dalilah came in.

"Master," she said. She stood in the doorway, which he had left open according to the Law, which said that a man and a woman who are not of the same family may not be alone in the same room with the door closed. Curious, he thought—now of all times, in her final illness, she has gone back to being a woman who is not part of the family. He didn't understand why this should be, but he didn't want to think anymore about it.

"What do you want?" asked Shylock. "Can't you see that you're disturbing us. Leave us alone."

Dalilah cringed at his harsh words, and it occurred to him again how small and thin she was. "The food is ready," she said softly.

Shylock stood up. "I'll come back later," he said to Amalia, and touched her hands, which felt hot and dry. She opened her eyes and tried to smile. The skin was tight over her cheekbones, and for a moment he had the impression that he was seeing the skull beneath the skin, the eye sockets, the nasal hollow, and a grinning, fleshless mouth. Then her face was back again, the lips attempting a smile that was more like a grimace.

"Rest now," he said quietly and touched her cheek tenderly. "Sleep a little. I'll be back soon."

Shylock ate listlessly, and the food did not taste right. He didn't know whether this was because Dalilah hadn't prepared the fish properly, the way Amalia did, or if he had simply lost his appetite. Only the knowledge that food was necessary to maintain life forced him to put one piece of food after another into his mouth with his fingers. Then he went up to his room and purified himself and said the evening prayer more rapidly than was actually permitted, just so he could get back to Amalia more quickly.

She was asleep when he came into the room. He sat down on the chair again. Amalia groaned in her sleep. Perhaps she wasn't really sleeping at all—perhaps it was one of those brief periods of dozing that are nothing at all like healthy, restorative sleep. A few minutes passed, and then she woke up again and had to cough. Shylock sat there for a long time listening to Amalia's rapid breathing and the clattering of crockery from the kitchen. It got darker and darker in the room. A couple of people went past outside the window, and although he couldn't see who they were because it was too dark, he could hear their footsteps and their voices clearly enough. It was Meir Parenzo and his brother Chaim. They seemed to be discussing a book. Meir said, "You can't compare it with . . ." but then their voices died away and he couldn't catch any more.

It was quiet in the kitchen now. Dalilah came and stood there uncertainly. Eventually she said, "It's time to sleep, master."

He raised his head and looked at her. Her face was just a blur over the burning oil lamp that she was carrying. He rubbed his eyes and said in a tired voice, "You go up and sleep in Jessica's bed. I'll stay with Amalia. If I need you I'll wake you."

He watched her light the lamp on the cabinet, take out her nightdress, then bend over Amalia and kiss her hand, and then she disappeared.

Now they were alone, he and Amalia, in spite of the open door. He looked at Amalia's face and thought of how Leah had looked before she died, familiar and yet very unfamiliar, as if her soul had no longer been in her body. He took hold of Amalia's hand and just sat there. He could hear voices from the Campo, and lots of people were still awake. He didn't know whether Amalia was asleep, he didn't know if she could hear him, but still he began to speak to her as he used to speak to Leah. "Tubal Benevisti came to see me today. He wanted to persuade me to accept the offer the Venetian merchants have made to collect three thousand ducats to free Antonio. But I can't. Can you understand that, Amalia? I just can't do it, never mind what happens. They have done more to me than a human being can bear."

She didn't answer, and her breathing was now very quick and shallow. "Amalia," he said a little louder, then again, frightened, "Amalia!" She didn't hear him. He wondered if he should send Dalilah to fetch Marta, Amalia's sister, but the idea of having that old hunchback in the room and listening to her wailing made him feel sick. He held Amalia's hot hand. She's still alive, he thought. Perhaps the Everlasting One, blessed be He, has relented and won't take Amalia away from me as well just yet. Why do I always realize what it is I want only when it is too late? I should have done things quite differently. I should have left the Ghetto with Amalia. . . .

Amalia groaned and opened her eyes.

"We could have gone to live in some other city," he said, as if he had simply been in conversation with her the whole time. "Why didn't we just go away and settle down somewhere else under assumed names? You needn't have been a divorced woman, and I needn't have been one of the *Kohanim*."

"Yes, perhaps we should have done that," said Amalia, so quietly that he could hardly hear. "But now it's too late."

"Should I take you to the hospital in the Ghetto Vecchio?" asked Shylock.

She tried to shake her head. "No, Shylock, it's too late for that too. Let me die here in peace, in this house, where I've spent most of the nights of my life. I only want one thing of you, Shylock. Let Jessica know that I was thinking of her at the end of my days. Let her know that I loved her with all my heart, regardless of what she may have done. The Everlasting One, blessed be He, made me barren. But He was merciful and gave me two daughters to care for." Exhausted, she fell silent and closed her eyes.

Shylock waited patiently until she had gathered her strength and looked at him, and then he asked, "What did we do wrong, Amalia? We loved her, didn't we?"

"We loved her too much," said Amilia. "She was something quite different and special for us, she wasn't the link between generations. We thought about her too much, and not enough about Dalilah. We made Jessica weak by giving her too much love, and we hurt Dalilah by not giving her enough love. The middle way, Shylock—we never found the middle way, neither you nor I. . . . Promise me that you'll let her know. . . ."

Her voice trailed off, getting weaker and weaker, until her words were just a murmur.

He squeezed her hand as a sign that he had understood. His eyes filled with tears. He made no effort to hold them back or wipe them away. Leah, he thought, Leah, it was the same with you. Don't be angry, Leah, I've never forgotten you, but Amalia has looked after me faithfully for many years, and my heart is aching. I don't want to lose her.

He dipped a cloth into a bowl of water that was standing on the cabinet and wiped the sweat off Amalia's forehead.

She looked at him with gratitude, almost tenderly, but he felt that she was slipping further and further away from him. "Go and call Dalilah," she whispered. "And then pray for me."

Dalilah knelt by Amalia's bed and held her hand. Shylock felt too weak to stand, and sat facing southeast, in the direction of Jerusalem. He pulled the lamp on the cabinet nearer to himself and started to read the prayers for the beginning of the Day of Atonement. He spoke slowly and clearly and waited after every sentence for Amalia to whisper a few words after him. He read as if in a dream, and, suddenly, he felt just as he had before, when he had read the prayers over his mother, or for his sister Jessica, who had died of a fever, and then finally for Leah. All these occasions merged with one another, the places became mixed up and Amalia's voice became confused with Leah's. He tried to concentrate on the words, which were supposed to bring him comfort, but he felt nothing, absolutely nothing, and he was incapable of thinking a single clear thought. Only occasionally did a word penetrate his consciousness, a single, meaningless word, and it was not until he said the *Sh'ma,* the most important of all the prayers, "Hear, O Israel," which he had to say seven times—*Sh'ma Yisrael, adonay elohenu adonay ekhud*—that he felt himself breathing once more, felt the beating of his heart and was aware of his voice coming from his mouth, and so he read until he heard Dalilah scream.

He turned round and saw that Amalia was trying to sit up. Her face was torn with pain, but instead of the last words of the *Sh'ma Yisrael,* a gush of blood came from her mouth and stained her nightdress. Dalilah had pulled her hands back in her shock, and was staring at Amalia in horror, holding her breath. Amalia sank back and closed her eyes. Her hands twitched once or twice more, and then they didn't move again. The bright red flecks on her cheeks disappeared. Her lips were drawn into a gentle smile and her face looked relaxed, almost contented. The lines on her face seemed to smooth out and the skin that was stretched across her cheekbones seemed to loosen. Her mouth was open as if she wanted to say something. Dalilah pulled the coverlet up to Amalia's chin to hide the blood. Shylock would have liked to touch Amalia again, that face, those hands, but he was one of the *Kohanim,* forbidden to touch the dead, just as he was not allowed even to be under the same roof as a corpse.

Dalilah burst into loud tears. Shylock lifted her up and led her out of the room, to give the soul time to leave the body. "Go over to Menasheh Padoani of the Charitable Brotherhood," he said. "He'll look after all that has to be done."

Dalilah wept, tore her hair, and made a ritual cut, a *k'ri'ah,* on the left-hand side of her dress, rending her garment as if her mother had died. "Go," he repeated, and he took his coat and left the house with her.

It was cold outside and not particularly dark. The sky was full of stars. There was no one to be seen on the Campo, and apart from his own footsteps, no sound of anyone either. The noise of his steps resounded and were tossed back as an echo from the walls of the houses, as if he were walking along in a deep ravine. The empty Campo looked ghostly and mysterious. Shylock went down to the bridge and stared into the canal. He sank to the ground and leaned his back against the wall of the house belonging to Manuel Todesco, the cantor. He could feel even through the material of his clothes how cold the stonework was. To his left rose the bridge, in front of him on the other side he could see the door to the house of the Torah scribe, Simone di Modena. From somewhere in the Ghetto Vecchio came the cry of a night bird, and from one of the houses on the far side of the canal he could hear a baby crying. But nothing affected him, none of this had anything to do with him; it was all foreign to him, and he was very alone.

Only when he heard rapid steps on the Campo did he look up. Figures were hurrying across the open square and disappearing into his house. Shylock stood up, wiped the dirt off his coat, and walked unsteadily across. The lamp still stood on the cabinet in Amalia's room. He stood there and looked in through the window. In the half light he saw that Menasheh Padoani and a couple of other men from the *Compagnia della carite della morte* had arrived.

Menasheh Padoani put a cushion under Amalia's head and held a feather underneath her nose to make quite sure that her soul had left her body. The coverlet slipped to the ground, and the blood on Amalia's nightdress was now a black stain. After the men had said the prescribed prayers, Menasheh spread around the floor some of the straw that he had brought with him, and with the help of two other men from the brotherhood, lifted Amalia out of the bed and placed her on the straw. Dalilah fetched him a white cloth from the chest of drawers, and he covered the dead woman with it. Then he said something to the girl that Shylock couldn't make out—he could only see his lips moving. Dalilah brought a candle and one of Amalia's silver candlesticks. Menasheh Padoani lit the candle and placed it by the dead woman's head.

Dalilah left the room. Shylock knew that she would be going upstairs to drape cloths over the mirrors in the salon and in Jessica's room, and then she would pour away any water that had been standing in the house and in which the angel of death might have washed his sword. And indeed he saw her come back and take the bowl of water away from the chest. He heard the door open and the water splash onto the street. A few moments later some more water was thrown out—that would have been the jug of water he had used to wash his hands, which Dalilah had now fetched from his room. And then a third time, the water from the kitchen.

When a group of women arrived to wash the body, put on the white shroud, and sit and mourn by the body, Menasheh Padoani came out, and Shylock let himself be led, numbly, to Rav Shlomo Meldola, the rabbi. He would stay there until Amalia was taken to the cemetery at the Lido the next day. He would not even be allowed to accompany her on her final journey.

Rabbi Shlomo offered him a place to sleep in his tiny study. Shylock lay down fully clothed on the hard bench. The rabbi had left a candle for him. Shylock stared into the flame. Leah's face appeared before him, clear and distinct, but then it changed before his eyes and became paler and narrower, lines appeared round the eyes and the mouth, the eyelids drooped, the sides of the mouth dipped down until it had become Amalia's face. The shadows cast by the flame danced on the walls, shadows like writing, containing a warning that he tried in vain to decipher.

He blew out the candle and turned to lie on one side. He had never felt so old and so drained of strength. The words that Job had answered Eliphas with came into his mind, and he whispered the passage to himself: "Remember that my life is wind; mine eye shall no more see good. The eye of him that hath seen me shall see me no more; thine eyes are upon me and I am not. As the cloud is consumed and vanisheth away, so he that goeth down to the grave shall come up no more. He shall return no more to his house, neither shall his place know him anymore."

Leah, he thought, Amalia, and just as the image of the two women had merged into one another, their names would from now on be one name. And just as he had been unable to weep when Leah had died, his eyes remained dry this time as well.

Chapter 18

Dalilah . . .

We buried amalia a week ago, and the mourning period when we have to sit *shivah* is over—no one will come again to sit and mourn with us. No one will bring us food anymore either, and from today I have to cook again. Luckily I remembered yesterday to put some beans in to soak, so that we've got something other than bread.

Things are bad for me. How could they not be? While we were sitting *shivah,* I mourned for Amalia, but there was always someone else there, from dawn until dusk. And now the house is empty. I never knew that a house could be so empty. I miss Amalia every minute of the day. It wasn't easy during her illness, but at least she was still there. She told me what to cook, she told me what to buy, she told me what jobs I wasn't to forget. And when there was something I didn't know, I could always go in and ask her. Now, for example, I'd love to ask her how to prepare these red beans the way the Spanish Jews do them. I've had them in to soak overnight, the way Amalia always did, and today I've boiled them with a lot of onions, a bit of leek, some celery, and some carrots. But they tasted quite different the way Amalia did them. What sort of fat was it that Amalia always put on the beans—olive oil or goose dripping? I was like a silly child when she was still alive, and now all of a sudden I'm supposed to be the cook and know everything. Why didn't I pay attention? I always just did what I was told to do. As if I had never wanted to grow up.

Should I run quickly over to Marta and ask her if she knows? No, I don't think so. I've never liked her much, and in the week when people came to sit *shivah* there were times when I could hardly bear her. The master will have to eat the beans as they are. We'll see, maybe a bit more salt will help.

You can hear voices and shouts from outside on the Campo, and out there life still goes on. The day after the funeral Joshua da Costa's daughter-in-law had a baby, a boy. The circumcision will be the day after tomorrow. Why didn't the Everlasting One, blessed be He, rather take old Sarah da Costa and leave Amalia here for a bit longer with me? But you mustn't think things like that. Suddenly I can't stand the emptiness of the house anymore, and I go out onto the Campo.

There are women with buckets crowding around the old cistern to fetch water, and by the second of the water cisterns there are tubs with washing in them. The wife of Chaim Luzatto, the shopkeeper, and his daughter are doing the washing today. We always did our washing in the kitchen where we could boil water, and then we threw the soapy water straight into the canal. Well, Amalia did a lot of things her own way. I go for a slow walk along by the houses. The sun is shining and it's a pleasant day, with plenty of people thronging the Campo. It's odd—a human being has died, but the sun goes on shining as if nothing had happened. Things are going on all around me too, as if nothing had happened. I feel like an outcast.

We get more sunshine than a lot of people in Venice. In Sestiere or in Cannaregio there are lots of little lanes that are so narrow that no ray of sun can ever penetrate them. It's suffocating there in the summer and cold in the winter. Where we are, the houses are all built around the great Campo and every house gets the sun. In the afternoon Amalia often used to put a chair outside the door and sit there mending clothes or sewing in the sunshine. And Jessica and I often used to take our embroidery and sit there with her. Amalia . . .

The smell of vegetable soup, cabbage, and slightly burned polenta is coming from the kitchen of the Brotherhood for the Care of the Sick. A group of boys are sitting on the ground in a circle in the corner by the Ponte di San Girolamo. I don't need to see them properly to know that they are playing dice. When we were children, Jessica and I, Amalia bought us some dice, against the master's will. He doesn't like games of chance. We used to play when he was in the countinghouse, or secretly in our room before we went to sleep.

In front of the house of Isaac dalle Torre, Zipporah is sitting with her little brother Shlomo. He's blind. She is reading him the same passages from the Bible over and over again until he knows them by heart. Little Shlomo suddenly lifts his head and points over toward the bakery. Now I hear it too. Chaim di Modena, the baker, gives a great roar, then the door is flung open and Moyshe, his son, hurtles out holding his hand against his cheek. Chaim di Modena lashes out very easily, everyone knows that. I don't think Amalia ever hit us. At least, I can't remember her ever having hit us.

There are such a lot of people on the Campo so late in the afternoon. And still I feel alone without Amalia. As if I were the only person and all the rest were ghosts. Or as if I were a ghost amongst people. I walk to the Canale degli Agudi and sit down by the water. Whenever you have worries, Amalia often used to say, look into the water and let your thoughts flow with the current. You'll see that it will help. You just have to look at the water for long enough, and you'll be peaceful and calm. Oh, Amalia, how calm I'd be if I could only see you. . . .

There were lots of people at her funeral—I hadn't realized at all how well thought of she clearly was. There were three boatloads of us when we left the Canale di Cannaregio. I can't remember the journey across the open lagoon. I sat there with my head bowed, staring at Amalia's coffin. It was only when we got to the bridge at San Pietro di Castello that I was scared into looking up, because people on the bridge were shouting down and shaking their fists at us. We are not even allowed to carry our dead to their graves in peace, said someone behind me. But at least they didn't throw any stones or pour water down on us as we went under the bridge.

After that it didn't take long for us to reach the Lido, and our cemetery is not far from San Nicolò. Tubal Benevisti was already waiting for us at the entrance. I thought he would be. After all, he's been a guest in our house many times. But I was surprised to see Joshua da Costa there with his sons and his daughter-in-law Rachel. His other daughter-in-law was at home because she didn't dare go out when her confinement was going to be so soon. The *parness* even made a speech about the value of piety and virtue, and what a good, God fearing and hardworking woman Amalia had been. Then he said that he hoped the Everlasting One, blessed be He, would look with favor on the fact that even though she had had to bear the burden of childlessness herself, she had brought up two motherless girls.

Now a cluster of boys of various ages has just come rushing out of the Scuola Grande Tedesca yelling and shouting. You can see how happy they are that lessons are over. Their teacher, Aaron ben Avram, is dragging himself along painfully on his sticks behind them.

Yes, the *parness* talked about two motherless girls. But only one of them was at the funeral, and that was me. I stood next to Marta, Amalia's sister, her only relative in the Ghetto. Marta was crying loudly and without any restraint, so that sometimes you couldn't hear what the *parness* was saying because her sobs were drowning him out. Water was running from her eyes and her nose as well. Eventually it was Rachel da Costa who went over and put her arm around Marta's shoulders. When they made the ritual tear in Marta's clothes, the *k'ri'ah,* on the right-hand side, as appropriate for a sister, I touched the tear on my left side, which is what you do for the death of a parent. Then the coffin was lowered into the earth. When I threw my three handfuls of earth into the open grave, right after Marta, I started to cry as well, so hard that I could barely bring out the words: "Dust thou art and to dust shalt thou return. Then shall the dust return to the earth as it was, and the spirit shall return unto God, who gave it."

After we had all washed our hands, to remove impurity and in token of the fact that we were innocent of the death of the departed, we said the sixteenth Psalm. Manuel Todesco, the cantor, said the *kaddish,* the prayer for the dead, because it is an act of charity to say the *kaddish* for a woman who has died without any male relatives. Then we went home. For the whole way from Cannaregio to the Campo, Marta insisted that I should support her and help her along. It wasn't very nice. It's hard to support someone who is limping, and you can hardly see where you are walking. But all the time I kept saying to myself: she's Amalia's sister, she's Amalia's sister. That made it easier for me.

I had already prepared our room—the one where Amalia had died—for people to come and sit *shivah.* Jehuda had helped me. He had brought in some low stools, and, between us, we moved the bed into his old room to make a space for the mourners. Someone—I think it was Rosa, the wife of Shimon ibn Lazar—brought boiled eggs and lentils, and we ate.

The master came to this meal. He sat on one of the low stools, his face like a rock. I noticed that he had made a tear in his coat, on the right-hand side and quite small, so that you might have thought it was accidental. But I knew perfectly well that his coat hadn't been torn before.

Tubal Benevisti sat down next to him and whispered a few words to him, but I didn't catch what he said. I was sitting against the opposite wall, next to Marta. She was telling everyone who was prepared to listen how wonderful, virtuous, and provident Amalia had been, even as a small child. Her mother had brought up the two girls alone, as their father had died young, of consumption, just like poor Amalia, may her memory be a blessing to us. She told about how Amalia had helped her mother with everything, had never said a harsh word against her mother or her sister, how she had been a positive angel, and as beautiful and strong as a summer's day. And then she started on about Amalia's husband. Leone had been a good enough man, she said, but he had never amounted to anything here. And since she hadn't given him any children, he'd divorced her and sailed off to the New World. That was a bad time. And then she started crying again. If Leone had still been here, she sobbed, he could have looked after me. I'm deformed—the Everlasting One, blessed be He, has given me this burden to bear. Amalia was a great comfort to me and always helped me out.

Amalia never mentioned that at all. Well, she wasn't the kind of person who chattered all the time. Certainly not about good works. I've heard her say often enough that *mitzvoth* have to be done in secret without anyone knowing, otherwise they just serve your own vanity and are worthless before God. But I didn't have time to think about it for too long because Marta had started again about how hardworking and virtuous Amalia had been, even when she was still only a child, and how kind and loving she had been to her elder and deformed sister.

I would rather have sat somewhere else and thought quietly about Amalia, but Marta insisted that I should sit next to her the whole time. And, of course, she told everyone at least three times a day about how Amalia had persuaded the master to take me in, a little orphan girl not yet four years old from a family no one knew anything about. And she always ended the story with the words: You owe her your eternal gratitude, Dalilah. And the women listening nodded in acknowledgment that she was right.

I nodded too and said, "Yes, Marta, your sister was a good woman, may the memory of her be a blessing to us." And to myself I thought: Oh, Amalia, if only you were here now. What idea can Marta have of how much I *really* owe you in gratitude?

People were there constantly while we were sitting *shivah.* Someone always brought some food for us, and in the mornings and evenings men came from the Scuola Grande Tedesca, so that there was a *minyan* of at least ten men to pray with us. Tubal Benevisti read the Book of Job aloud to us, with beautiful expression, and Rabbi Shlomo Meldola read from the Lamentations of Jeremiah. It was very solemn and it made me cry again.

On the fifth day of the *shivah* period, a merchant from the Rialto came—Isaac Levi, a man that the master had sent me to with messages once or twice in the past. I recognized him at once by his sticking-out ears—there isn't anyone else in the world whose ears stick out so much. He brought the news that the Christian merchants had raised the money to pay Antonio's debt and release him from prison. There was great relief in his voice. All the men got very excited and wanted to talk to the master about it, but he refused, and said no, not today, not now, he didn't want to talk business during the period of mourning. But I saw that later on he went out with Tubal Benevisti, and then I heard their steps on the stairs. Tubal Benevisti left the house without coming in to us again, and he wasn't there for the prayers in the evening. I didn't see him on the sixth or seventh days either.

The master wasn't obliged to sit *shivah*. Amalia wasn't his sister and she wasn't his wife, but he did it anyway. He often said the *kaddish* for her too. And the whole time he sat there stony faced. I kept on looking at him from the side, and I thought about what Jessica had said: He should rend his garments and weep, as you do when a child has died. He isn't the first man to have lost a daughter. I could hear her words so clearly that I caught myself looking around for her. The master didn't mourn for her as if she had died, like the Torah scribe Simone di Modena did when his daughter ran away from the Ghetto to marry one of them. The master hasn't mourned for Jessica, I thought, but he is mourning for Amalia. But perhaps he's thinking of Jessica anyway.

This morning when I was at the bakery buying some bread, I heard that the master has insisted on justice. Rachel da Costa was saying that he isn't prepared to take the three thousand ducats from the Venetian merchants. Her father-in-law has apparently tried to talk to him twice, but he won't listen. Rosa, the wife of Shimon ibn Lazar, was there and she said: May the Everlasting One, blessed be He, punish him for his arrogance. And Rachel da Costa added: We must all pray that we don't all have to pay for his sins.

The trial is the day after tomorrow. I can't talk to the master about it, however heavy my heart may be. He just refuses to talk to anyone. Over the midday meal I tried very carefully to broach the subject: I heard a rumor today, I said, about Antonio. . . .

He gave me a really hard look and said: I don't want to hear about it. Keep out of things that don't concern you. Not another word! Do you understand? And after that he went straight back to his countinghouse.

I miss Amalia so much. How happy I was before, how easy my life was! I get up, brush the dust off my skirt, and set off for home. Sarah da Costa, the crippled wife of the old *parness,* is sitting in the upstairs window and my wicked thoughts about her come to me again. While I am looking up at her, Rachel comes in and wipes the spit away from Sarah's mouth. I am too far away to see exactly what she is doing, but I've seen them often enough to know that Rachel is wiping the cloth over the open mouth and then the neck of the old lady. I can't remember a time anymore when Sarah da Costa was healthy, but Amalia often used to say that she had been a strong woman, a beautiful woman who never said an unkind word about anyone. And when she said that, there was pity and sympathy in her voice.

But now Amalia is dead and Sarah da Costa is still alive.

I turn around quickly and run into the kitchen. The house is just as empty as it was before, and the beans still don't taste the way they did when Amalia cooked them. So I'll add a little bit more salt.

It will be some time yet before Shylock comes back from the countinghouse. I'll lie down for a little while on the bed in what used to be Jehuda's room, where I am still sleeping until someone can come and help me get the bed back into our room, the room that is now just mine. I'm not going to ask anyone to help, and I'd rather wait until the end of the full month's mourning. Perhaps Amalia's soul still hasn't quite managed to cut itself free of this earth, perhaps she comes back at night. Nobody can be sure. I'd prefer not to sleep in there for the time being.

What does the master really want? To cut a pound of flesh from Antonio's body? To use a knife to cut into a living person? I've got to make myself think of something else quickly, or I'll be sick.

I think I've put too much salt into the beans.

Chapter 19

SHYLOCK LEFT THE DOGE'S PALACE where the trial had taken place. The light struck him so brightly that he was dazzled and had to shut his eyes. He groped for one of the columns to support himself, then stumbled along to the next. The stone beneath his hands was rough and cold, but his fingers were even colder. He still felt numb and unable to form any clear thoughts, while phrases and scraps of phrases went round and round in his head. My justice. You shall have your justice. When thou sittest to eat with a prince. They speak according to their wilfulness. A pound of flesh. You shall have your justice, Jew. Three thousand ducats. I offer him six thousand. You shall have your justice. Here is the bond. Put a knife to thy throat if thou be a man given to appetite. But no jot of blood. "I will leave my complaint upon myself; I will speak in the bitterness of my soul. They speak according to their wilfulness to cause harm and turn things as they will." A pound of flesh, no more and no less. Mark, Jew. No jot of blood. If you should spill one drop of Christian blood your life shall then be forfeit. There, now you have had your justice, Jew. Take it. A pound of flesh, no more and no less. But no jot of blood.

Shylock stopped, leaned against a pillar, and waited until he could get his thoughts straight in his head. They rose up like ships in the fog, appearing for a moment on the horizon and then vanishing. He took no notice of the astonished looks of the passersby, who assumed that he was drunk, and he didn't hear their mockery or their laughter. He waited until the fog in his mind gradually went away, and he could see in front of him, even if it was still blurred, the outline of the Piazza San Marco, the Torre dell'Orlogio, and the passage through which he would have to go. He set off.

Nor did he see Dalilah, who was standing a little way away from him in the shadow of one of the columns, and had been watching him the whole time. She didn't dare to come closer, nor to leave. She stood there like a statue and couldn't take her eyes from the figure of her master, who had lurched like a drunkard from one column to the next, his lips moving soundlessly. Only when he had crossed the piazza with weary and uncertain steps and had disappeared into the passageway by the clock tower did she tear herself out of her trancelike state and follow him, keeping a distance between them.

Shylock took no heed of where he was going—he just went on, away from this court, a court he had entered with such certainty, where he had hoped to find justice and where people turned justice upside down. His feet were moving as if they didn't belong to him. The skies were gray, the stones were gray. When thou sittest to eat with a prince, he thought, consider diligently what is before thee, and put a knife to thy throat if thou be a man given to appetite. Now I understand, Tubal, now, at last, only now it is too late. Why do I only ever understand things when it is too late. Why? What was it you said, Tubal? You think you have right on your side, but in the end you'll find out that it is only a Jew's right.

The sentence pronounced by the young judge still rang in his ears: The words expressly are "a pound of flesh," thus it says in the bond. But take care, Jew, that you spill no jot of blood. Your bond speaks just of flesh. And if you wish to cause the death of any Christian citizen, then your life shall be forfeit. So mark, Jew, not a jot of blood.

At that moment it became clear to him that he had lost, that his justice was worthless, then it was exactly as it was written: "They speak according to their wilfulness to do harm, and turn things as they will." But this time the words of the Holy Scriptures were no comfort to him.

"I believed that I had right on my side, but in the end it was only a Jew's right," said Shylock, without noticing that he had spoken aloud. A couple of street urchins coming past with a barrow load of wood saw the crazed-looking man who seemed to be talking to himself. "It's a Jew who's gone mad! Pity they don't all go mad!" One of them barged into him. Shylock stumbled and fell face first into the filth of the street. The street urchins whooped and went on their way. The rattling of the wooden wheels could be heard for a long time.

Shylock lay there dazed, defeated and laid low, like Job. His complaint rose up in front of him, not like a thought, but like a picture. He imagined he could see letters in the dust of the street, perfectly clear, although everything else was blurred: "Wherefore then hast brought me forth out of the womb?" he read. "Oh that I had given up the ghost and no eye had seen me! I should have been as though I had not been, I should have been carried from the womb to the grave. Are not my days few? Cease, then, and let me alone, that I may take comfort a little, before I go whence I shall not return, even to the land of darkness and the shadow of death. A land of darkness as darkness itself; and of the shadow of death, without any order and where the light is as darkness."

Then he noticed that someone was pulling on his arm, lifting him to his feet, and brushing the dust from his coat with quick, careful movements. It was Dalilah. "I waited for you outside the court," she said. "Come along, master, I'll take you home."

Like a helpless child he let the girl lead him. She took his hand and led him around any obstacles, pushed him along when his steps became slow, and supported him when he had to cross a bridge. He put one foot in front of the other as if he were a wooden puppet, with no idea of where he was. The houses were foreign to him, the streets were foreign, he was a stranger in their city. Where was the girl taking him? Only when they reached the Ponte di San Girolamo did he recognize where he was. Home. But this word had lost its meaning too, and was no longer the safe refuge that it used to be.

Shylock stood in front of his house, his arms hanging lifelessly at his side, while Dalilah opened the door. She took off his red hat and helped him carefully out of his coat, the way a mother would help a child, and then she led him up the stairs to his room. There she lit him a light before she pushed him down into a chair, took off his shoes, and led him to his bed. He fell onto his bed and closed his eyes. As if in a dream he heard her leave the room, go downstairs, and open the front door of the house. Then it closed, and he was alone.

Leah, he thought. Amalia. Man is born alone and dies alone, and in between he sometimes just imagines that he is not alone.

He lay on his back and stared at the ceiling, across which yellow-gray shadows were flickering. Faces rose up in front of his eyes that he didn't recognize, but which were still familiar to him. Men, women, children. They moved forward in an endless, sad procession, carrying wretched bundles—old men supported by other old men, women pressing newborn babies to their meager breasts. They all filed past him in an endless line. He saw from their open mouths and from the despair in their eyes that they were lamenting and crying, but no sound reached his ears. A gray, sad, and seemingly never-ending procession. And then he picked out faces that he knew amongst them—his father, his mother, his sister Jessica, Leah, Amalia. He tried to get up from the bed and join in the procession, but his limbs refused to obey him. It got dark all around him, and he let himself slip into the darkness.

He woke again when the door was opened downstairs. Hurried footsteps came up the stairs, then Tubal Benevisti came in carrying a large basket. He put the basket down, sat on the edge of the bed, and took Shylock's hand as you might take the hand of a sick man, to show your sympathy.

"Everything has turned out the way you said it would, Tubal," murmured Shylock at last. "I thought I had right on my side, but it was still only a Jew's right."

Tubal nodded, and ran his hand over Shylock's fingers, which were still very cold.

"A young lawyer presided," said Shylock hesitatingly, "so young that he didn't even have a man's voice yet. First of all he seemed to grant the justice of my case, checked the bond and found that it was in accordance with the laws of Venice. I was fooled and was already congratulating myself inwardly and looking at the fear in Antonio's eyes. But then he said: A pound of flesh, no more and no less. But take care that you spill no jot of blood. If you should spill one drop of Christian blood, your life shall be forfeit. Tubal, I am only a Jew, who is granted his rights by being cheated out of them."

"I know," said Tubal. His voice was gentle, and he stroked Shylock's hand. "I've already heard about it all, my friend, you don't need to tell me any more."

"Three thousand ducats have been lost, and you gave me a thousand of them. How am I to pay you back?"

"Don't worry about that, Shylock. You know that I am not a poor man."

Shylock turned his face away as he continued, "And even that isn't the worst. Have you also heard about Antonio's demand that I should allow myself to be baptized?"

"Yes," said Tubal. "Yes, I heard that as well." Shylock looked his friend in the face for the first time. Tubal nodded. "That's why I'm here," he said. "I would have come anyway, even if Dalilah hadn't come to fetch me, because I had everything ready. You will have to run away, Shylock, my friend. You have no choice."

"I won't run away," said Shylock. "Let them complete their work, let them kill me. What is happening to me is just as Job says: 'Though I were perfect, yet I despise my life. This is one thing, therefore I said it, He destroyeth the perfect and the wicked. If the scourge slay suddenly, He will laugh at the trials of the innocent. The earth is given into the hand of the wicked and He covereth the faces of the judges thereof.'"

"Shylock," said Tubal angrily, "the Everlasting One, blessed be He, gave you your life, and only He has the right to take it away from you. It is your duty to stay alive, never mind what has happened. None of that can be changed. But you are alive. Wake up, Shylock. You have to save yourself. You are not the first Jew who has had to leave his homeland to stay alive, and you won't be the last. May the Everlasting One, blessed be He, preserve us from any more misfortune."

"I was born in the Veneto, I grew up in the Veneto," said Shylock. "I've become a person of respect here in Venice and it was here that I lived with Leah, may her memory be a blessing upon us." He hesitated, and then added in a slightly lower voice, "And I lived with Amalia as well, for a few years."

Tubal nodded again.

"Did you know?" said Shylock.

"I'd guessed," answered Tubal.

"Did you go with her on her last journey?" asked Shylock.

"I did," said Tubal. "Many people went with her on that journey—she was a well-respected woman. You would have been proud of her to see so many mourners paying their respects."

"Tubal," said Shylock, "you must seek Jessica out and tell her that Amalia loved her and was thinking about her in her last hours. It was her dying wish, and you will have to fulfil it, as I can't." Once again he saw Amalia's face in front of him, torn by pain. "Jessica was guilty toward her too," he said angrily. "Amalia could not bear her betrayal. It broke her heart."

"I'll try my best to fulfil Amalia's wish," said Tubal. "Let us not talk about Jessica—what's done is done. I just want to say one thing. You were guilty toward Jessica too. You didn't arrange a marriage for her at the proper time, which was your duty. But don't torment yourself, my friend. It is written: 'A man's heart deviseth his way, but the Lord directeth his steps.' Now you have to think of your own escape."

Tubal took a leather bag out of his pocket.

"Here, I've brought you money, and two letters. One of them is addressed to my friend Isaac ben Eliezer, who lives in Rome. He will take you into his house and help you build up a new life. He's a good and upright man. The other one is addressed to Joseph Nassi, who fled from Venice to Constantinople years ago. If you think it better to move into the Ottoman Empire, he will help you. There are plenty of flourishing Jewish communities there where you can build up a new life for yourself. But you will absolutely have to take a new name, just in case you have to avoid being pursued."

"I'm an old man," cried out Shylock despairingly. "It is written: 'Now my days are swifter than a post; they flee away, they see no good.' How am I to start a new life at my age?"

"You are only on the threshold of old age," interrupted Tubal. "And no one can tell how many more days the Everlasting One, blessed be He, will grant you. Take heart,

Shylock. He, who has taken so much from you, will also give you the strength for a new life."

"I will not take any money from you," said Shylock. "I still have some hidden. When Dalilah is asleep we can fetch it. But it isn't as much as a thousand ducats, and I shall still be in your debt. Only God knows whether I shall ever be able to repay you. I am sorry that you have lost money through my fault."

Tubal smiled and put the bag down on the bed. " 'If a man see his neighbor and he sinketh in the flood, or if a wild beast shall carry him off, or if he fall amongst robbers, then it shall be his duty to save him,' " said Tubal. "That too is written. You mustn't stop me from carrying out a *mitzvah*, or the guilt will be upon you. And now get up, Shylock, my friend. You have to set off today, as soon as night falls. I've brought you different clothes so that you won't be recognized immediately. It's all arranged. I'll take you to a fisherman who will take you as far as he can in his boat." He laughed, though there was no humor in the laugh. "When it's a question of baptism they are very quick off the mark, our princes and nobles. It's possible that there might be a knock at the door in the early hours tomorrow morning, and they'll have come for you."

Shylock stood up obediently. He looked at the blue *zimarra* and the feathered cap that Tubal took out of the basket and put on a chair. "I shan't even look like a Jew," said Shylock in a dull voice. "How will my Jewish brothers be able to recognize me?"

"Until you get there," said Tubal, "never mind whether it is Rome or Constantinople, nobody is supposed to recognize you as a Jew. Quickly now, let's pack the things that you absolutely need."

"Dalilah can do that," said Shylock, but Tubal shook his head.

"No, Dalilah mustn't know. She mustn't be a witness to your escape in case they ask her where you are. She's not much more than a child, and you can't give her that kind of burden to carry."

Silently Shylock packed the little blue velvet bag with the phylacteries, the bag that Leah had made for him and had embroidered with a Star of David even before they had been married. The material was already fragile. Then he packed his prayer shawl and prayer books. After that the friends went together to the Scuola Grande Tedesca, to pray together one last time. Shylock hardly dared look around him. It all looked different, it all sounded different when you knew it was the last time, the last farewell. He looked over to Joshua da Costa's place. The *parness* was there, praying. Slowly Shylock went over to him and held out his hand. The *parness* took it and looked questioningly at Shylock. Shylock just nodded. That was their farewell. Nothing more was needed.

Even when he and Tubal at last sat down to eat their evening meal together that Dalilah had prepared for them, Shylock had the feeling that he was eating herring for the last time, and bread for the last time, and cheese for the last time. And when they said the prayers after eating, he suddenly thought that this could be the last time too, and the thought came as a shock.

He sent Dalilah up to bed early. Then he and Tubal took a last walk across the Campo, over the Ponte degli Agudi, and down to the Canale di Cannaregio. Only when they reckoned that Dalilah was asleep did they walk back slowly. After they had taken the money from its hiding place, Shylock packed some food, put on the strange clothes, and tiptoed quietly out, leaving the house in which he had spent so many years.

The boat was waiting at the Canale di Cannaregio and the fisherman was a young, strong fellow with an open and friendly face, a man you could trust.

"Don't forget to pass Amalia's last words on to Jessica," said Shylock, as he took his leave of Tubal Benevisti. "And one more thing. On the anniversary of Leah's death, go to the cemetery and say the *kaddish* for her. And on the anniversary of Amalia's death as well, please."

Chapter 20

A COACH HAD TAKEN JESSICA and Lorenzo from Belmont to Padua. Lorenzo would happily have stayed longer, but at Jessica's insistence he had agreed to leave his friends Bassanio and Antonio. "Very well," he had said, "we'll travel to Padua, to Tia Rosalia, my aunt, and we'll stay there for a while. She hasn't any children, so perhaps we can settle ourselves in and stay with her until everything has blown over and been forgotten." By "everything" he meant my background in the Ghetto and the trial, thought Jessica as she took her shoes off. By "everything" he meant my poor father.

Tia Rosalia's maid had brought hot water up to the little room next to the one they slept in, had filled the bathtub, put in some scented oils, and was now helping Jessica to undress. "You may go now," said Jessica, when she was standing in her underclothes. "I should like to be alone." Jessica still found it uncomfortable to show herself naked in front of strangers, even if the person concerned was only a maid.

The maid, a young thing with a cheeky face, curtsied and left. Jessica wasn't sure if she had seen contempt and malicious amusement on the girl's face, or whether she had just imagined it. Did the girl maybe know that she was Jewish? Then she told herself firmly: Stop that kind of speculation once and for all. In the eyes of justice and the law you are an Italian noblewoman, regardless of what you might feel inside.

Jessica sank back into the warm water. She was alone for the first time in days. For the first time since that evening when Portia, Bassanio, and Antonio had arrived at Belmont, excited and in a festive mood, she didn't need to pretend, didn't need to force herself to laugh. What a dreadful evening that had been.

The warm water relaxed her, and she slipped deeper into the tub and closed her eyes. Images rose up before her, just as if she were in the theater.

On the richly decorated stage stood a table, underneath a chandelier with a huge number of lit candles, and in front of several high and narrow windows with dark-red velvet curtains. Around the table, on chairs with high, straight backs and red-and-white striped upholstery, sat five players, three men and two women.

The first man was young and handsome, with long narrow fingers and a full red mouth. Whenever he spoke, you could see his white teeth. He was wearing a yellow silk shirt and a blue waistcoat, with a red scarf knotted round his neck. He had almost never looked so handsome, thought Jessica, as handsome as he does now, sitting in front of me on the stage. My heart aches at how beautiful he is.

The second man was Bassanio, coarser-looking than Lorenzo, with a sharp nose and thin lips. Especially his upper lip, which was not much more than a straight line.

When he laughed, he showed huge teeth, almost as big as a horse's. He was wearing dark-green breeches, and under his white waistcoat he had a pale-green shirt. The third man was older than the other two and a little on the portly side. That was Antonio. On his self-satisfied face, the face of an elderly baby, could be seen his satisfaction at having won the case against "the Jew," which is what he always called him.

Jessica sank even deeper into the water, but the two women did not disappear; she could still see them, and had to watch them whether she liked it or not. One of the two women was Portia. She was still dressed up as a lawyer and seemed disinclined to change her clothes for the time being. She had clearly enjoyed playing the role too much to want to part with the costume. And now she was obviously revelling in the admiration of the three men.

She isn't actually very beautiful, thought Jessica, but if you're rich and aristocratic, that obviously isn't very important. Especially when you are Christian by birth.

Next to Portia sat the second woman. Jessica couldn't avoid looking at her. The second woman was young and beautiful and she had two faces. She showed a laughing face to the audience, but Jessica could see her other face perfectly clearly, a face on which you could see horror at all she was hearing. Why has she got that false smile? thought Jessica. Why is she lying? Why doesn't she scream out in her pain? Why didn't she say anything when Antonio called her own father "that Jew"?

"And he had to sign a deed of gift declaring that you are his heir," Bassanio was just saying to Lorenzo. Why is he saying that? thought Jessica. I am my father's daughter, I'm the one to inherit.

Lorenzo laughed out loud, a laugh that usually she loved, but which this time caused her pain. "I knew he'd have to leave everything to us," he cried out. "I knew it! No more poverty—that Jew has got what he deserves!" He raised his goblet and said to Portia, "My thanks to the beautiful and wise advocate!"

Bassanio and Antonio raised their glasses as well and shouted, "Yes, to the beautiful and wise advocate!"

Wait! That's not how the play is supposed to go, said Jessica in her bathtub. Lorenzo mustn't say "that Jew." Nobody should really, but certainly not Lorenzo. Has he forgotten that "that Jew" is my father, the man to whom I owe my existence, who brought me up? Does he perhaps want *me* to forget? She turned her face away, but in front of her closed eyes the play went on.

The second woman, the one with the two faces, smiled. Why are you smiling? asked Jessica. Don't you know what your father is having to suffer just now?

Portia raised her hand and said in her disguised voice, "You shall have your justice, Jew, and more than you wished. A pound of flesh, no more and no less. But take care that you do not spill a single drop of Christian blood, or your life shall be forfeit."

"You should have seen his face," put in Bassanio enthusiastically. "First of all, he'd been so confident, and then when he realized what was happening he got paler and paler. Like a beaten dog, he tried to grab at the last bit of bone, the three thousand ducats, but Portia took them away from him as well. What a clever wife I have! With a wife like that what a happy future I can look forward to!" He put his arm around Portia's shoulder and drew her to him possessively. Then he said thoughtfully, "I still don't quite understand why he wouldn't take the money that the Venetian merchants had collected. And certainly not why he didn't grab it when he was offered double that during the trial."

"He wanted flesh," shouted Antonio. "He's a devil! He wanted my flesh!"

And then Jessica heard the two-faced woman speak, "Even when I was still living with him," she said, and looked at the others in turn, "even when I was still living with him he said he would rather have Antonio's flesh than the money."

Why did you say that? thought Jessica, horrified. To make them like you? So that you belong?

The two-faced woman gave no answer. She picked up her glass, and Jessica saw her face contort into an ugly laugh.

She would have liked to smash the glass out of her hand and shout: Is that what you wanted? Did you want to destroy your father's life? Go on, eat the preserves, eat until you're sick. Buy flowers, buy them, but they'll never please you. And what is a life of riches and elegance worth if you always have your father before your eyes? What use are concerts when you can hear your father weeping behind the music? Tell Lorenzo, tell him!

But the other one shook her head. No, I shan't tell him. Stop accusing me, I didn't want all that to happen. I wanted to be free, I wanted feasts, a life in comfort. I wanted to get away from the Ghetto. . . .

Yes, said Jessica, that's what you wanted, and what has become of all your wanting?

It is written: "A man's heart deviseth his way, but the Lord directeth his steps."

Dinner was served. To celebrate winning the case, a lamb had been slaughtered. Everyone set to with a will, eating and drinking and stuffing themselves full, even the two-faced woman.

Have you forgotten the lamb that you always had at the New Year festival in your father's house? asked Jessica. Have you forgotten how happy you were on those days?

The two-faced woman turned her head away, and with a smile of satisfaction Jessica watched as she put her hand over her mouth, jumped up, and ran out into the corridor, where she leaned against the wall and was sick.

Serves you right, said Jessica, just as she and Dalilah often used to say to one another when they were children.

At this moment, the maid came back in with a fresh linen towel in her hand to help Jessica out of the tub and to dry her.

When she had finished dressing the maid was already calling her for the meal. Still churned up inside, Jessica went downstairs slowly. Lorenzo and his aunt were waiting for her at the foot of the staircase.

Tia Rosalia was a stern woman, tight-laced under her dark *gamurra,* over which she wore a *cioppa* that was also dark, with a long train. Her face was very pale, almost white, and the corners of her mouth dipped contemptuously downward as she saw Jessica. She was a large solid woman, and beside her Jessica looked like a child, subjected to hard looks as she was openly inspected. Jessica bowed and did not dare to raise her head again.

Not until they had taken their seats at table and Tia Rosalia had engaged Lorenzo in a lively conversation about some relatives whose names Jessica had never even heard before did she cautiously raise her head. Her glance fell on a painting that hung on the wall behind Tia Rosalia, a portrait of a man in dark but elegant clothes. The fur collar of his *zimarra* was painted so naturally that Jessica would have liked to get up and touch it with her fingers, she was so convinced that she would be able to feel the individual hairs.

"That is a portrait of my late husband," said Tia Rosalia, who had followed Jessica's look. "He was a town senator, a much respected nobleman. Our family has always provided senators. My father, for example, was a senator in Venice."

Jessica lowered her head again. She knew that Tia Rosalia's comments were intended to annoy her. After all, what could she have replied? How nice! And my father is a pawnbroker in the Ghetto.

The maidservant brought in a dish of beans, but they tasted bland and uninteresting, and suddenly Jessica remembered the red beans that Amalia had always cooked—beans done the way the Spanish Jews eat them. If we had our own home, she thought, I could show the cook how to prepare them. I wonder if we shall ever have our own home? Lorenzo likes being a guest, it doesn't bother him. And suddenly she thought: Why should it bother him, anyway? He's just gone on living his life the way he always did. He'll meet up with his friends, whether it's Bassanio or someone else, he'll have these friendships with men, which are so much nobler than love for a woman, and I'll be a prisoner in this or that palazzo. I'm not free. She looked at Tia Rosalia. Was Rachel da Costa, the daughter-in-law of the *parness,* really any worse than Tia Rosalia?

As she cut up the meat that had been set before her, dipped the bread in the sauce, put it into her mouth and chewed it, she had a picture of the kitchen in her father's house and imagined that she could smell the cooking, could hear her father saying the blessing, *ha-motzi,* and could hear too how, after the prayer for the end of the meal, Amalia and Dalilah would say "amen."

Today was Friday, the eve of the Sabbath. Jessica looked out of the window and saw that it was just beginning to get dark. The Ghetto rose up before her inner eyes, the Campo. She could see the rabbis from the different synagogues crossing the square, checking that all the shops had really closed and that every Jew had concluded his business before the Sabbath, the day of rest, had begun. She heard them telling people to light the Sabbath candles. And now the trumpeter, a Christian, paid by the Jews, who sounded the signal for the start of the Sabbath, came into the middle of the square and raised his trumpet to his lips. He sounded the signal three times at intervals of half an hour, starting two hours before the beginning of the Sabbath, so that everyone knew when to start bringing any business dealings to an end. Half an hour before sunset the Sabbath began, and the commandment of rest and keeping it holy came into force. At this time, every woman in every Jewish house had to light a lamp with at least four wicks so that it would burn as far into the night as possible. And on the table, which had been spread ceremonially with a white cloth, was the *challa*, the white Sabbath loaf, covered with another white cloth.

The picture that Jessica had seen every Friday evening now came up before her eyes: Amalia, who lights the two Sabbath candles, places her hands over her eyes and says the blessing: *"Baruch ata adonay elohenu, melekh ha-olam, asher kiddeshanu be-mitsvotav ve-zivanu lehadlik ner shel shabbat."* Praise to Thee, O Lord our God, King of the World, who has sanctified us with His laws and has commanded us to light the Sabbath candles. She saw Amalia and Dalilah standing in front of the table in their Sabbath best. She saw them welcome her father when he came back from the synagogue, lead him to the table, and serve the celebration meal. She heard her father say the blessing and Amalia and Dalilah repeat the words, then she saw them raise the kiddush beakers to their lips, and after that begin to eat. And suddenly she envied them the peace of the Sabbath, while she herself was here, putting the food into her mouth amongst strangers.

Suddenly she felt a longing that was physically painful, which pressed against her eyes from within. I've exchanged the confines of the Ghetto for palaces, she thought. I've exchanged dark colors for bright ones. I did it of my own free will, and I have to take the consequences. My sons will never know how close you can feel yourself to be to another person when you can smell them; they'll never experience the feeling of warmth you get when you wake up and imagine the morning prayers being said in every house. They'll never know their grandfather, "that Jew." Perhaps they'll never even find out that their mother has always been in her heart of hearts, a girl from the Ghetto. My sons. Her monthly cycle was three weeks overdue. She knew what that meant. Hannah Meshullam had told her.

She thought again, as she had done so often, about how young she was, and how many parts she would have to play between now and the end of her days; now that she had cast off so violently the role that had been given to her when she was born, and the thought chilled her, as it always did.

But then she heard Lorenzo say, "Tia Rosalia, I shall be going out again with my wife. I want to show her Padua and introduce her to my friends."

Tia Rosalia pulled a face, but she didn't offer any objection. Jessica knew what she was thinking. A married woman belongs at home. But she was so relieved at the prospect of going out with Lorenzo, wandering through the town and listening to his stories, that she could not suppress a smile.

"I'll put on my other *cioppa*," she said. "Wait for me." Elated, she ran up the staircase. Perhaps she had been too gloomy about the future. Perhaps Lorenzo would love her the way she wanted him to love her once she was the mother of his children. And perhaps her new role, as a mother, would bring her the happiness she had dreamed of. She hoped so. After all, happiness had to be somewhere.

Chapter 21

Dalilah . . .

I'M STANDING IN THE KITCHEN washing my hair. With cold water, to clear my head, because I need a clear head more than anything else. Then I shall take the scissors and go up to Jessica's room so that I can cut my hair in front of the mirror. Even shorter than it is now. Not only so that I'm not recognized. Short hair is better to stop you getting lice when you are traveling. Now as I'm cutting it, strand by strand, I'm trying to recall everything that happened this morning. It's important that I don't forget. Not a single word of what Tubal Benevisti said to me.

The master has disappeared. This morning, when I woke up, he was no longer there. I can understand what he's done, though I haven't any idea where he's gone. Yesterday evening I heard him go out again with Tubal Benevisti, but then I must have fallen asleep. At any rate, when I woke up this morning I saw that he wasn't there anymore.

I dressed quickly and ran over to Tubal Benevisti at once. He looks quite different in his ordinary coat, I thought. Not nearly as elegant as he usually looks. And his face looked older than I remembered it looking. A man who was quite familiar, but who suddenly looked to me like a stranger. Where is my master? I asked while I was still standing in the doorway. I was completely out of breath from running.

I don't know, Dalilah, he said, and took me into his salon. I had never been in his apartments before, and for a moment I stood stock-still. So many books! He offered me a chair and said: I don't know, and it is better if you know nothing too.

I sat on the chair, right on the edge, and hardly dared to look around. So many books! Even more than there are in Rabbi Shlomo Meldola's study. I felt really inhibited being surrounded by so many books. How clever he must be, if he's read all these, I thought. I was so astounded by them that I didn't listen to him at all. But then, when he raised his voice a little, I realized that he had asked me something. I gave a start and looked at him.

He smiled and said: I was asking what plans you have for your future, Dalilah.

Future? I hadn't given it any thought at all yet. Why should I have? For the whole of my life one day after another had come and gone, for the whole of my life I had got up in the morning and gone to bed at night. For the whole of my life Amalia had told me what to do, I'd looked after the master and Jessica. Nothing out of the ordinary ever happened, apart from my visit to Jessica, of course. But otherwise? I had always assumed that life would carry on like that. I hadn't had any reason to think differently.

Suddenly, when Tubal Benevisti asked me the question, I realized that the master's fate would affect me too. And suddenly I felt a surge of anger against him. And against Jessica. And although it sounds stupid, even against Amalia. They all made decisions about what they wanted to do, I thought, and each one did what they thought was most important for them, and none of them gave any thought to those who had to bear the consequences of their actions.

What are you thinking, child? asked Tubal Benevisti.

I told him what was going through my head. He smiled. You are right, he said. But listen to the words of one of our scholars: "My days are like a shadow that declineth, says the Psalmist. Does that mean that life is at least like the shadow of a tower, or of a tree, a shadow that will endure? No. It is like the shadow of a bird which flies past, and when the bird has flown past, there remains neither the bird nor its shadow." He looked at me in a kindly manner and asked me: Are you going to reproach the bird for casting a shadow?

I didn't understand entirely what he meant. He must have noticed that, because he went on: Your master didn't want to hurt you, but he just wasn't able to protect you. When a storm comes, the tree shakes and the birds' nests fall to the ground.

I understood that a little better. And the eggs break, I said. Is that just?

He smiled and said: We cannot understand the justice of the Everlasting One, Dalilah. And often there are no longer any eggs left in the nest, just young birds who are forced to realize that it is actually time for them to fly away.

Suddenly I remembered what Amalia had once said to me, on the day before Rosh Hashanah, when I had asked her about my mother. Dalilah, she had said, you don't need to be afraid. You are a good girl, you'll be able to cope with your life—perhaps better than Jessica will, who has all the things you envy. Believe me, you are strong and you have much love in you, and the Everlasting One, blessed be He, will make up for the suffering you will have to go through.

I wanted to get up and leave, but Tubal Benevisti held me back. Dalilah, he asked, do you want to work for me? Shall I take you in?

No, I said, I think it's time for me to fly away. I shall leave Venice.

You could go to Jessica, he said. I'm sure she would be happy if you went to her.

I didn't have to think very long about that, and I shook my head. No, I said, I don't want to live with them, with the Christians. I want to stay with the people I belong to. I'm not a white mouse in a litter of gray ones.

He looked at me in surprise, and so I told him what I wanted to do without having thought it out first. But the moment I put it into words I knew that it was the right thing. Because suddenly my lion appeared before my inner eyes, the winged lion of Judah. And I felt as if I had been moving toward this point for my whole life, without knowing it. I want to go to the land of our fathers, I said. There are Jewish communities there, in Jerusalem, in Zefat and in Tiberias. I've often heard of them, and I'm sure there must be others as well. And since he did not answer me at once, I added quickly: Hardworking hands and a willing heart are welcome everywhere. I don't know whether I was trying to convince him or myself.

He nodded, stood up, and fetched a small bag from a chest and gave it to me. You should not leave without money, Dalilah. Tie the bag to a belt underneath your clothes so that no one can see it.

I had to smile, because Amalia had said the very same thing to me. And then he did something else that Amalia had done. He placed his hands on my head and said: *Yes-imekh elohim ke-Sara, Rivka, Rahel, ve-Leah.* May the Lord make you like Sarah, Rivka, Rachel, and Leah.

I pressed against him. Thank you, I said, thank you. I thanked him twice, once for the money and once for the blessing.

When I had already reached the door, still a little confused by everything that had happened, he added: Your route will be through the Ottoman Empire. Don't forget that there are Jews in all the big cities. Find out where they are, they will help you on your way. And if you ever change your mind, Dalilah, you can always come to me.

I nodded and left him. On the way home I thought about my plan and wondered how I could best put it into operation. I dropped in on Jacopo Romano, the cobbler, Jehuda's father. Jacopo was in his workshop, his hand bandaged and his arm strapped up, giving Jehuda instructions.

We've heard what happened to your master, said Jacopo when I came in.

I took some money from the bag that Tubal Benevisti had given me and put the coins on the table.

That is for the boys' clothes that Jehuda brought me, I said to Jacopo. I'd like to keep them, to help me on a long journey. Is that enough?

Jacopo took the coins and put them away. More than enough, he said. May the Everlasting One, praised be He, protect you and keep His hand over you.

Jehuda was looking at me the whole time. What a handsome lad he is, I thought, and he's slowly becoming a man. Suddenly it occurred to me that his lips no longer looked as red as before. But his eyes were as beautiful as ever, except he was looking very sad. I knew what he was thinking: It was you who was allowed to go to Belmont, to Jessica, and now you are leaving the city again. You are free, and I have to sit in this workshop. And suddenly another realization came into my head: To be alone, to have no family, that was a kind of freedom. I tried to smile at Jehuda, but I am not sure whether he didn't see triumph in my face instead, because he turned his head away and said: Peace with you, Dalilah, may the Everlasting One, praised be He, protect you and keep His hand over you. He lowered his head. How sad he looked.

Once outside again I took a deep breath, and I felt that I had accomplished something important. I don't just mean that I had paid for the clothes and had no more debts left.

My hair is very short now. It looks prickly on my head. Like the prickles of the hedgehog that I saw on my way to Belmont. Only black.

I'll sweep up the hair so that I can burn it later. Cut hair and fingernails mustn't be left lying around or else someone might use them for black magic against you—that's what Amalia and Jessica kept on telling me.

There is a short, bright flame when I throw it into what is left of yesterday's fire. And it stinks.

I fetch my pack from its hook in the hall, where it has been hanging since my journey to see Jessica, and look for some provisions. Apart from a hard crust of bread and some cheese there is nothing left. The master must have taken all the food with him. But that doesn't worry me. I've already got some experience in traveling. I know how to get food on the way.

Then I change clothes. How long ago was it when I went dressed as a boy to find Jessica? Two weeks? Three weeks? Or four? I don't know anymore. It seems like a year ago, but only because Amalia's death came in between. Amalia . . .

I go over into our room and look round. The bed in which Amalia and I slept for so long is still in the next room. I shan't sleep in it again. And I shan't be there when Marta and all the others visit Amalia's grave at the end of the *sheloshim*, the month of mourning. Amalia's Sabbath candlesticks are standing on the cabinet. Amalia, you would certainly have wanted me to have them, now that Jessica no longer lights candles on Friday evenings, wouldn't you? I'll always give them pride of place, I promise. I'll take your light-gray shawl as well, to wrap them up in. And as something to remember you by. And my prayer book. I shan't take anything else. I don't need anything else.

I go upstairs and into Jessica's room as if in a trance. I have to say my good-byes. That's the bed Jessica and I slept in together for many years. That's the table we used to play dice on when we were children, secretly, so the master didn't find out. This was where we used to tell each other stories in the evenings, comic ones or ghost stories. I could always tell stories better than Jessica. I draw back the curtain and light comes in. Suddenly I see Jessica before me. Jessica as a child. She is beautiful, she is laughing. Sing, Dalilah, she says. Come on, sing, I want to dance. And I sing the songs we used to sing when we were children. Tears are running down my face, one drops onto my hand. I stop singing. Jessica was forever wanting to dance and play. She always wanted to run away from the Ghetto, to do things and see things. I think I was much quieter than she was.

Jessica won't sleep in this bed again either. I wonder who will move into this room? I wish anyone who lives here in the future more happiness than we had. But perhaps it was happiness and we just didn't notice. Maybe.

Then I open the door to the master's room, but I don't go in. My eyes are still stinging. In the light that comes through the open door I can only see shadows. That's where he always stood, in the light of his oil lamp. He stood there, his prayer shawl around him, the phylacteries tied to his left arm with the *shel-rosh* around his head. I open the wardrobe door and feel along the shelf there. Yes, he's taken the blue velvet bag with the phylacteries, and his prayer shawl and his prayer books. That's good, I think to myself. It would have been bad if he'd lost his faith as well as everything else.

Last of all I go into the salon. The blue of the curtains is shining and so are the gold borders. I run my hand over the velvet for the last time and press my face to the material. I shall never see these curtains again. But I shan't need them either. I am going off in search of another shade of blue. I'll be setting off soon on my way to the east, to the lands where the sun rises in the morning. I think I'm looking forward to it. Yes, I *am* looking forward to it. The world can be so exciting when you dare to leave the old familiar paths.

What did you tell me, Amalia? The Ghetto means protection? Yes, that's true, but it also means restriction. I know that. And something else, Amalia: If all those misfortunes hadn't happened to us, if you hadn't sent me to find Jessica, I would never dare to leave the protection of the Ghetto now. When a storm comes it shakes the tree, and the birds' nests fall to the ground. That's what Tubal Benevisti meant. And I'm ready to fly away.

When I leave the house I'll look all around the Campo and impress every detail on my mind. Perhaps one day, when I'm old, I'll have to tell my grandchildren, or somebody else's grandchildren, about how we used to live in this city with all the canals. Our Ghetto was an island, I shall say, surrounded by water. You don't know what the Ghetto is? Oh, it's a prison or a place of safety—it all depends what you want it to be and what you want to do. The Ghetto was set up in April 1516, according to their calendar, that means in the month of Nissan in the year 5275. In the space of three days every Jew in Venice was brought here, to these houses on the Campo, on which the sun shines when the weather is fine. Because the new foundry was there, they called it the Ghetto Nuovo, even though it was older. And the new Ghetto was set up near where the old foundry was, and that's why it's called the Ghetto Vecchio, the old Ghetto, even though it's actually newer.

Our Ghetto was an island, bounded by canals, and there were only two bridges. One of them, the Ponte di San Girolamo, led into the city, and the other, the Ponte degli Agudi, led to the Ghetto Vecchio, where mostly Sephardic Jews lived, and we used to call them transpontines, the ones who lived across the bridge. But it's the Ghetto Nuovo I want to tell you about. I'll tell how the houses were all crowded closely around a square that we called the Campo, crowded so closely that you could hear the voices of other Jews, and it was like a piece of music, which began with the morning prayer, still solemn, and then developed, swelling to a crescendo, until it died down again after sunset with the *ma'ariv*, the evening prayers.

Once upon a time, I shall say, there were two girls who lived in one of those houses. One of the girls had fine brown hair and light-gray eyes, and the other had black hair, dark eyes, and a squint. One of them was rich and beautiful, the other one was poor and ugly. But they had one thing in common—they were both motherless. And they loved each other. When they were children they played dice in secret and went roaming around the city. And when they grew up they both left the Ghetto. You ask me why? Children, children, that is a long story, a very long and very Jewish story.

About the Book

SHYLOCK AND HIS DAUGHTER, Jessica, whose relationship with one another is the starting point for Mirjam Pressler's book, are both characters in Shakespeare's play *The Merchant of Venice*, which he wrote at the end of the sixteenth century, around 1594–6—not very many years after the period in which the novel is set.

In fact, Mirjam Pressler reminds us quite often, and in a number of different ways, that her book is based on a Shakespeare play. Some of the dialogue—especially Shylock's words—are quotations from *The Merchant of Venice*, and there are other less direct reminders as well. For example, one of Shakespeare's favorite devices, found in a number of his plays, is to have girls disguised as boys, or women as men. In *The Merchant of Venice* itself both Jessica (briefly) and Portia adopt such a disguise, and in the novel this happens both with Dalilah (who is not one of Shakespeare's characters) and with Portia (who is).

The idea of playacting itself is also present all through the book. In the last chapter in which she appears, Jessica goes over a whole sequence of events in her mind, just as if she were watching a play on a set—and it is a play in which she herself is a character. This is an important section because it lets us see her analyzing herself and her own actions quite objectively, in the same way that we might watch and analyze someone's actions in a play.

Shakespeare uses the idea of "plays within plays," but he also makes the point that all of life can be seen as if it were a play:

> All the world's a stage
> And all the men and women merely players:
> They have their exits and their entrances
> And one man in his time plays many parts . . .

Those famous lines are not from *The Merchant of Venice*, but all through Mirjam Pressler's novel, Jessica is preoccupied with the idea of whether she should or should not play the part that has been assigned to her by God or by Fate. She decides that she will not play that part, and her decision to go against what has been laid down for her at birth is both bold and difficult. She is also aware that any one woman will play many different parts as she goes through life and, at the end of the book, Jessica knows that she will soon be taking on yet another role—that of a mother. The reader may wonder how Jessica—who never really had a mother—will cope with it. Dalilah, on the other hand, plays a variety of parts within the story: that of a street urchin (which she even replays to entertain her friends afterward), that of a slightly simple boy when she goes to find Jessica, and a boy again when she leaves the Ghetto.

The Merchant of Venice is in some ways a difficult play for a modern audience to read or to watch, though it has given us just as many famous phrases and proverbs as any of Shakespeare's plays. For example, "It is a wise father that knows his own child," or "a good deed in a naughty world." Shakespeare tells various different stories in the play, and introduces us to a range of very different characters, some of whom are taken up by Mirjam Pressler in *Shylock's Daughter* and given a life of their own that goes much further than in Shakespeare's play. She also provides a whole range of new characters.

In the main story in the play, Antonio, the "merchant of Venice" of the title, borrows money from Shylock, the Jewish moneylender, so that he can give that money to his young friend Bassanio, thus helping Bassanio in his quest to marry the beautiful heiress, Portia. Antonio hates Shylock—he tells us so, and Shylock confirms it—and at least some of the reason for this is anti-Semitism on Antonio's part.

Indeed, Shylock is referred to simply as "Jew" by other characters, and the conflict between Jews and Christians is important. Historically, moneylenders were often Jews because Jews, although prohibited from many professions, were permitted to lend money for interest, whereas Christians were not. Antonio's dislike of Shylock as a Jew is therefore not rational, though he and others consider it valid on the simple grounds that anyone who is not a Christian must be an enemy.

Antonio borrows the money and Shylock, goaded about the fact that he charges interest, offers to lend the money free of interest, but asks for a pound of flesh as security. That is, if the merchant ships that Antonio is counting on to bring him back a good profit fail to return, Shylock can have a pound of Antonio's living flesh. Meanwhile, Shylock's daughter, Jessica, has become involved with another of Antonio's young friends, Lorenzo, and the couple elope and marry, having taken—the word is really "stolen"—some of Shylock's gold and jewels.

Antonio's ships, part of the great trading fleet of Venice, are indeed all lost, and Shylock therefore demands his pound of flesh, insisting on his rights ("I crave the law!" he says) and refusing even double the payment when Antonio's friends offer this to him. However, Portia, by now married to Bassanio, disguises herself as a lawyer and, after first seeming to support Shylock's claim, points out that Shylock is allowed a pound of flesh, but not a drop of blood. How can Shylock have one without the other? Accordingly, he cannot have his pound of flesh and he has already rejected the money. The Doge orders (prompted by Antonio) that Shylock be fined, that he must become a Christian, and that his remaining property must be left to Lorenzo (and Jessica) when he dies.

Shakespeare's pictures of the various people involved are not straightforward and can be interpreted in different ways. Lorenzo is either an attractive young nobleman or a shallow idler, interested in a pretty girl with a rich father who, because he is a Jew, can be robbed without too many qualms. Jessica may be breaking away from her home out of romantic but potentially thwarted love, or she might on the other hand be either silly or treacherous, or both. Most difficult of all is Shylock himself—one of the best known figures in Shakespeare. He can be seen in the play either as a victim, properly protesting that Jews are exactly the same as everyone else ("If you prick us, do we not bleed?" he asks), and utterly destroyed at the end, or he can be seen as a potentially murderous old miser, who cares more about his money than his daughter ("O my ducats! O my daughter!").

Over and above these basic problems, Shakespeare leaves a lot of other questions unanswered. Why does Shylock make the curious proposal about the flesh? Why does he not take the money when double is offered? What motivates Jessica to run off with Lorenzo? Does it trouble her that she is robbing her father and abandoning her faith?

Mirjam Pressler gives us some of the answers, but in doing so she offers us a new story, which raises a number of new questions—some of them very modern, and some of them (as Dalilah says right at the end of the book) very Jewish. To do this, Pressler brings in several new characters, as well as helping us interpret the Shakespearean ones. Antonio, Lorenzo, Bassanio, and Portia are all in Shakespeare's play, as are Jessica, Shylock, and Tubal Benevisti (briefly). Even Shylock's dead wife, Leah, is mentioned. But Lorenzo's relatives (like the arrogant Tia Rosalia), most of the other people of the Ghetto, and especially those in Shylock's household, are not in the play: Amalia, Jehuda, and, above all, Dalilah, Shylock's "other" daughter and probably the most important character in the book. Hannah Meshullam and her family are also new, and they answer the simple question of how an Italian aristocrat could ever have met the moneylender's daughter in the first place.

If Shakespeare's play is often ambiguous—capable of having different meanings—Mirjam Pressler also gives the reader plenty to think about, and there are indications of this even in the title. *Shylock's Daughter* clearly refers to Jessica, but Dalilah, the girl he has adopted or at least taken into his home, is in many ways a better daughter to him. Even the place and time in which the book is set are ambiguous. We are told at the outset that the setting is Venice in 1568—but also the Venice Ghetto in 5327–8. Both of those designations of place, and also the rather strange-looking set of dates, are important.

Venice nowadays is a tourist center, tucked away at the top of the Adriatic Sea in the north of Italy, at the sea edge of a plain (called the Veneto), with the Alps and Northern Europe above it. It continues to attract visitors in vast numbers because of its position on the sea, because of its canals (especially the Grand Canal), and their gondolas, because of its palaces, squares, and the business area known as the Rialto, and, most famously of all, because of St. Mark's square, the *Piazza San Marco*, with the church, bell tower—the *campanile*—and the palace of the Doge, the ruling duke of the old Venetian republic. There are still plenty of pigeons and seagulls too. But if Venice is now a tourist city, it was once vastly more important, and in the period when the novel is set, in 1568, it was still the center of a powerful independent republic. Admittedly, by the end of the sixteenth century that power had really begun to decline, but it was still important and independent.

At its height, the Venetian Republic controlled not only the land of the Veneto and part of the Balkan coastal area but, more importantly, it also controlled the sea, sending out its warships and its traders from its prime position commanding the Adriatic, with access to the Mediterranean, and controlling the routes to the Levant, the Middle East, and beyond. Ruled by the Doge and a council of aristocrats, it took and established military bases at important strategic points, like Crete and Cyprus, and its merchant ships traded over a huge area, taking Venetian goods (glass, lace, and other items) and bringing in foreign and exotic goods for distribution throughout Europe. To be a merchant of Venice was important. However, Venice was close to another large and threatening power—the Turkish Ottoman Empire—and it fought against that empire many times.

Many reasons caused Venice to lose power in the end. The opening up of the New World, and also of routes to the Far East around the Cape of Good Hope, turned the Mediterranean into a commercial backwater; and in military terms, the power of the Turkish Empire grew too strong. But in 1568, Venice still proudly held her title of *la Serenissima*— "her serene highness," the Queen of the Adriatic—and the Venetian fleet would still have a final great victory over Turkish forces at the sea battle of Lepanto in 1571.

1568 is a Christian date, reckoned from what was taken to be the year of the birth of Christ. But we are also told that the book is set in 5327–8. These are dates from the Jewish calendar, the year reckoning of which is dated from the presumed time of the Creation, which was thought to be 3,760 years before the supposed year of the birth of Christ. There are thirteen months in the Jewish year (some of them are named in the book), which begins in September/October, and it is important that the events of the book straddle two years. The Jewish New Year, Rosh Hashanah, is a variable date depending upon the new moon around the end of September, and it is a feast day. But after it and into the New Year itself comes Yom Kippur, the Day of Atonement—another very important holy day, a "holiday" in the old sense and a day of fasting. New years are always new beginnings, and 5328 is a year of decisions and new situations for all the main characters. According to Jewish tradition, however (and Shylock himself tells us this in the book), during those first days of the New Year it is decided in Heaven who is truly righteous and who is truly wicked. Those in between—that is, most of humanity—have the transition period to do their best and to repent of their sins. The period between those very important Jewish holidays plays an important part in the book, so that the Jewish dates are as significant as the Christian one.

Much of the book is set not just in Venice, but, specifically, in the Ghetto—or rather, in the two Ghettos: the Ghetto Nuovo (meaning "New Ghetto," but which, as Amalia explains, is actually older) and the "Old Ghetto," the Ghetto Vecchio, which came a bit later. The word "ghetto" is still familiar today, and it has an extended meaning: It is now applied to any area where an ethnic group is kept to itself, usually nowadays for reasons of social or economic pressures (we might refer to "black ghettos," for example). Originally it was used for an area of a city where Jews had to live segregated from Christians. London and Rome, for example, had such Jewish quarters before the name "ghetto" was applied to them.

The connotations of the word "ghetto" are nowadays completely negative, and this has much to do with the imprisonment of Jews in ghettos, especially in Eastern Europe in towns like Warsaw or Lodz or Vilnius, and ultimately their murder by the Nazi regime in the Second World War. But although these specific and restricted Jewish quarters existed in several cities far earlier than 1516, the word comes from an area of Venice that was established as a Jewish quarter in that year. The word itself is probably an abbreviation of *borghetto,* meaning "little borough," "little district" (*borgo* is Italian for a small town), although no one is quite sure, and in the book, Amalia seems to link it with the metal foundries (*gettare* is the Italian word for casting metal, although it is not pronounced the same way as ghetto).

As Amalia also makes clear in the book, the idea of a ghetto was not always seen completely negatively. In the early ghettos, Jewish communities were at least afforded some (though hardly complete) protection, and they could have some degree of administrative autonomy, their own community councils, and could carry out their own religious practices, some of which are described in the novel. But it is still segregation, imposed on one group by a larger one, with the otherness—the *apartheid*—made clear by enforced dress regulations. We are shown here how Jews are regularly attacked or mocked outside the Ghetto because they have to wear distinctive clothing, and yet that idea was suggested by a church council in 1215. When Jehuda goes out without his red hat to watch the burning of the books, nobody realizes that he is a Jew, of course, so nobody attacks or mocks him. And of course, Christian forces enter the Ghetto itself to confiscate the Hebrew books.

Having established themselves in Europe at a very early stage, Jews found themselves gradually driven out of most western European countries by the later Middle Ages. England was the first to expel them in 1290, and Jews (from Spain or Portugal) did not really begin to return, more or less unofficially, until around Shakespeare's time. Whether Shylock's creator had ever *met* a Jew is debatable (especially an Ashkenazi Jew).

France expelled the Jews a century after England, and the last and most notable expulsions were those from Spain and Portugal, where Jews were expelled after 1492 if they refused to be baptized. At the end of the fifteenth century the Spanish Inquisition was set up largely to make sure that those who had converted were actually true to the new faith. These converts were called Marranos, and many of these also fled from Spain and Portugal.

Northern Italy, especially the Venetian Republic, was one of the few places in which Jews could—within a set of rules laid down by various bodies in the Republic—resettle and join an established Jewish community, even if that community was restricted to specific parts of the city after 1516, and even if limitations on numbers were often set. Venice was independent and could even defy the Pope to some extent. Other Jews fled farther east, and one place that offered them shelter was the Ottoman Empire—partly to annoy the Christian powers in the west. It is no surprise that Shylock, and later Dalilah, in Mirjam Pressler's book eventually go in that direction. There were also Jewish settlements in the ancestral homeland, the territory called Palestine by the Romans, notably in Safed, now Zefat, in Galilee, and also at Tiberias.

Venice was home to two groups of Jews. First the *Ashkenazim*, Jews originally from central Europe, and secondly the *Sephardim*, from Spain. In this second group we can also include those Jews—usually merchants—who came to Venice from the Levant, from the Middle Eastern communities. This broad group felt themselves culturally superior. Levi Meshullam, the highly respected doctor, is a Sephardic Jew, which illustrates the point. In some ways they were differently (and indeed better) treated than the Ashkenazi Jews.

However, Jews were always a potential target for racial hatred and attack, not only on religious grounds from the dominant Christian society, but also because of rumors, such as that mentioned in Mirjam Pressler's novel that they were in league with the enemy, the Turks. The book has many parallels with the modern world. Tubal Benevisti points out that Shylock is neither the first nor the last Jew to have to leave his home, and the idea of *diaspora*, dispersal, is of great importance in Jewish history.

In 1555, and at other times as well, Jewish books were burned by Christian zealots, and the public burning of the books here in St. Mark's Square (watched with horror by Jessica and with mild interest and presumably approval by Antonio) reflects not only the history of the sixteenth century, but more recent times, such as on May 10, 1933, when Hitler's Nazis burned books by Jewish and other anti-Nazi writers. There is a famous comment, attributed to the German writer Heinrich Heine (who was also a Jew) in the nineteenth century that once people start burning books they will soon begin to burn people. In Jewish culture, books—and not just the holy books—are of massive importance and are treated with reverence because they embody tradition itself. As Jehuda points out, words are sacred things and cannot really be destroyed, and Shylock and the other Jews do manage to save a number of their books. The reader of the novel is left wondering, however, whether Lorenzo—who is away from Venice at the time—would have attended the burning if he *had* been there.

What answers does Mirjam Pressler give to Shakespeare's open questions? Shylock is goaded into the contract with Antonio (here it is suggested by Antonio himself rather than by Shylock), and his despair at the loss of his daughter leads him to become obsessed with revenge—an obsession that those close to him try to curb, however understandable it may be. It accounts for his apparently bloodthirsty insistence on the pound of flesh, and the refusal to take the increased money. Jessica is indeed guilt ridden for stealing her father's property and unsure that she has done the right thing, either regarding her father or regarding her religion, tradition, and upbringing.

But at least Shylock is not entirely ruined at the end, nor is he forced to abandon his religion. We do not get a completely clear picture of the Venetian nobles, but the shallowness and greed of Lorenzo and Bassanio come across strongly, as well as their unthinking (its casualness is important) anti-Semitism, even if Lorenzo does seem to love Jessica for herself as well. Antonio is a bit pathetic, and Portia, the wise beauty of Shakespeare's play, is rather *too* full of herself after the defeat (or trickery?) of Shylock in court. Jessica puts Portia into perspective naively but significantly, thinking: Portia is not really *all that* beautiful, but when you are rich and Christian by birth, you don't need to be.

Shakespeare critics and Shakespearean actors have interpreted Shylock in all kinds of ways. Here, he is a sympathetic, even tragic figure, far less the miserly pawnbroker (and certainly not a bloodthirsty caricature) than a figure of almost puritan austerity and tradition. But he is also a very lonely man who tries to hold on to his only daughter, Jessica, partly because she reminds him of his dead wife, Leah, whose presence is still real to him. He is unable to marry Amalia because of Jewish law—a law that even prevents him from seeing her to her grave, but to which he has kept all his life. Shylock is insulted by the Christian noblemen even when they need him, and eventually he tries in vain to get his revenge for the theft of his daughter (as he sees it).

Shylock follows tradition so firmly because he sees it as a way of maintaining order in a chaotic world. He speculates at one point, with Amalia, that they might in the past have gone against the law; but they did not, and it is difficult to see how Shylock could ever have done so. However ambiguous Shakespeare's Shylock might be about his money and his daughter, in the novel the loss of his daughter is the worst thing that could happen to him, robbing him above all of his participation in the future generations of Israel. This drives him over the edge so that he refuses (even though it might harm the whole Ghetto) to temper justice with mercy. Just as in Shakespeare, he sees the revenge he wants as precisely what the Christians would do to him if the circumstances were different.

Jessica is very young, although, as we learn, she could (and indeed ought to) be married, in an arranged match made by her father. She feels that she doesn't belong in the Ghetto, however, and breaks away from it by stealing from her father and marrying Lorenzo after voluntarily (although very uneasily) accepting Christian baptism. This means that there can be no going back for her. Her desires—apart from Lorenzo—are, however, all for material things. She craves parties, flowers, rich dresses—things forbidden to Jews under the clothing laws (and seen by her father as an expression of vanity, though she calls it miserliness on his part). Clothes preoccupy her, and she wants always to be a beautifully dressed woman; she is entirely feminine. Dalilah is able to dress as a boy, to adopt masculine characteristics when necessary. Jessica would be quite unable to do so (in fact, she does so in Shakespeare's play when she elopes and is mightily embarrassed by it, even though Lorenzo rather enjoys her disguise). She could never really adapt in a way that would seem to make her less feminine, which meant that she could ultimately only break away by becoming a wife.

The open question with which Mirjam Pressler leaves the reader is whether Jessica can ever be really happy, or whether she will go on thinking of her betrayed father and, indeed, go on being a child of the Ghetto, cut off from her traditions, forever. Shakespeare lets her sum up her whole confused position when she says:

> Alack, what heinous sin is it in me
> To be asham'd to be my father's child!
> But though I am a daughter to his blood,

I am not to his manners. O Lorenzo,
If thou keep promise, I shall end his strife,
Become a Christian, and thy loving wife.

She is quite determined, nevertheless. Shakespeare's Jessica seems at least to be happy at the end of the play, but in the novel (where we see much more of her), although she leaves the Ghetto and gets what she thought she wanted, the price she pays is enormous. Jessica may have become a Christian noblewoman, but when she takes a look at herself, she is now the woman with two faces. She learns a far harder lesson than Dalilah does.

The Venice Ghettos (and the other ghettos) did offer some protection, but they were also prisons where, nevertheless, the Jews remained vulnerable. The attack and the stealing of the books show just *how* vulnerable the Jews could be. It is interesting that all the main Jewish characters have, by the end of the book, left the Ghetto. Amalia does so through death, and Tubal Benevisti is, we know, a traveling merchant in any case, with contacts around the world. Shylock *has* to leave. Dalilah and Jessica choose to do so, each in her own way. Although a ghetto could be for any minority or oppressed group, Dalilah says that the story we have all just read is "a very Jewish story." The main characters also all show different responses to the idea of the ghetto that reflect aspects of Jewish history. Amalia accepts it and even sees advantages in it; Shylock is forced to move away from the place where he grew up, forced to wander; Jessica compromises of her own free will with the ghetto makers; and Dalilah's aim is a Jewish homeland.

Dalilah, Shylock's foster daughter, is the real central character of the book, and also the foil, the counterpart, to Jessica. The point of view from which the reader sees the events happening alternates between chapters, and while we are shown things happening to Jessica and to Shylock more or less objectively (with some insights into their minds), several chapters take us directly into Dalilah's thoughts. Jessica talks about herself playing different parts, but Dalilah (with whom Jessica playacted as a child) is actually far better at it. She can disguise herself, she can tell stories, she can improvise and adapt—and perhaps adaptability is better than compromise. But then again, Jessica is in love, and the slightly younger Dalilah, though attracted to the equally young Jehuda, is not.

Amalia, who has brought up the two girls, tells Dalilah quite rightly that she is a stronger character. Dalilah learns a great deal, and her attempt to persuade Jessica to return is very important. She learns things: that there is a world outside the restrictions of the Ghetto, and—very importantly—that Christians too can be poor and struggling, but decent. Jessica's Christian world is composed of aristocrats, for whom every day is like a feast day, and whose behavior is strange and sometimes questionable. By contrast, Dalilah meets poor people on her travels.

At the end, Dalilah also leaves the Ghetto—through her own choice, although she has been pushed in that direction by events. But she stays within the traditions of her faith, heading eastward, following her dream of the lion of Judah (which is how she perceives the lion that represents St. Mark, the heraldic badge of Christian Venice). She looks forward to the time when, in the land of the Patriarchs, she will be able to tell later generations the story of the Venice Ghetto as something that is part of history.

—Brian Murdoch